BREAKOUT

SAN FRANCISCO STRIKERS, BOOK 1

STEPHANIE KAY

Shannon,
Last names are overrated!

~Stephanie Kay

Breakout

Copyright © 2017 Stephanie Kay
eBook Edition: March 2017
Edited by Chelsea Kuhel www.madisonseidler.com
Cover Art by Ben Ellis www.tallstorydesign.com
This is a work of fiction. Names, characters, places and incidents either are a product of the author imagination or are used fictitiously, and any resemblance to actual persons, living or dead, business establishments, events or locales is entirely coincidental.

With the exception of quotes used in reviews, this book may not be reproduced or used in whole or in part by any means existing without written permission from the publisher, Stephanie Kay. www.stephkaybooks.com
ALL RIGHTS RESERVED.

Warning: The unauthorized reproduction or distribution of this copyrighted work is illegal. No part of this book may be scanned, uploaded or distributed via the Internet or any other means, electronic or print, without the publisher's permission. Criminal copyright infringement, including infringement without monetary gain, is investigated by the FBI and is punishable by up to 5 years in federal prison and a fine of $250,000. (http://www.fbi.gov/ipr). Please purchase only authorized electronic or print editions and do not participate in or encourage the electronic piracy of copyrighted material. Your support of the author's rights is appreciated.

❧ Created with Vellum

She was never supposed to see him again...

Penny Connor was practical to a fault. Which is why the beautiful accountant was determined to enjoy her honeymoon — groom or no groom. After walking in on her fiancé with another woman, she called off the wedding and hopped a plane to Italy. She allowed herself one sizzling week, acting completely out of character under the Tuscan sun with a handsome stranger, before returning home to pick up the pieces.

Hockey hotshot Ethan Hartnell had quite the reputation living life on his own terms. Being traded to the San Francisco Strikers, due to his questionable behavior was a fresh shot— his last shot. One he couldn't afford to mess up. Everything was going according to plan, until he walks into a local bar and sees the woman who ran away from his bed in Tuscany.

Which is exactly what she plans to do when they see each other again— but this time he's not going to let her get away so easily.

Please sign up for my newsletter for upcoming releases and exclusive excerpts. You can also email me at stephanie@stephkaybooks.com or find me on Twitter or Facebook. For more information, please visit my website, www.stephkaybooks.com. You can also join my reader group on Facebook, Stephanie Kay's Sassy Readers. We discuss books, romance, dessert, and hockey butts.

DEDICATION

To John, my amazing husband
Without you agreeing to get married in Gretna Green, this book never would've happened.
Thank you for dragging our four rolling suitcases through six train cars, while I hobbled behind you, because I insisted we get on the train in first class so we wouldn't miss it, even though our seats were in second class—it's a miracle you still wanted to marry me after that!
Thank you for encouraging me to write every day and pushing me to pursue my dreams.
Let's be honest, it's really so you can get me out of your hair and go hiking.
I love you more than words can say, even when you drive me crazy... which is daily, in case anyone was wondering.

ACKNOWLEDGMENTS

There are so many people to thank that I don't know where to start.

To Susie Warren, my fabulous critique partner, thank you for the great—and speedy—feedback. Your suggestions made this book what it is, so thank you for the multiple read throughs and for letting me bounce ideas off of you.

To Chelsea Kuhel, my awesome editor, thank you for polishing up my writing and catching every word I missed. And I'm so sorry for not listing you in the acknowledgements in Unmatched. See what happens when I don't list the acknowledgements in the version of the book I send to you!

To Iveta Cvrkal, proofreader extraordinaire, thank you for finding every comma I missed...I hate commas!

To Ben Ellis, my fantastic cover artist. This one might be my favorite, and I'm sure I'll say that about the next one, too.

To Samantha Wayland for getting me hooked on hockey. Bet you didn't think I'd get this obsessed this quickly! Can't wait for our next hockey road trip, you know, for research purposes. Maybe we can run into another AHL team on the road and recognize them by their outstanding asses.

To Aven Ellis, for helping me try not to over-analyze everything. I'm a work in progress.

To Karen Stivali, for writing the perfect blurb.

To Penny Watson. My contemporary romance career wouldn't exist without you ordering me to write this book based on a Facebook post. I might still be working on that historical that will never see the light of day.

To my new and fantastic beta readers, Elaine and Sita. Your comments helped immensely and I'm glad you enjoyed Penny and Ethan's story.

To the Hearties. Thank you for welcoming me into this group of amazing hockey romance authors and for answering all of my questions. I'm sure I will pester you all with each book.

To my mom. You and Dad showed me how to have a successful 40+ year marriage through laughter and affection. You've also shown me that even in grief, you can become the strongest woman I know. So glad you are finally able to travel the world and have a social life I envy!

To my amazing in-laws, thank you for letting me watch your hysterical Italian family for the last 10+ years. I still think about that first Christmas Eve. After everyone gorged themselves on seafood for dinner, my mother-in-law asked if anyone was hungry, and the family sat down to a lasagna she just had in the fridge and dove in…at eleven p.m.

To my family for always encouraging me to go after my dreams and for your unwavering support, even if most of you don't read romance novels…I'll forgive you for that last indiscretion.

And of course, to my husband, John, for more reasons than I can count. You were the one who encouraged me to get back to writing when I was laid off from my day job in 2008. Probably so I would leave you to your books and guitars. Chicken has dried out on the grill and sweet potatoes have been burned because I was working on a scene instead of focusing on dinner, but you never complained…well, not that loudly. And you agreed to let me live out my romance dreams and get married over the anvil in Gretna Green, Scotland, even if you did refuse to wear a kilt. Thank you for loving my craziness and putting up with discussions about the characters in my head not doing what I want them to.

And to my readers, thank you for taking the chance on a new author. I hope I make you laugh out loud and follow your heart.

Please sign up for my newsletter for upcoming releases and exclusive excerpts. You can also email me at stephanie@stephkaybooks.com or find me on Twitter or Facebook. For more information, please visit my website, www.stephkaybooks.com. You can also join my reader group on Facebook, Stephanie Kay's Sassy Readers. We discuss books, romance, dessert, and hockey butts.

CHAPTER 1

Crawling around on her hands and knees in her office was never a good way to start the day. If anyone walked in, they would see her ass up in the air, and her shoes kicked off next to her desk. Definitely not office appropriate. Penny's hair slipped from her clip as she crawled toward her credenza, the uncooperative curls at it again.

She bit back her frustrated laughter, and blew a wayward blonde strand out of her eyes.

"Where is that damn clicker?"

She'd already dug through the files on her normally immaculate desk. Nothing. Her lack of organization caused her cheek to tick. She had a presentation in an hour for a new and extremely important client, and instead of going over her notes one last time, she was on the floor looking for her damn PowerPoint remote.

She peeked under the cabinet.

Lots of dust—gross. And the clicker.

She felt a twinge as she shifted on her right knee. Six months ago, she'd wiped out at her drunken bachelorette party. The bachelorette party that never should've happened. But after surprising her fiancé at his office, the morning of the party, and getting her own surprise when she'd walked in on his boss gyrating in Michael's lap—the woman's moans reminiscent of an episode of *Wild Kingdom* on Animal Planet—Penny had needed to numb the pain with martinis. A lot of martinis. And shots. She couldn't forget the shots.

Damn cheating bastard.

That night, she hadn't confessed to her friends that she'd called the wedding off. She couldn't dwell on a cancelled wedding, a cancelled future, when she was tossing back shots and dancing until her knee gave out.

She'd learned many valuable lessons that evening.

Never wear a veil in a bar.

Never take three shots in a row, just "because you went to college."

And "dropping it like it's hot," isn't that hot when you end up sprawled out on the dance floor in pain.

She'd put a serious dent in her pride that night. At least from what she could recall.

She shook off her memories. It was over, and she had to stop thinking about the plans they'd made. Plans she'd counted on.

Her ex-fiancé was a forgotten memory. Not totally forgotten. But she was working on that.

Her honeymoon—well, that was another story.

Stop it.

She was completely distracted, but she was nervous about today, and her brain was flitting off in random directions. Hence, the messy desk and disappearing clicker. She stuck her hand under the credenza, grasped the offending clicker, and sat back on her heels.

The less time on her knees the better. She always feared it would dislocate on her again. And she did not have time for that right now.

She stood up and sank down into her chair, grabbing the

Alexander file. She was prepared, but one more run-through would make her feel better.

She crossed *clicker* off her list and scanned her notes. Robert, her boss, was looking to promote someone to Accounting Manager, and she'd been with the company for five years. The position should've been hers last year, and she hoped she hadn't been overlooked because she'd been in wedding mode. Another way Michael had screwed her while he was screwing someone else.

She was determined to land this account and that promotion. She'd done a detailed review of everything she could find on Mr. Alexander and his company, since she would be handling his personal and business accounts. She read through everything one last time, making notes in the presentation so she didn't forget anything.

Today had to be perfect.

* * *

"To Penny, may she finally get the promotion she deserves," Amanda said as she toasted with her lemon drop martini later that night at Byrne's grand opening.

Lexi lifted her glass. "Yes, to Penny. It's about time."

"Let's not get ahead of ourselves. Today was just an initial meeting. I'm hoping the guy signs on, but even with that account, I might not get promoted," Penny said to both of her friends. Today couldn't have gone better. Well, that was a lie. Mr. Alexander could've signed the contract instead of informing her that he was meeting with two other firms and she'd hear back in a week or two.

"We should celebrate with a cookie bomb, too," Lexi said, and Penny chuckled.

"You and that freaking dessert," Amanda said.

"Adam promised to keep it on the menu," Lexi said, glancing

toward the bar where her boyfriend, Grant, sat talking to his best friend and the bar owner, Adam Byrne.

"I don't have the promotion yet, you guys. I don't even technically have the *client* yet."

Lexi took a sip of wine. "But you will. Mr. Knight can't keep holding you back or he'll eventually lose you."

"Damn straight," Amanda stated, with a fist pump. "You could always go out on your own."

"Too many risks in that," Penny said. Not that she hadn't thought about it. She'd weighed the pros and cons multiple times—every time someone else was promoted.

"I'm sure you have the checklists to confirm it, but you could take a chance. It could work," Amanda said.

"Or it could be a disaster. I'm sure I'll get promoted eventually," Penny muttered, ignoring her friend's checklist dig. Making lists was important. How else could she make sure she examined every option and didn't miss anything?

"Well, I still say you're going to get it. I think this calls for a round of shots," Amanda said, her gray eyes twinkling.

Penny knew that *look*. It'd gotten her into way too much trouble over the years, especially six months ago. Well, not *the look* exactly, more like the line of shots that followed.

"Definitely no shots for me tonight. It's a work night," Penny said.

"Fine. I'll go grab another round of drinks." Amanda slipped off her stool and practically floated to the bar, her hips swaying as she walked.

So unfair. Perfect hair, petite body. If Amanda wasn't one of Penny's best friends, she'd be tempted to trip her. But Amanda was also graceful, so she'd probably stand back up as if nothing happened.

Penny, on the other hand, had the grace of a newborn gazelle. No, not a gazelle. They were typically agile. She was like the gazelle for the first few seconds after birth. All arms and legs. No coordination. Not that a gazelle actually had arms...

"I'm glad the meeting went well. I know that Robert has been hinting around that he's ready to promote, and you're the obvious choice. We all know he doesn't want the hassle of looking for someone outside of the company." Lexi was the office manager and took care of all HR at Knight and Welling, so she would know.

"I really hope that I get it. I've been feeling stuck, like he was never planning to move me up." She fiddled with the stem of her glass. It was so damn frustrating.

"You deserve this, and Robert should recognize that. How many accounts have you brought in this year?" Lexi asked.

"At least four large accounts, and a handful of individual accounts. He even mentioned positive changes coming soon when I spoke with him after my meeting today. And this would be our biggest client." But she hated getting her hopes up, only to have them crushed.

"The job should be yours," Lexi said.

"I hope so."

"I have a good feeling about this."

Amanda came back with more martinis in hand. "What did I miss?"

"Just talking about work stuff."

"Boring. How about we talk about the hot guys in this bar? I think the pickings are even better than usual. Adam mentioned hockey players. Lexi, you're here all the time. Point them out," Amanda said.

Lexi laughed. "I'm going with that group of guys over there. The asses are a dead giveaway."

"Are you scoping out other guys?" Grant asked, coming up and wrapping his arms around Lexi's waist, and kissing her.

"Definitely not. Your skater's butt is more than enough for me," she said. Grant played in a rec league with Adam.

"Glad to hear it. And yes, Amanda, Adam played in the AHL with a few of the Strikers, so some of the guys are here tonight," Grant said, and Penny looked toward the bar. It was a hot looking group.

"Hey, Harty. Over here," one of the guys called out.

Penny took a sip of her drink and scanned the bar, her gaze stopping at the door, where *Harty* stood, and her heart dropped to the floor.

No. It wasn't possible.

He wasn't looking at her, his face was turned to the side, but she caught the hint of the crooked smile she knew so well.

Memories flooded her, and she was back in Tuscany. Back to her sham of a honeymoon. She'd needed to get away from everyone after Michael's betrayal and the trip to Italy had already been booked and paid for. She still couldn't believe she had gotten on that plane and gone to Italy on her own.

But it had been worth it. She had met *him*.

They had crossed paths during a tour of a vineyard near Montalcino. He'd sat beside her at the long farmhouse table for lunch, and as the wine flowed, so had their conversation. He'd been so easy to talk to. His laugh had captured her, intrigued her. He laughed without a care in the world, and at that moment, she'd coveted his unbridled happiness.

And a couple nights later, after too many bottles of wine, one thing had led to another, and…and she had just needed to forget her life at home, her called-off wedding. Liquid courage, they called it, and boy had it delivered. For every moment of the next week in Tuscany, he had been there, making her smile. Making her forget. She could still taste the wine-drenched kisses.

It had been a fling. A fantastic fling, but a fling nonetheless. They hadn't even exchanged last names.

"Penny?" he asked, his shock most likely mirroring hers. Of course, hers was more of a panicked shock.

"Ethan? What are you doing here?" Her voice came out on a crack. How the hell was he here?

"I should ask the same of you," he said, his voice tight.

"I live here. You know that. But why aren't you in New York?" Penny asked, her hand clutching her martini glass so tightly that she feared she'd snap it.

"Penny, what is going on?" Lexi asked, shifting closer to her. Penny's gaze darted between her friends and Ethan, concern and question in their eyes.

"Umm. I should go. Big day tomorrow," Penny said, setting down the fragile martini glass and clutching her bag. She had to get the hell out of there.

"Penny. Wait, is this Italian Ethan?" Lexi whispered, her eyes wide.

Oh God, here it comes. She couldn't face their questions now—or ever. The woman obsessed with making lists and checking them twice—or three—or thirty times, had thrown pros and cons to the wind and had a week-long fling with a stranger in a foreign country. It so wasn't her. Hell, she still couldn't explain it to herself, let alone anyone else.

Fuck. This wasn't supposed to come back and bite her in the ass. She lived here. He told her he lived in New York. He was currently on the wrong coast for that to be true, so what else had he lied about? Panic was firing on all cylinders now.

"Penny," Amanda said, dragging her name out in clear question.

"I should go. Sorry. Lexi, I'll see you at work tomorrow," Penny said, giving Ethan one last look before rushing out of the bar, the questions yelled at her fading to silence as the door shut behind her. She shivered in the crisp night air, her coat forgotten as her fight or flight instinct kicked in. Tonight, she'd gone for flight.

What the hell had just happened? She walked briskly down the street, praying for either a sinkhole to open up and swallow her whole or a cab to stop. Frankly, it was a toss-up as to which one she'd prefer.

"Harty, get your head out of your ass," Nels Seibert, assistant coach for the Strikers, called out the next morning during practice when Ethan missed an easy shot.

Shit. He had to get it together. He skated back to the bench, sliding in next to their captain, Ben "Cheesy" Chester.

"What's up with you, man?" Cheesy asked.

"Nothing. Rough night," Ethan said, still in shock from seeing Penny fifteen hours ago. Not that he was counting. He'd known running into her was a possibility, but in a city of over eight hundred thousand, what were the odds that he'd run into her at the reopening of Adam's bar? It should've been slim—extremely slim. Practically non-existent.

Yet there she'd stood, steps from him, her green eyes bright, her cheeks pale in panic, and her hair. Fuck, her hair. He'd wrapped the curly length in his hand, the early Tuscan sunlight turning it to spun gold as he'd brought them both to shattering orgasm that first morning together. Shit. He couldn't think about that now. Hell, it'd played on loop last night as he'd tried to drink the image away. He'd woken up with a headache and a tented sheet this morning as a result.

He didn't have time to think about that now, which of course meant that he could only think about that. About her. It'd been six months since she'd slipped out of *her* hotel room in the early morning hours, just a note saying thanks for a good time, that room service was on its way up with breakfast, and to not forget checkout at eleven. Shock hadn't even begun to explain his feelings in that moment.

And now she'd turned up unexpectedly, screwing with his head. And he still didn't know her last name. He'd had no idea when he'd been in Italy, when he'd told her he lived in New York, that his days on the East Coast were numbered. The trade had been a complete shock. He was still getting over it. They were both living in the same city and apparently had mutual friends. The world was not that small.

His plans last night had been to have a few drinks with the guys and head home, resting up for tonight's game against his old team, but he'd had no desire to go back into the bar after he'd seen her. Her friends had whispered *Italian Ethan*, and he'd bet money that the guys would razz him about breaking hearts when he'd just returned to the city, so he'd headed to his new townhouse, and played bartender on his own.

He didn't have time for this. Seibs was right. He needed to get his head on straight and focus. It was the first time he was playing his old team in his new house, and he had to be on fire.

"Tonight's a big game. You going to be ready?" Cheesy asked.

Ethan heard the *you better not fuck up*. It was silent, but it was there. His reputation had preceded him. Not that he'd expected anything else, but he was damn tired of his game not doing enough of the talking. Yeah, he was a party boy—had perfected it over the years—but he played to win—always.

Tonight would be no different, except he'd be stealing pucks from guys he'd played with for years instead of passing to them. He'd played for New York for six years until they'd traded him this summer with one year left on his contract. He'd known the reasons, but it didn't stop him from being pissed about the trade. He'd expected to play the rest of his career in New York, but it was true that no matter your skill level, you were never safe from a trade.

New York had one of the best teams in the league, so he

needed to get his shit in gear. He'd gone to the Playoffs for the last five years with them, and they'd made it to the final round a few years ago. The Strikers—they were a different story. Sure, he was playing on the top line now, when he'd been second—sometimes third—line in New York, but the Strikers had a consistency issue with the Playoffs, missing it for a few years, and being bumped first round last year.

While Stanley was still elusive, Ethan was used to winning and making a deep run in the postseason. Now he'd just be happy for the Strikers to get there. The team looked good this year, but it was still early.

It sucked being traded to a second-tier team, but those were the cards he'd been dealt, and he had to suck it up and help his team to victory, especially tonight. Less than two points wasn't an option.

"I'm good, man," he said, focusing back on the ice. They were working penalty kills. Hopefully, that special team wouldn't spend too much time on the ice tonight. New York currently had the top power play spot, while the Strikers penalty kill was ranked in the middle of the league.

Practice wrapped up, and he headed to the locker room.

"Nervous about tonight? Afraid they'll finally be able to bang you up because you're the enemy now?" Max Bastian, top line defenseman chirped, his French accent still thick even though he'd been playing in the States for almost a decade.

"Funny, Baz. Real funny," Ethan grumbled.

"Don't worry, I'll protect you," Baz said, beating his hands on his chest like an overgrown gorilla—which was a pretty accurate description. Baz had kept his bushy beard for years. It wouldn't surprise Ethan if something was living in that ragged mess.

"Good to know," Ethan said, shaking his head.

"And don't forget to shoot at the right net. You know, since you're on our team now," Connor Horton said, his cheeks flushed as the guys ruffled the kid's hair. Ah, to be a rookie. Still figuring out your place and your chirps.

"I'll keep that in mind, Timmy," Ethan said, before heading to the showers. His determination to prove he belonged here would get him through the game—the season. At some point, his skill and dedication to the game had to overshadow every stupid thing he'd done off the ice.

* * *

"Top line, huh. No one else available?" New York's captain, and Ethan's one time roommate, taunted as Ethan faced off against him at the start of the game.

"Really funny, man. Nice to see you, too," The chirping had started as soon as the teams had hit the ice tonight during the warm-up, a mix of shoulder bumps and heckling were how hockey players showed their affection, and Ethan wouldn't have it any other way. With international play and trades, you always ended up playing with someone you might've hated before. He could only hope that his new teammates felt the same. Bringing home a win tonight would definitely help on that end.

"It's good to see you. I will apologize in advance for kicking your ass tonight," the captain said.

Ethan gripped his stick, the ref held out the puck, and Ethan focused on the small rubberized disk. "We'll see about that," he said, as he dropped his stick to the ice and won the face-off, knocking it back to Cheesy, and then they were skating up the ice toward Ethan's former goalie.

Being on the ice was always a rush, the cool air across his face, his legs pumping as he zeroed in on his goal. Out of the corner of his eye, he caught his old captain trying to snag the puck from his new captain, and he tapped his stick on the ice, letting Cheesy know he was open.

The puck hit his tape and he deked around his former teammates, shooting the puck toward the goal. It clanged off the pipes, but the goalie didn't grab it, so Ethan snagged the rebound and knocked it between the goalie's legs.

The goal horn sounded and his new teammates crashed into him in a bruising hug. Not that he could feel it through all his pads.

"That's right," Sully called out, tapping Ethan's helmet.

"Damn straight," Baz cheered, his hug extra exuberant.

"Great shot," Cheesy said, with a hug and a tap on the helmet.

Ethan didn't fight his grin as he skated up next to his old captain and former roommate. "You were saying?"

His friend laughed. "Nice shot, man. But we're still taking you down."

"We'll see about that," he shot back.

And three hours later, when they'd beaten New York soundly, a painful five to two, Ethan was still grinning as his team cheered around him.

CHAPTER 2

Penny glanced down at the clock on her computer. She needed to get to Robert's office. And she needed to stop thinking about the man who refused to leave her thoughts, with his gorgeous blue eyes and sexy crooked smile. Stupid non-symmetrical smile.

Dammit! Just stop!

She'd escaped home Friday night and brushed off every text from Lexi and Amanda, promising details later. They had questions, but she had no desire to answer them, yet—if ever. Okay, they were her best friends. She'd answer them. Just not yet.

But it was Monday and she worked with Lexi. She was shocked that Lexi hadn't been waiting at Penny's office door at eight on the dot, but Lexi's daughter, Abby, had a doctor's appointment. Penny hoped it was just routine, but she was grateful that Lexi wasn't in yet.

She was still in shock at seeing Ethan. What were the freaking odds? And as a fan of logic problems, she was still trying to puzzle this one together. At least she knew his last name now. She'd googled that shit as soon as she'd made it home. Ethan Harty had turned out to be Ethan Hartnell. Professional hockey player just traded from New York over the summer. Known party boy who'd gotten into more trouble than, apparently, his team thought he was worth.

No thank you.

She'd stared at image after image of him, always with a different—gorgeous—woman. Nope. Definitely not for her. Not that he wanted to be with her.

She pulled herself back to the present. She did not have time for this. Or anything for that matter since she was going to be late to her meeting her with her boss. Robert had hinted at changes coming in the staff meeting this morning, but he'd been vague. She hated vague. It left things open to assumptions and over-analyzations.

She grabbed the hard copy of the Riggs file—she'd already emailed Robert the electronic file—and her tablet, smoothed down her dress, and made her way upstairs to his office.

She gave Jane, Robert's secretary, a smile as Jane told her to go in.

"Penny, come in, come in." Robert Knight waved her toward one of the chairs in his office. "Just one second."

He pressed the intercom on his phone. "Jane, can you let me know when my nephew gets here?"

"Sure." Her response came through the phone.

Robert turned back to Penny. "You wanted to talk about the Riggs file, right?"

She opened the folder, pulling out a few documents. "Yes, I found a few discrepancies that I wanted to review with you before going back to the client."

They spent the next fifteen minutes going over the account. "Great work, Penny. You're always so thorough."

"Thanks." She shuffled the paperwork back into the folder, closing it.

"One other thing. I have a new accountant starting next week and was hoping you would show him the ropes."

"Sure," she replied, trying to hide her frustration. Another new hire to train. She was getting sick of being the go-to girl, stuck as a senior accountant, never moving up.

"Great. Knew I could count on you to help out. And I should mention that it's Alan's son," he said.

She held back her bristle. Great. The other owner's son. Should go well.

"Your nephew is here," Jane buzzed in.

"Please send Ethan in. We're just finishing up," Robert said.

Ethan? She shook her head. Clearly, she was hearing things since he was still on her mind, niggling in the back, berating her for skipping out on him with a note.

"Hey, Uncle Robert." The familiar voice rolled over her. Her heart raced, and her palms started to sweat. No. This was not happening. Oh god, he was her boss's nephew. But he was a professional athlete. Why was he related to her boss? How did she not know this already? She internally shook her head, her thoughts making no sense. Professional athletes had families, too. She just hadn't expected to be working with one of them. Maybe she could get out of the office without actually looking at him.

"Hey, Ethan. Come in. Come in. This is Penny Connor, one of our top accountants." Fuck. So much for escaping.

"Penny?" His tone was filled with shock. Hell, she was shocked, too.

She turned, rising from her chair. Her gaze locked with his, and she didn't miss the question—and irritation—in his gaze. She could really go for that sinkhole right about now. Flustered, she jabbed her hand out. "It's nice to meet you," she said.

He stared at her palm for a split second before engulfing it with his. She would not think about the heat spiraling through her body as their hands met, but she couldn't stop her sharply indrawn breath.

"Nice to *meet* you," he said, squeezing her hand tightly. His expression was blank, and he didn't out her.

"It's so great to have him back on this side of the country," Robert continued as if he couldn't sense the awkwardness flooding his office. "You watch hockey, Penny?"

"Umm. No," she said, tugging her hand free.

"Ethan plays for the Strikers. Just traded a few months ago. First time visiting the office."

"Oh, that's nice." She turned back to Robert, anything to stop looking at Ethan.

"You know. It's funny, actually. The two of you were in Italy around the same time. How crazy would it have been if you'd met?" Robert interjected.

"Yeah, crazy," Ethan whispered, and Penny couldn't resist looking at him again. His gaze held barely banked anger, and a coolness she'd never seen before. And she felt like an asshole.

She swallowed hard. She needed to get out of Robert's office before she embarrassed herself by fessing up to the truth or throwing her arms around Ethan's neck.

Shit. Where had that thought come from? She didn't want to hug him. She wanted to escape, with her dignity intact—well, what was left of it.

"Did I mention that to you before, Penny?" Robert asked.

"No. No, you didn't," she said, finding her voice again. "Well, again, nice meeting you." She stepped back, and hit the door with an *umph*, the doorknob digging into her spine as the Riggs file spilled to the floor. She'd have a bruise there tomorrow. At least she hadn't dropped the tablet. Jesus. She was a mess.

"You okay, Penny?" Robert asked as she dropped down, gathering the papers and shoving them out of order into the folder.

"Yep, fine," she said, rising and pressing the file to her chest, a pathetic armor. "I should get back to work now." With a quick nod to Robert, and a tight smile to Ethan, she escaped Robert's office.

As she left the office, she heard Robert tell Ethan they could leave soon. She walked down the hall, refusing to run. Holy shit, what had just happened? *Deep breaths. Deep breaths.* She repeated the mantra in her head as she briskly walked down the stairs—but not too briskly—that's how accidents happened.

Heavy footsteps sounded behind her, and she knew it was him.

"You're making a habit of running away from me," he said. That stupid voice rolling over her, doing things to her body that it had no right doing. Fuck, this was not going to end well, but he kept popping up in her life, and she had to face him at some point.

She'd just wished it'd be some point in the future—the far-off future.

Karma was an evil bitch.

"Penny, stop."

She paused in her flight and turned to face him, hating the tight line of his lips. Remembering the bright smile that he'd shot her when he'd sat down next to her at that vineyard all those months ago. The crooked grin, that playful laugh—no, that week had been a fantasy, and it was better to push it from her mind.

"Umm, hi, Ethan."

"So, you do remember me?" His tone was irritated, his sharp eyes glaring.

Why the hell had he sought her out if he was just going to sneer at her? Sneer was a harsh word, but his expression was close.

"Of course, I remember you. I'm just in shock. How the hell are you related to my boss? How did I not know you were related to him? How is this happening?" she said, dropping her head, grasping the file closer to her chest.

"I was going to ask you the same thing. And he's my mother's brother, if you want to get technical. We've been estranged." He paused. "Not that I need to explain myself to you."

"No, you don't. Crap, I'm pretty sure I complained about my job to you. This is a disaster. Please don't say anything to him," she said, looking back up at him.

"That's all you can say to me?" he asked.

"I—I'm sorry. My brain isn't fully functioning right now. I'm still in shock."

"You said that already. I'm surprised you don't have a list made up of possible responses for seeing me again." His lips tilted up in the corner, the hint of a smile, before they flattened again.

"Of course I don't have a list. I was never going to see you again." She didn't miss his flinch. She should've made a list. Should've been prepared for anything since running into him the other night—and running away. Plenty of time to make a list.

"That much was obvious when you left me in that hotel room, with a damn note," he gritted out. "And now, here you are, working for my uncle. Hanging out at a bar owned by a guy I've known since I was a kid. How is that possible? The world is not that small."

"Wait? You know Adam, too?" She tightened her grip on her tablet and folder to stop her need to fidget.

"Yes. We went to the same high school. Actually, he'd graduated before I started, but I used to go to the high school hockey games when he was playing."

"Oh, yeah, small world." Her laugh was pained. "Umm, he's best friends with my best friend's boyfriend, and they invited me. Can we not do this here?" she asked, wishing he'd just leave, but seeing that he wasn't, she refused to have this conversation in the hallway, where anyone could walk by. She'd been office gossip fodder for long enough. It was just starting to die down, and she refused to feed the monster anything else.

"I would think you'd want everyone to see that you know your boss's nephew. Pretty sure one of the few things you mentioned about work, when we were in Italy, was that you were due for a promotion," he said. It'd been one of the few things he'd gotten out of her about their real lives. She'd wanted to keep reality off the table, but had let some aspects of her job slip. Too bad she also hadn't mentioned she was an accountant or that she worked for his damn uncle.

He cursed his pride when the color drained from her face. God, he could be an asshole. He blamed it on his shock at seeing her in his uncle's office.

He'd recognized her as soon as he'd walked into Robert's office. Her curls pulled up in a twist, a few strands kissing the neck that he'd lavished attention on in Italy. Her skin softer than any he'd ever touched. His lips tingled to trace along her hairline, and he clenched his jaw.

Fuck. How was she here? What were the goddamn odds of her working for his uncle? Not that he planned to do background checks on women he slept with, but it was something to consider. He'd hadn't thought that through—or anything through in Italy—when he'd found out she lived in his hometown. They may not have exchanged last names, but she'd told him she was from San Francisco the first day he'd met her. At the time he'd had no plans to leave New York, so he'd mentioned having some family there, but said that he hadn't been home in years.

"How can you think that of me?" she gasped.

"I honestly don't know what to think," he said. "Where's your office?"

"A few doors down, but you're not coming into my office," she said. The color was slowly coming back to her face, but she was still pale.

"I want answers…so we can do that here or in your office," he said, unsure of what he wanted. He should turn around and walk back to his uncle. What did it matter that she worked for Robert? It's not like Ethan had plans to visit an accounting firm that often. But he needed to know why she'd skipped out on him. That never happened. Call it ego, or anything you wanted, but he needed answers.

"Follow me," she said, spinning on her heel and heading down the hall.

He should've walked away, but instead he trailed behind her, attempting to ignore the determined swaying of her hips and the tightness in her shoulders. It looked uncomfortable and awkward as hell as she power-walked toward her office. She opened a door and gestured for him to enter, shutting it quickly behind him.

She let out an audible sigh and turned to face him, her tablet and folder still clutched to her chest.

He plucked the armor from her hands and set it on the desk. "Why did you leave?"

"What?"

He dove right in. "That morning. Before I woke up. Why did you leave?"

"It was easier that way," she said softly, her gaze on her hands, her cheeks starting to pink.

"You knew it was our last day. I had more things planned, and I woke up to a note reminding me that check-out was at eleven. Pretty cold, Penny," he said, hating the bitterness in his tone. He'd never let a woman affect him the way she had—well, not in years. He'd been surprised that she had when he'd woken up in the cooling sheets, a crisp folded note on the pillow where her head had been only hours before.

"I'm sorry. It was just supposed to be a fun time, and I didn't want to do the whole sad goodbye where we claim we're going to call each other but never do. I mean, not that you had any intention of it being more than just that week, but…" she trailed off, and he read her loud and clear.

Not that he could fault her. They'd been honest from the beginning. A week of glorious sex, and they would go their separate ways—no phone numbers or last names or forwarding information. But it still stung waking up alone in her damn hotel room. She wasn't supposed to linger in his mind during the rest of his trip in Italy or pop up in his brain when he found out he'd been traded to her hometown. That was not how this was supposed to work. And he was pissed at her and himself for even having those thoughts. Not that he'd let her know about that.

"I can't believe I didn't hear you packing or leaving. It was your room."

She fiddled with her fingers, another sigh slipping past her lips.

"Could you at least look at me?"

Her gaze darted up, and her embarrassment was vivid in her eyes. He just had no clue why she was embarrassed. Was it because of what they'd done? Not that five days of the best sex he'd ever had should be embarrassing.

"I packed everything the last night before you came back to my room."

"Wow. So you knew you were going to bail before we slept together that night. Why didn't you just kick me out of your room when you were done with me?" Jesus, he needed to rein in the bitterness. She couldn't get the better of him, even if the signs blatantly pointed to that being the case.

"That's not why I packed early. I thought it would be easier to be ready to go because I didn't know what you had planned for my last day. I didn't decide to leave that morning until later. I'm so sorry, Ethan. I thought it would be better that way."

Her explanation did not make him feel any better.

"You keep saying that. So, you truly had no idea who I was? That Robert was my uncle?"

She glared at him, standing straighter. "Of course not. I didn't even know you played hockey. I mean, you have all of your teeth," she said.

His laugh was harsh. "Way to stereotype, Penny."

"Sorry. I'm a little flustered. I never thought I'd see you again, and now I've seen you twice in the last week in places I never imagined running into you."

"You've imagined seeing me again?" he asked, unable to stop the question from coming out of his mouth. He was mad at her—pissed —and yet he needed to know. It was ridiculous how she tied him up in knots. He needed to focus on his anger, get his answers, and get the hell out of this enclosed room before he did something insane like grab her and see if her lips were as sweet as he remembered.

Goddamn knots.

"No, I didn't," she said, and he refused to read more into her words. "Now, I do have to get back to work. Robert is probably wondering what happened to you." She inched around her desk, probably wanting the large expanse between them.

"Yes, I should go. And good luck getting that promotion you wanted," he said, turning to leave.

"Umm. Could you not mention to Robert that we know each other?"

"In general or carnally?" He couldn't stop himself, and her cheeks flared red.

"Seriously? Just don't tell him anything. You should go," she said.

"Goodbye, Penny. At least I get to say that this time." He wrenched open the door and stepped out into the hall, her gasp fading as the door shut behind him. The parting jab was unnecessary, but he apparently turned into a vindictive toddler around her. Fuck, he had issues.

He returned to his uncle's office, catching the smirk on Robert's face. "What?" he asked.

"Want to tell me what that was about?"

"What? I just had to run to the bathroom."

Robert chuckled. "Right. The bathroom. You know I'm not a senile old man, right?"

"You are looking a little old," Ethan shot back. Not that Robert looked that old. He was Ethan's mother's younger brother. The man's smirk increased his wrinkles.

Damn. He'd been obvious running after Penny, but she hadn't given him much of a choice.

"Bite your tongue. I'll have you know that I work out five times a week, and I'm in the best shape of my life. I bet I could keep up with you on the ice," Robert said, grinning.

"Yeah. I doubt that, but you're welcome to come to an early morning skate with me," Ethan teased, hoping to steer his uncle away from Ethan's recent disappearing act.

"I'll pass on that. Now, do you want to tell me why you ran out of here?"

"It's nothing. You ready for lunch? I'm starved."

"First time you've visited my office and you're already hitting on my employees?" his uncle said, shaking his head. "That was fast."

"I thought she was someone I'd met before," he replied.

"Thought you said you had to go to the bathroom," Robert said, his brow arched.

"Just drop it," Ethan grumbled. "Now I thought you were taking me to lunch. Can we go?"

"You signed another multi-million-dollar contract, and you won't pay for lunch. Ungrateful nephew," Robert muttered.

"Come on. It's on me, of course."

"Damn straight."

Ethan laughed and followed his uncle out of his office. Of the few family members he tolerated, his uncle was at the top of the list—the very short list.

CHAPTER 3

The tension flowed out of Penny's body as her foot connected with the bag. It felt so energizing to kick something.

"Bad day at work?" Amanda asked as she bounced on the balls of her feet.

"You don't know the half of it."

"Jab, cross, jab!" the instructor yelled from the front of the room.

Penny turned away from Amanda to repeat the move, feeling the power of her punch vibrate through her arms.

Kickboxing always made her feel better. There was just something so relaxing about beating the shit out of the bag. You could imagine anyone's face, and over the years that face had varied. Right now, it was Ethan.

Jab, right between his blue eyes. Eyes that reminded her of the Mediterranean Sea. She took in a shallow breath, willing the memory away.

Cross, right to his gut. But he didn't have a gut. Just a stomach she could do laundry on. Probably because he was a freaking hockey player.

Dammit!

Uppercut, right to his crooked smile. Maybe she could straighten it out. But no, it just laughed back at her.

Uppercut, jab, uppercut, jab. The moves rolled through her head as she continued to punch. Sweat trickled down her back.

"Let's move on to uppercuts," the instructor yelled out.

Hadn't they already been working on uppercuts?

What the hell! Focus Penny, focus. He was ruining her workout.

Today had been a disaster. After he'd left her in her office, her mouth gaping like a fish at his last remark, she'd been useless. Luckily, she'd gotten most of her work done before lunch, but that wasn't the point. He was invading her every thought. Every time she heard a knock on her office door, or a low voice coming down the hall, her heart raced, and her nerves went haywire. She could not function like this.

She growled as she punched the bag again.

She couldn't get a moment's peace, and it was all in her freaking head. She hadn't seen him since that morning in her office, but he hovered over her shoulder. Figuratively, of course. Which was almost worse than literally. She was a damn mess.

She felt the flush travel up her skin, as if he was standing right next to her. Felt his fingertips tracing a line down her back, instead of the sweat currently making the journey down her spine. *Sweat.* Oh, he had made her sweat. Under the hot Tuscan sun. It sounded like such a cliché, she wanted to vomit.

His hands travelling down her body as he'd made love to her over and over again. She could still picture his tongue skating across her skin. A moan crept up her throat, and she shook her head trying to clear it before it escaped through her lips.

"Punch, then a side kick." The perky instructor was at it again. "C'mon ladies. Ten minutes left. Show me what you got," she yelled.

Stop interrupting, Penny wanted to yell back. *I'm having a moment over here.*

An erotic moment that she should have stuffed into the back of her mind, never to be retrieved. She wished she could blame the hot flashes on her kicks, but as soon as she raised her leg, she felt the air conditioning waft over her heated core. And then she remembered how his breath had whispered over her flesh before his tongue had wiped all coherent thoughts from her mind.

Son of a bitch!

She was going to melt into a puddle in the middle of her class in about five seconds. Or maybe in six seconds. Six sounded like sex.

What the hell! She could even make numbers dirty. Numbers were not dirty.

If someone had access to her thoughts they might lock her away. It was like a goddamn tennis match. Back and forth and back and forth. From one end of crazy to the next.

What move were they even on at this point? She quickly glanced around and noticed that the kicks had stopped. Only cross jabs.

Jab, jab, jab. She hit the bag repeatedly, her breath coming in short gasps as she tried to focus on the workout. She stared intently in front of her as she punched, her feet stabilized on the floor. She could feel the vibrations in her shoulder as the bag swayed.

"Whoa," Amanda said.

"What?"

"Why do you look about ready to go a few rounds with something other than that poor bag?"

"It's just been a rough couple of days."

Amanda laughed. "Okay, Sugar Ray, how about we discuss it over Chinese?"

"Chinese? Doesn't that defeat the entire purpose of the workout?"

"We have to replenish the calories we just burned. Do you know nothing about how exercise works?"

"Thank you, Jillian Michaels." Penny rolled her eyes. "I must have missed that article in *Shape* magazine."

"It was the cover story."

"I'm not sure what kind of magical scale you have at home, but I don't think mine works that way. But of course, I'm in. I've been dreaming of Chinese."

"Right," Amanda said slowly, "because that's what it looked like you were thinking of before you started punching the shit out of that bag. Sure you weren't dreaming about Ethan?"

"What?" She froze, and then the bag slammed into her, knocking her back and she lost her footing. Her knee twinged a little as she went down, and she shook her head, glaring at the swinging bag.

"Definitely about Ethan," Amanda said with a grin, as she reached out a hand to help Penny up. "Still can't believe he was at the bar. You know, he darted out after you. I'm assuming he never caught you."

He did? Penny ignored the thrill that rocked through her. No. He'd just wanted to yell at her, which he'd done in glorious fashion earlier today. She was definitely not telling Amanda that right now. She'd fess up over dinner. In the quiet of her own home, where Amanda's outbursts wouldn't be witnessed by strangers.

Penny ignored the proffered hand and got up, swiping at her ass and straightening her shirt. "Leave me alone. I've had a bad week, and today was a nightmare. Can't you just let me work out in peace?"

"Okay. This calls for reinforcements. And we will discuss your behavior or whatever the hell is up your ass over takeout."

"What kind of reinforcements? And will there be wine?" If she was going to suffer through an interrogation, she might as well have a buzz.

"I'm calling Lexi. I'm sure Grant can watch Abby. Obviously, this is an emergency," Amanda said, that stupid grin still in place.

"Don't make a big deal about this," Penny grumbled as they walked back to the locker room, and Amanda quickly grabbed her phone, tapping out a message.

"She'll be at your place in fifteen," Amanda said, clearly proud of herself.

Fuck. Her plans of gorging on carbs and disappearing into a bottle of wine by herself vanished. She refused to pout, but she was not looking forward to this at all.

It was a short walk back to her townhouse, one of the few reasons she used to convince herself to attend the class at least once a week. She needed to ramp it up to at least twice a week, but she had so many legit reasons to skip it. TV, her Kindle, her sweats…all viable motives to stay home.

"Don't you just feel so refreshed?" Amanda asked, as she followed Penny through the front door of Penny's townhouse a few minutes later, and headed for the kitchen.

"Normally yes, but you two are going to grill me, so refreshed isn't exactly what I'm feeling right now," Penny said, grabbing the menu—not that she needed it. It was going to be an orange chicken and rice night. White rice, that was slightly healthier than fried rice, right?

"If you provide us with the info we need then we won't need to grill you. Apparently, more is going on than you've told us, so you're going to fess up. I'll grab the first shower," Amanda said, before heading down the hallway to the bathroom. "Don't forget to order me an eggroll."

"I don't think you deserve an eggroll," Penny muttered, pulling up the restaurant's info on her phone. She quickly placed their order and then plopped down on the couch.

Penny was still trying to figure out how to tell her best friends that the man she'd had crazy rebound sex with was her boss's nephew, when Amanda came back down the hall ten minutes later.

"Your turn."

"Money's on the counter," Penny replied as she escaped to take a quick shower. She focused on thoughts of orange chicken and rice and refused to let Ethan creep into her mind.

"Food's here. And so is Lexi," Amanda yelled just as Penny made her way back into the living room ten minutes later. "Now, what is going on?"

"Yes. What is going on with you? Is it Ethan? Did you track him down?" Lexi asked.

Penny put her wet curls up into a clip. "Can I make up my plate first? I'm famished."

Amanda laughed. "Of course. You definitely worked up an appetite. I can't remember the last time you were so energetic in class. But be quick about it, no stalling."

As Penny filled her plate, Amanda and Lexi settled around the coffee table.

"Is this going to cut it, or do we need something stronger?" Amanda asked, holding up a bottle of wine.

"I hope not, and I do have to work tomorrow. Wine should be fine."

"Okay." Amanda filled her own plate, snatching up an egg roll.

"You know you can have mine," Penny said.

"I don't know why you don't like these. They're so good."

Penny wrinkled her nose. "No thanks. Too much green stuff inside." She really wasn't a fan of vegetables.

"Just tastes like fried yummy goodness to me. Your loss. Anyway. So, what's going on?"

"With what?" She knew she shouldn't stall.

"Umm, with you beating the shit out of that bag tonight. You getting flustered when I mentioned Ethan. I know you've been holding out on us, and that hurts, Penny," Amanda said, feigning pain.

"I'm just a little frustrated."

"So, spill. You get me for at least an hour and then I should probably head home. Grant is great with Abby, but I don't want to miss bedtime," Lexi said, and Penny's chest squeezed.

"I'm so happy for you, Lexi. Grant is amazing," Penny said. It'd only been four months since Lexi had gotten her shit together and worked everything out with Grant, and Penny wanted that. The love in their eyes whenever they saw each other or talked about each other. She'd thought she'd had that with Michael. That was a lie. She knew she hadn't had that. But she'd thought they'd be happy together, until it had come crashing down around her. Shit, her life had done that a few times in the last few months.

"Yes, he's amazing. Now stop stalling and spill your guts," Lexi said.

"Yes, you blew us both off about Ethan, and we want to know what is going on," Amanda chimed in.

She had to stop stalling. They were her friends—her best friends. They'd been there to pick her up off the floor—literally, at her bachelorette party, and Amanda still offered, almost daily, to run Michael over with her car.

She'd tried to put her life back in order after she'd returned from Italy, but things were still strained with her family. And Michael. He needed to stop trying to get in touch with her. She'd spoken with him when she'd returned from Italy, telling him it was over. But he still called. And called.

And then there was Ethan. Fuck, this was a nightmare. She pinched herself, but the only result was a bruise on her arm and a reality she didn't want to face. When Amanda and Lexi had picked her up from the airport, she'd looked like a puffy, messy fright from all her crying. They'd consoled her over comfort food and wine that night, assuming she'd still been upset about

Michael, which had angered them even more. Their shock when she'd told them about Ethan almost made her chuckle. Not that she'd told them everything.

"So, um, yes, that was Italian Ethan and, funny story, he's pissed because we didn't really say goodbye. I kind of left him a note saying thanks for a good time and that check-out was at eleven," she said, shoving a piece of orange chicken in her mouth, munching away like nothing was wrong. Until this moment, she'd kept that little nugget from her friends, and she held back her laugh as they both gaped at her.

"Seriously?" Lexi asked, dropping her fork.

"Wow. That's kind of brutal, Penny. I'm sort of impressed," Amanda said.

"Amanda, really? You're impressed?" Lexi asked.

"She was sad and finally threw caution—and her lists, most likely—to the wind and had some fun. She needed it," Amanda said.

"I agree, but that note might've been a bit much. You really said that check-out was at eleven?" Lexi asked, shaking her head.

"I sent him room service to soften the blow," Penny said, playing with her wine glass. Yeah, it hadn't been her finest moment, but she'd panicked. She did that a lot around him.

Amanda chuckled. "Baller move, Penny. So not like you."

"You know I felt bad. You saw me come off that plane. I just didn't know what to do about him, so I bolted instead of talking to him," Penny said.

"Which is exactly what you did when you saw him in the bar," Lexi said.

"I know. Ethan said the same thing today."

"Today?" Amanda asked.

"You saw him again? Today?" Lexi asked.

"So, another funny story. He's Robert's nephew."

"Robert? Like our boss, Robert?" Lexi asked, her eyes wide.

"Umm. Yes," Penny stuttered.

"No, that's not possible. How is that possible?" Lexi asked.

"Yes, how the hell is that possible?" Amanda piped in. "Wow. Fate is freaking crazy."

"I wouldn't call it fate. Just horrible, horrible bad luck," Penny grumbled.

"So how did you see him?" Lexi asked.

"I was in Robert's office earlier today, and Ethan walked in to take his *uncle* out to lunch."

"Oh shit," Amanda said.

"Oh shit, is right. When Robert introduced us, I claimed not to know Ethan and then Robert joked about how we'd both been in Italy at the same time and wouldn't it be funny if we'd run into each other."

"Oh crap."

"It's not funny," Penny said, glaring at Amanda, while Lexi just stared, her mouth hanging open.

"Damn. I can't believe I missed seeing him. And, wow. What are the odds?" Lexi said.

"I'll tell you what the odds are. They should've been freaking minimal, like non-existent," Penny bit out, knocking back the rest of her wine and holding out her empty glass to Lexi. "Load me up. I need it."

"Yeah you do," Amanda said between chuckles.

"This is not funny," Penny grumbled.

"Then what happened?" Lexi asked.

"I escaped, and he followed me. Started asking me questions and accusing me of knowing who he was when we were in Italy. I stupidly talked about my frustrations at not being promoted a few times. I had no idea he was related to my boss. Jesus. How the hell could this happen?"

"Wait. He accused you of knowing who he was? What, that you slept with him so he'd put in a good word for you with

Robert? That's ridiculous," Lexi said, sitting up straighter, her anger apparent.

"That bastard. How dare he," Amanda said.

"I set him straight on that and asked him to leave. He made a parting jab that he finally had the chance to say goodbye to me, right before he slammed my door. What if he tells Robert?"

"Hopefully he won't. Honestly, he sounds hurt," Lexi said.

"Oh please. I'm sure it's just his pride. He's basically a celebrity. I googled him and he always has a new girl on his arm. Who would skip out on a star hockey player, *player* being the correct term. Hopefully he's not vindictive, but I have no idea. I'm dreading tomorrow. What if he shows up again?"

"Then you ping me, and I'll rush to your office and kick him out," Lexi said.

"I can't believe this is happening," Penny said, shaking her head.

"We'll figure it out. And I doubt that he'll show up at the office that much. The season started two months ago, and this is the first time you've seen him, so he probably doesn't stop in to take Robert to lunch all that often," Lexi said.

"I hope you're right."

Penny dug back into her orange chicken. She didn't want to talk about Ethan anymore, let alone think about him. He was a wild card she hadn't planned on and that freaked her the hell out.

"I'm grabbing the first round," Colin O'Sullivan said Wednesday night when they walked into Byrne's.

"Damn straight you are," Baz said. "Your pull-up performance was weak today."

"Yeah, yeah. You edged me out by one, but a bet is a bet," Sully said, making his way toward the bar.

They had two nights off, after playing—and winning—back-to-back games. Morning practice had been pushed back a few hours, so Ethan had agreed to a few drinks with some teammates. He should've known they'd head to Adam's bar.

The scene of the incident.

He would not look around the room to see if Penny was here. No. Absolutely not. And he would not think about running into her at his uncle's office earlier this week. What were the fucking odds of that? He was still having trouble processing that one. And he still felt like an ass for accusing her of knowing who he was in Italy. Her shock had been as clear as the glass around the rink when she'd seen him for the first time since Italy in this very bar last week.

His gut reaction had been to accuse, and he wasn't proud of that. Or his parting shot in her office. Usually, he wasn't a disaster like this. Fuck. Why did she throw him so off balance?

"So is she here?" Sully asked, when he brought over their drinks.

"Is who here?" Baz asked, quickly scanning the bar.

"That girl from last week. The one who ran out of here when she saw you," Sully said.

"Why am I just hearing about this? You chase another girl off, Hartless?" Baz asked.

Fuck. He hated that nickname. He'd been hoping to leave it in New York. Most guys called him Harty, but Hartless came out whenever his dating life did. It's not like he set out to hurt anyone. Every woman he dated knew the score going in. And he really didn't want to talk about Penny with the guys. He was still trying to figure out what to do with the fact that she worked for his freaking uncle.

"Ah, yeah. Ran into some girl I dated. It was nothing," he said, trying to brush it off. "So, last night's game was awesome. I think we're really gelling as a team."

"Nope. You're hiding something, and it sounds like it's a doozy," Baz said.

He never should've agreed to come out tonight. Especially to this bar. He didn't want to think about Penny, but he'd spend all night looking over his shoulder. Why did she do this to him? Her ditching him in Italy and bolting every time he'd seen her since should make her feelings and intentions clear. She wanted nothing to do with him.

He refused to believe that was why he was interested. But it had to be. He'd rarely pursued anything that wasn't a sure thing.

The whole situation was insane. Shit. This was a disaster.

"Hey, Hartless, give it up already and fill me in," Baz said. Ethan glared at the guy. He was the worst gossip on the team, and Ethan had no desire to give him any fodder.

"She's just some girl I met over the summer before I moved here. Didn't expect to see her again. No crazy story." Had that come out as nonchalant as he'd hoped?

"Looked like a lot of drama to me," Sully said.

Ethan shrugged. "Just shock. Nothing more."

"Not sure I'm buying what you're selling," Baz said.

"Not sure I care. Now, doesn't Sully owe us drinks?" Ethan asked, trying to change the focus away from him.

"Did you know she lived here?" Sully asked.

"Yes. Just didn't plan on seeing her again."

Baz laughed. "Hartless probably broke her heart. Not nice, Hartless. Not nice."

"She looked pretty shocked to see you," Sully said.

"Yeah. So, did we come here to drink or gossip?" Ethan asked. He'd given up the pretense of being subtle.

"You have much to learn, my boy. We can do both, but I'll let you off the hook for right now because I'm a nice guy. Although

I make no promises after a few beers," Baz said, with a loud laugh. "Sully, go grab a round."

"I wonder if Adam knows her. I should ask," Sully said, a grin on his face.

Ethan glared. "How about no."

"Are you sure? Maybe she's a regular," Sully said.

Ethan bit back his groan, refusing to give up any more information. They didn't need to know that Ethan could find Penny any time he wanted to. He just wouldn't be inviting the guys to lunch with Robert any time soon. Not that lunch with his uncle was a normal occurrence, even if he'd made plans to do just that in a few days.

"You don't need to do that," Ethan said.

"He who doth protest too much, or some shit," Baz said, his grin wide.

"Doth protest? Who says that?"

"I'm hooking up with a grad student. She's studying Shakespeare or something," Baz said.

"Wow. So, she's slumming it with you," Ethan teased.

"I'm very intelligent behind my rough exterior," Baz said, running a hand down his long beard. At least the guy had put all his teeth back in tonight.

"So, Sully, how about those beers?" Ethan asked.

"On it. Baz, if you get anything out of him, I expect a full report," Sully said before heading to the bar.

"You two are like gossipy old hens," Ethan muttered.

"Old hens? Who says that?" Baz barked out.

His grandmother used to say that. Man, he missed her. She would've loved Penny. He paused. Where the ever-loving fuck had that come from? Yep, he was a mess.

"What did I miss?" Sully said, breaking into Ethan's downward spiral a few minutes later.

"I think we've lost him again to the girl who doesn't mean anything," Baz said, and Ethan glared at both of them, snagging a beer from Sully's hand and gulping down half the pint.

"You good?" Sully asked.

"Just thirsty."

"So, I think we should play a game," Baz said.

Ethan eyed his teammate warily. "What kind of game?" He heard his fair share of stories about Baz and the man's pranks and games that never went well for anyone aside from Baz.

"We need to get you out of your doldrums after being bailed on by the mystery woman," Baz teased.

"This probably isn't going to end well," Sully said, echoing Ethan's thoughts.

"Probably not," Ethan grumbled.

"Come on. Have some fun. You clearly need it," Baz said. "How long has it been since you've had any fun? Wait…when was the last time you got any?"

"I've been busy. It's been a crazy few months, the trade, moving, the start of the season," Ethan said, surprised he hadn't ticked that list off on his fingers. That was something Penny would've done. He bit back his smile. Her love of lists was epic. He'd invaded her lunch in Siena, the day after their vineyard meeting. She'd been nibbling on gelato as she flipped through her heavily flagged guide book. The pink bits of plastic on almost every page.

He'd watched her remove a pink flag as she walked up the steps to the church, and he hadn't been able to stop himself from asking.

She'd told him that after she visited a landmark or museum, she removed the flag. That her goal was to remove every flag before she went home. How else would she have known she'd succeeded in seeing everything?

It was oddly adorable, and he'd offered to help her clear that book. They'd started with the cathedral in Siena and visited every museum she'd flagged over the following days. It'd been the start of an unforgettable week. One that had ended with her bailing. She'd removed the last flag that final afternoon so he should've seen it coming. Fuck. It wasn't supposed to sting.

"Ethan, you in?" Sully asked.

"What?"

Baz laughed. "He was thinking about her again. That glazed look is a dead giveaway."

"Screw you, man. No, I wasn't."

"There he goes, doth protesting again," Baz said, wiggling his brows at Ethan's glare.

"Whatever. So, what's this stupid game?" Ethan asked.

"A game of numbers. And how many you can get," Baz said.

"I'm passing the Hartless nickname over to you," Ethan said.

"Stop pouting and stalling. You playing this game, or not?" Baz asked.

"You haven't explained it yet," Ethan said.

"There seem to be some good pickings here tonight," Baz said.

"And…" Ethan trailed off, not trusting Baz's grin.

"The game is two parts. First, the last guy to get a number has to take a shot and buy the next round," Baz said.

Okay, that was no biggie.

"And you can't tell her you're a hockey player, and if she guesses and gives you her number, it doesn't count," Baz continued. "And if she guesses you're a hockey player, you have to also do a shot."

"These shots keep adding up," Ethan said.

Baz smirked. "Only if you lose."

"Practice could suck tomorrow, but I'm in," Sully said.

"Fine," Ethan muttered, already thinking of ways to knock back a few loser shots and escape home, without the guys razzing the hell out of him. Odds of Ethan succeeding on that front were basically nil.

"I'll be back." Baz said in his best Schwarzenegger impression, which really wasn't all that bad, as he headed into the crowd.

Ethan finished his beer, and grabbed another one. This was not going to end well. But at least they weren't talking about Penny anymore. Shit. And there went his plans of not thinking about her.

CHAPTER 4

Penny skimmed through a few emails Thursday morning. She had a full day, and the new accountant was going to sit with her shortly. It'd been over a week since she'd run into—and away from—Ethan in this very building. Dammit. She didn't want to think about him, but she couldn't stop the panic. Her heart raced at every deep and vaguely familiar voice she heard in the hall outside her office this week. And then she chastised herself because he had no reason to be at her office, on her floor, especially since Robert's office wasn't even on her floor. Shit. She needed to put Ethan behind her.

The ringing of her desk phone jerked her out of her thoughts, and she picked it up before checking the caller ID.

"Good morning, this is Penny Connor."

"I can't believe you finally picked up."

Of all the times to not look at her caller ID. She'd barely spoken to Michael after Italy. She'd moved on within a week of her return and never looked back.

"I told you not to call me," she bit out.

"I wanted to see how you're doing. I miss you."

"Why are you calling me, Michael?"

"Can't I call to check up on someone I care about?" he asked. He was laying it on thick.

"Care about?" she scoffed. "Why are you really calling me?"

"I miss you and wanted to talk."

"You already said that, but we have nothing to say to each other." She squeezed the bridge of her nose.

"We had over five years together, and you're going to just end it?"

"It was seven years. And I believe you screwing your boss one week before our wedding ended it," her voice rose.

"It was a mistake. You'd just been so busy with the wedding, and I was so lonely," he whined.

"You're unbelievable. Are you trying to blame me for the fact that you couldn't keep it in your pants?" she said through clenched teeth. "You really are a fucking asshole, you know that?" It felt so good to say that.

"Penny, please."

"No. You don't miss me. You're calling me because you want me to convince my father that you aren't a douchebag so you can make partner. You selfish bastard. As if I would ever do that."

"That has nothing to do with why I'm calling. I'm so sorry about what happened. It will never happen again. I still love you."

She snorted. "How the hell can you say that you still love me? You slept with another woman. With your boss."

"It was a mistake, and I promise it will never happen again. Have dinner with me tonight?"

"Are you insane? Absolutely not. It's over. Stop calling me." He could whine and apologize and promise never to hurt her again, but she wasn't buying it. Even though her parents had asked her to not be hasty in calling off the wedding, her father was still pissed at the drama and embarrassment Michael and

Veronica had caused. While he'd been unable to punish Veronica since she was already a managing partner, Penny's father had stalled Michael's road to partnership. Penny guessed that was his way of being supportive, even if he hadn't initially supported her decision to call off her wedding.

"Do not call me again," she bit out, hoping she wasn't yelling loudly enough to be heard outside of her office. She slammed the phone down, cursing her racing heart. For someone she thought she'd loved and was planning to spend the rest of her life with, he really pissed her the hell off.

She felt like an idiot every time she thought about Michael. In the last few months, she'd started remembering times where he hadn't been honest with her, or how he'd been cagey toward the end. How had she not seen it?

Because she hadn't wanted to see it. Michael was the perfect fit, the logical choice. While she would never work for her father, like her parents wanted, Michael would. He would be an extension of her and make her parents happy that the business would continue in the family.

She turned back to her computer, ignoring her phone as it rang again, her spreadsheets calling out to her. Numbers always made her happy. Sweet, dependable, rational numbers. No emotion, just straightforward calculations. She smiled and pulled up the next account. At the end of the day, numbers were numbers, and they didn't sleep around or piss you off by honing in and exploiting your weaknesses.

* * *

"Come in," Penny said, just after lunch, when there was a knock on her door. She was calmer. Numbers that added up correctly did that for her.

"Hi Penny," Robert said as he entered her office with a man she didn't recognize. This must be the new employee she was supposed to train. Alan's son. "I wanted to officially introduce you to Kevin."

She rose from her seat, stretching out her hand. "Hello, and welcome aboard. It's nice to meet you." He grasped her hand, giving it a quick shake before releasing his grip and offering a wide smile as his eyes roved down her body. Great. A creep. Exactly what she needed after the morning she'd had.

"It's very nice to meet you," he replied. He was tall and lean, and his expensive suit hung off his broad shoulders. He was good looking and he knew it.

"Penny is one of our top senior accountants and is a wealth of information. Any questions you have, she will be able to answer," Robert said. Penny puffed up at his confidence in her. It felt good to be valued, even if she was stuck in the same position.

"Thank you, Robert. And yes, I am here for any questions you may have," she said, smiling at both men.

"Kevin is all set up in the system so I thought he could shadow you for a few weeks, and we will slowly start to give him clients. If you could oversee the accounts for at least the first month and then we can evaluate and hopefully send him off on his own," Robert said.

"Of course," she replied.

"I will let you two get acquainted, and I look forward to having you with the company, Kevin," Robert said.

"Thank you, Robert," Kevin said before Robert left the office.

"You can pull a chair over, and we can get started," she said as she gestured to one of the chairs in front of her desk.

"Sure," he said as he moved the chair, and they both sat down.

"Why don't you tell me your background and then I'll have a better idea of where to start."

"Sure. I got out of college a few years ago. I've worked for a few of those tax prep firms since it always came so easy to me. And now I'm here. Dad wanted me to learn the ropes." He sprawled out in his chair, hands behind his head as he watched her.

Two seconds in and he was already throwing around his connection. This was going to go well.

"Right. Alan is your father. Okay. How about I just go through my normal day and a few files and if you have any questions, let me know." And then she'd bang her head on her desk as soon as she was alone. This guy had zero actual experience and was the owner's son. A cushy job for a kid that probably had no business sense. Entitlement at its finest.

It was unfair for her to judge him that quickly, but she had a feeling it was going to be a long day.

* * *

A few hours later, Penny was grateful that the day was over and she hadn't given in to jamming a pen in her eye. Although, she'd thought about it repeatedly as he'd continually asked the same questions. She shoved a notepad in front of him and suggested he take notes, but he'd said he was a terrible note taker and much better at hands on. That statement had been followed by a leering look at her cleavage again. And then she'd contemplated sticking a pen in his eye.

Probably wouldn't have gone over well with the boss. *His father.*

"Did you have any questions?" she asked as she shifted away from him, and collected the papers scattered on her desk from the last file they'd reviewed.

"Would you like to go out for a drink?"

She swiveled back. "I'm sorry. What?"

"Come have a drink with me. So we can get to know each other even more. You know, like co-workers bonding," he said, his eyes focused on her mouth. She willed away the need to squirm.

"I'm sorry, but no thank you," she said as politely as possible.

"Are you single?"

"Not that it's any of your business, but yes, I am."

"So, have a drink with me?"

"It's the middle of the week and I do not date co-workers."

"It's not a date. Just drinks." And the way he was looking at her, possibly more. He skeeved her out.

"No thank you," she said.

"Your loss," he replied as he pushed back from his chair and walked toward the door. "See you tomorrow."

"Can't wait," she mumbled as the door shut behind him, and she banged her head on the desk.

"Ready for lunch?" Ethan said as he popped his head into his uncle's office the following day.

"Sure," Robert said, his questioning eyes matched his earlier tone when Ethan had called to extend the invitation.

What? He couldn't grab lunch with his favorite uncle? And of course he'd swing by the office to meet him first. He hadn't missed the humor in Robert's voice when Ethan had offered to swing by the office first, and not wait for his uncle at the restaurant down the street.

"Great. There's this new sports pub that opened down the street a few months ago. Byrne's," Robert said.

Of course he'd recommend that place. The site of Baz's terrible numbers game from the other night. The game that Ethan had soundly lost. He'd taken the ribbing, but trolling for numbers no longer held any appeal. He knew why, he just wasn't ready to give it a name yet. But she had one. And he wasn't sure how he felt about that.

"Sounds good," Ethan said as they made their way down the stairs to the first floor. He turned the corner and bumped into someone. The familiar soft floral scent wrapped around him, and he knew exactly whose shoulders he now gripped.

"Penny," he whispered. She looked up with shock before stumbling back.

"Oh, I'm so sorry. Ethan, right?" Why did it sting that they were still playing this game? He shouldn't care. He was supposed to be mad at her.

"Yes. Penny, right?" He felt like an idiot since he'd already whispered her name, but hopefully his uncle hadn't heard him. He stepped back, letting his hands linger on her arms before he released her. Pink suffused her cheeks, and he ached to lean down and kiss her. He needed to stifle that ache. It had no place here. Or anywhere, for that matter.

"Yes. Sorry for bumping into you."

"That's okay. No harm done," he replied.

"Penny, how's it going with Kevin?" his uncle asked. Ethan caught a glimmer of irritation in her eyes before she masked it. Who the hell was Kevin?

"Fine," she quickly replied.

"I know you'll do a great job training him," Robert replied.

"Thank you. I'll do my best," came her tight reply, before she plastered a smile on her face. Now he really wanted to know about Kevin.

"I know you will. You always do," Robert said.

"Well, I should let you both get to lunch. Nice seeing you again, Ethan."

He almost blurted out the pleasure was all his, but he resisted. "No harm done. Nice to see you again, Penny." He might've lingered on her name, hoping for a reaction, but she gave them one last smile before skirting around them and heading down the hall.

Ethan wanted to turn and watch her walk away, but his uncle would definitely notice that, so he kept his gaze straight ahead as he followed Robert out of the building.

"Still surprised by your invitation. Not that I don't want to have lunch with you, but shouldn't you be carb-loading with the team? Big game tonight, right?" Robert asked after they got a table and placed their order at Byrne's.

Ethan itched to ask questions of his own. About Penny. And this Kevin guy she visibly wasn't a fan of, but he held back.

"I eat with them all the time. Can't I have lunch with my favorite uncle? You're the only family I see at this point," Ethan said.

"Have you talked to them since you've been back? It's been over three months since you moved home," Robert said.

"Not really, and I haven't seen them. Ally will be home on winter break soon, so I'll have to swing by then." And he was dreading his sister coming home from college. He wouldn't be able to brush off his family anymore. It'd been years since he'd been home. He'd paid for Ally to come out and visit him, which had been much easier once she was in college, but he'd steered clear of the city, only returning when his previous team played the Strikers.

He was over what his ex had done, but what he couldn't get past was his family, and playing nice with all of them was not on his list of necessities. He'd have to make a concerted effort to fix that since he was back home and excuses of being too busy and living on the other side of the country weren't going to fly now that they shared a zip code. Especially when Ally graduated in the spring. Unless he was traded again. Not that he wanted that. He was starting to find a flow with his teammates.

"I know it's rough. And the decisions they made, I vehemently disagreed with, but that was years ago. They miss you," Robert said. "You're not still hung up on Julie, are you?"

"Definitely not. She wasn't the one for me, and I've known that for years. But it still doesn't mean that I'm happy for them, after everything that happened," he said.

"I don't blame you for that, at all. But maybe grab dinner with your parents. Test the waters. Invite them to a game."

"I probably should. I'm surprised Ally hasn't demanded season tickets," Ethan said, and smiled, thinking about his hockey-crazed sister.

Robert laughed. "She might have mentioned it a few times to me since she found out you were coming home. Thought she'd hit you up for a handful of games and work her way up to the season. Especially if she stays here after graduation."

Ethan wished his sister would've just come out and asked for the full season. She shouldn't have to work her way up to asking him. He'd gladly hand them over. Their relationship had been strained until she'd gone to college, since he'd refused to come home. He was a horrible older brother, but he had his reasons.

"I'll let her sweat it out since she hasn't asked yet," Ethan said. He hadn't seen Ally since before he was traded. She'd already been back at school when he'd moved home. "And yes, we are playing Dallas tonight. They're top in the Conference right now, and they're freaking fast," Ethan said. The team had spent a couple hours this morning watching the last two Dallas games before they'd had their morning skate. The Strikers were just outside the playoff standings, but it was early December. Typically, the teams in the playoff spots now would be the teams that actually made it to the playoffs in April. Ethan was determined to get the Strikers in, so grabbing two points tonight was a necessity.

"You'll beat them, and I have no doubt that you'll turn the team around," Robert said.

"We better win. We need those points." Ethan's chest tightened. It was a foreign feeling, having a family member's support, but his uncle had always been there for him. He'd missed seeing him on a regular basis. One of the other perks of moving back to California.

* * *

An hour later, Ethan said goodbye to his uncle outside the restaurant. He would not follow him back to the office. Not search for the halo of blonde curls and hope he accidently crashed into her again.

He should still be pissed, brush her off, and never see her again, but all he wanted to do was talk to her, touch her. While it still irked him that she'd bailed without a real goodbye, they weren't supposed to be more than a fling. And the fact that she'd said it would've been too hard to say goodbye to him did things to his gut that he wasn't ready to acknowledge.

CHAPTER 5

The cool air seeped through her jacket as the players whizzed past her, and she looked for number twenty-two. Why she'd agreed to come to the game with Lexi and her family, she had no idea. Lexi hadn't even had to try that hard to get Penny to use the extra ticket they magically seemed to have. She wasn't buying that Grant got an extra one by accident. She didn't even like hockey. Well, to be fair. she didn't understand it. Maybe she could like it.

For now, she couldn't figure out what to focus on. They moved so fast and every time she spotted number twenty-two, he was gone before she realized it. Not that she was looking for him. Not that she was waiting for him to notice her. Why couldn't they have seats in the nose bleeds? Why did their seats have to be three rows from the glass, next to the penalty box, where she could stare across the ice at the player's benches and hope Ethan never spotted her?

She hadn't seen him since bumping into him, literally, at her office last week. The heat of his touch still burned in her skin. Her shiver had nothing to do with the crisp air in the arena. God, she wanted him to touch her again. Shit. She shouldn't have these thoughts. She couldn't have anything with him. Aside from being her boss's nephew, he was also an elite athlete. Always in the spotlight, for both good and bad reasons—mostly bad—and she had no desire to draw attention to herself. She had seen the pictures.

"Did you see that pass to *Ethan?*" Lexi asked. Penny cringed at the emphasis on his name. At least Lexi had stopped calling him Italian Ethan.

"How can you focus on anything? I don't know where to look," Penny said, ignoring the pointed question.

"You look at the puck. You know, that black disc flying across the ice. That's where all the action is," Lexi said, laughter clear in her voice.

Penny rolled her eyes. "Thank you, Captain Obvious. But there's so much going on, that when I try to find the puck, it's already gone."

Lexi chuckled. "It gets easier the more games you go to. You should ask Ethan for season tickets. I bet he'd give them to you. And did I see him at the office again this week?"

Penny kept her focus on the ice, kept her expression neutral. Why did it sting that he'd been to the office and hadn't stopped in to see her? Not that he had a reason to stop by her office. He had probably just swung by to have lunch with Robert. She didn't want him to seek her out. She shouldn't want him to seek her out. He should want nothing to do with her after how she left him in Italy. Not one of her most shining moments.

"He was? Probably just having lunch with Robert," she said, her gaze trailing after Ethan as he skated up the ice, the puck on his stick. Her heart was in her throat as he moved around the other players, his speed and agility impressive, moving the puck in and out of the legs of the other team, in complete control.

Fuck. That was hot as hell. His control and determination reminded her of the control she'd gladly given him in bed in Italy. His precise focus as he shot the puck at the net and scored a goal turned her on more than it should, and she feared she would bring the temperature of the arena down a few degrees with the heat boiling inside of her.

She shot out of her seat and clapped, the sirens and music at decibel piercing levels, popcorn and beer spilling from containers as everyone jumped up and cheered along with her.

Lexi leaned in and whispered, "The hug is my favorite part."

"What?"

"The hug. They slam into each other with such excitement. If I didn't have Grant, I'd totally be on board with being in the middle of that. I wouldn't even care about the sweat."

"I heard that," Grant muttered beside her.

Penny grinned, watching her friend turn to give her boyfriend a blinding smile.

"You know I love hugs. Especially when you're giving them," Lexi said, snaking an arm around Grant's waist.

He brushed a kiss to the top of her head. "You definitely don't want to be in the middle of that sweaty mess down there."

"Of course not," Lexi said. She turned back to Penny and whispered, "So hot."

Penny bit back her chuckle and focused on the ice. Ethan was wrapped in a hug with his other teammates. Back slaps all around and she caught his grin. Dammit. She was in more trouble than she wanted to admit. God, why was he traded to San Francisco? She was never supposed to see him again. That had been the only reason she'd snuck out of that hotel room with just a note. Fate was laughing her ass off at this one.

Penny sunk back in her seat as the players skated back to center ice. Ethan wasn't on the ice at the moment, and she craned her neck, spotting him on the bench, talking to the guy next to him, a smile still stretched across his face.

* * *

Penny settled back in her seat, pretzel in hand, for the start of the third period. The Strikers were down three to two. Grant grumbled about too many bad penalties and that they needed their stuff in gear—he'd started to say *shit*, but Lexi's glare had him stumbling over his words since Lexi's daughter, Abby, currently seated beside him, liked to hang on his every one.

Penny took a bite of her pretzel, just as the boards rattled in front of her, and she found herself staring into Ethan's intense gaze. Her mouth opened, the bite of pretzel tumbling out of her mouth and into her lap.

She held back her squeak and wrapped the slightly chewed pretzel piece into her napkin. Well, that was attractive. Her cheeks heated as the shock in his eyes quickly faded. He grinned back at her, and then shoved another player to the side, his stick jabbing at the ice.

He ducked his head down, pushing the other guy one last time, and then he was off, skating toward the opposing team's goalie. Holy hell, he was fast.

"Wow. He knows you're here now," Lexi said, laughing.

Penny glared at her friend, and took another bite of her pretzel. This time, she successfully swallowed the carby goodness before responding. "You are *not* funny."

"And the heat in that stare." Lexi pulled back, fanning her face. "I'm surprised the ice didn't melt. Those eyes. Whoa."

"I'm starting to get jealous over here," Grant said.

"Oh stop. I was referring to how he looked at Penny."

"Right," Grant drew out.

"You know I love you and your eyes the most. They are super yummy. Like chocolate," Lexi said, patting Grant's arm as he muttered something about Lexi only loving him for cake.

"You better not forget that, or I'll tell my mom to stop dropping off tiramisu," he said, grinning at them.

"You wouldn't dare," Lexi gasped. "Now, can we focus on Penny?"

"How about we not? I want to hear more about Grant's chocolate eyes," Penny said, biting back her chuckle. "I just picture Lexi trying to eat your face."

Grant's eyes darkened, and Lexi choked on a laugh. Penny knew her cheeks were a brilliant red. Well, that was awkward.

"Umm. So, anyway. I hope they get another goal," Penny said, focusing back on the ice just as a whistle blew.

"Dammit, your boy just took a penalty. Minnesota better not score on this power play," Grant yelled.

"He's not my boy," Penny whisper-yelled. "And what did he do?" she asked, watching Ethan argue with the ref as he skated toward the penalty box. The one she was a few seats away from.

"Two minutes for slashing," a voice carried over the loud speaker, and it was met with angry shouts and pointing fingers from members of the crowd who apparently disagreed with the call. She had no idea what a *slash* was, so she settled back in her seat and focused on her half-eaten pretzel.

She gazed at him under hooded eyes as he skated into the penalty box and sat down, anger clear on his face. She looked up at the jumbotron suspended above the ice and focused on Ethan. He propped his stick against the door and lifted his jersey to wipe his face, his gorgeous abs glistening for all the world to see—and looking massive on the large screen, a full six pack that she vividly remembered tracing with her tongue. She squirmed in her seat.

"Wow," Lexi whispered. "That's impressive."

"I'm still sitting here," Grant grumbled. Penny tried not to laugh, fearing what sound would come out since her heart was racing in her throat, and she was having difficulty breathing.

"It's impressive that he doesn't wear Under Armour under his pads. Wouldn't that chafe?" Lexi asked, but Grant wasn't buying it, if his snort was anything to go by.

Penny tore her gaze away from the large screen now that

he'd covered his impressiveness back up and took another bite of her pretzel.

"I think he's trying to get your attention," Lexi said, nudging her again.

"I'm sure he's not," Penny said, refusing to look in Ethan's direction.

"He's tapping the glass. Just look at him already."

Penny turned toward the penalty box, cursing their seats again. Cursing herself for agreeing to come to the game when she knew that she should avoid him for more reasons than just the fact that he was her boss's nephew. Or how he'd wormed his way into her heart and her head in Italy.

When she finally looked at him, he grinned and mouthed, "Hi." His helmet was off, and he raked a hand through his sweat drenched hair. Her fingers already itched to touch him again.

"Hi," she mouthed back, knowing that he wouldn't hear her over the loud sounds and music echoing through the arena. Who knew hockey games were so musical? How did the players even think with the loud rock music blasting?

Conversation wasn't possible, so they stared at each other for another thirty seconds before he put his helmet back on, took another swig from the communal water bottle—she tried not to skeeve out about that—and with one last tap of his stick on the side of the penalty box in her direction, he was back on the ice, snagging the puck and heading toward the net, while she was still trying to catch her breath.

"Oh my God," Lexi exclaimed as Ethan shot the puck to the back of the net, and tied the game.

"Two goals so far tonight. You might be Harty's good luck charm," Grant shouted, as the arena shook with excitement. "Maybe he'll get a hattie. I don't think he's had one since early last season."

"A hattie?" Penny asked, her gaze locked on Ethan as he

hugged his teammates again. Lexi was right. Hockey hugs were hot.

"A hat trick. If he scores three goals tonight, people throw their hats on the ice," Lexi said.

"Wow. You really are becoming a fan, huh?" Penny asked.

"We've watched so many of Grant's games that I couldn't help but learn," Lexi said.

"It's a rec league, babe. Not the same as the pros," Grant said.

Lexi snuggled into Grant's arm, and pressed a kiss to his cheek. "Still as fun to watch."

"I still don't understand the hats. What's the point? And what if you're really attached to your hat?" Penny asked.

"It's the price you pay, wearing it to a game," Grant said.

"You should try to talk to him after the game," Lexi said.

"And why would I do that?"

"Because there's obviously something going on between the two of you that you didn't finish six months ago."

"We had our fun, and it's over. I don't have enough fingers to count the number of ways that it would be bad to try to pick up where we left off," Penny said, hearing the sadness in her own voice. She hated that she wanted what she shouldn't, no matter how many times she told herself she didn't want anything with him.

"I'm sure you made multiple lists, but I think you should go for it. You never know what could happen," Lexi said with a smile, before she turned back to look at Grant.

"Yeah, disaster could actually strike," Penny muttered, her gaze back on Ethan. Shit. What was she doing? And why couldn't she stop herself? There were too many variables between them, his uncle, her ex. The ways that it could go horribly wrong were infinite.

"Lunch again?" Robert asked when Ethan popped into his office early Wednesday afternoon.

"I'm beginning to think you don't want to have lunch with your favorite nephew. I can head home," Ethan said, shucking his coat and laying it across the chair next to him.

"You know I'm always happy to see you. And that game last night, man, you were on fire. A hattie. I threw a hat at my TV," Robert said, walking around his desk to give Ethan a hug.

"Yeah. Think I'm finally getting my feet under me here. Took longer than I wanted, but hopefully I can pick up my points now. Don't want the Strikers to regret the trade," Ethan said, pulling back from his uncle to take a seat as Robert moved to settle back in his.

"How could they? You are working with a new team, new linemates. That cohesion isn't instant. They know your point history, your track record for thirty plus goal seasons."

"Well, I better pick up the pace if I want that this season." Ethan couldn't describe his happiness at his uncle's support. He needed some form of family support more than he wanted to admit. He shouldn't want it—shouldn't need it—but he did.

"You'll hit it. I have a feeling this is the right place for you. And the Strikers need you," Robert said.

"Let's hope management agrees with you since I only signed a one-year contract," Ethan said. His agent was already working on getting an extended deal, and Ethan hoped to sign one before the All-Star break in January.

"They will. Now, if you have a minute, I wanted to talk to you about your account."

"Sure. What's up? Do I need to sign something?" Ethan asked, grabbing a pen from the cup holder on Robert's desk.

"No, but I was wondering if you'd be willing to have your account managed by one of my senior accountants."

Robert had managed Ethan's books since Ethan signed his first large contract in New York six years ago. "Any reason why?"

"The firm is growing, and I'm spending less time actually accounting and more time running the firm. I don't want anything to slip through the cracks, and I would like to hand over management of your account to someone I trust implicitly," Robert said.

"If you trust them, then I'll defer to you. I know you always have my best interest at heart," Ethan said.

"Great. Let me call her in here," Robert said, tapping on his keyboard.

Her. Robert had multiple female employees, but Ethan couldn't stop the weird flutter in his chest at the possibility. He still couldn't believe she'd been at the game last night. He fought back a chuckle remembering her response when he'd slammed into the boards in front of her. He'd spotted her early in the first period, and it was possible that he'd nudged the Minnesota captain into the boards right in front of her on purpose. Not that he'd admit that to anyone.

Her cheeks had flamed dark red, the pretzel bite falling to her lap as she stared at him. Seeing her there had spurred him on, and he'd quickly turned his focus back to the puck, digging it out of the captain's legs and passing it to his teammate.

"Penny will be right up," Robert said, pulling Ethan from his thoughts. This ought to go well.

There was a brief knock on the door and Penny stuck her head in. "Hey, Robert…"

She looked so nervous. He hoped Robert wasn't just springing this on her.

"Come in, Penny. You remember my nephew, of course."

"Yes. Hello Ethan." She awkwardly held out her hand, her gaze darting between Ethan and Robert again.

"Good to see you again, Penny." He grasped her hand, giving it a squeeze and schooled his features when all he wanted to do was grin from ear to ear.

She pulled her hand free and sunk into the chair next to him, her hair brushing against his jacket that still lay over the back of the chair. That would no doubt hold her soft floral scent after she left. Hell, he remembered her scent so well, how it lingered on the pillow next to his, every morning that he'd woken up beside her in Italy. He would not admit to burying his face in the slightly cool pillow that she'd left behind when she'd snuck out. Or how he'd been tempted to take the pillowcase home with him as some fucked up souvenir.

Definitely not admitting to that. To anyone. He didn't even want to admit that to himself. Not his best moment.

"So, as we've discussed, you will be taking over Ethan's account. Just wanted you to officially meet before I send his files over," Robert said, bringing Ethan back to the present. At least she knew ahead of time.

"Yes, of course," she said, plastering on a tight smile as she looked at Robert.

"Great. I look forward to working with you," Ethan said, fighting back the urge to squeeze her hand and tell her it wasn't a big deal. Would working with him be that bad?

"Perfect. We are taking on new staff, and I'm going to have you shift a few smaller accounts to Kevin in the very near future, and I would like you to take on Ethan's," Robert continued. Ethan did not miss Penny stiffen at Kevin's name. Something was up with that and he had an overwhelming need to find out exactly what the deal was with that guy. And if he needed to have a talk with the punk. Penny inspired a protective streak in him that he'd never had for someone who wasn't family—that he didn't have for most of his family.

"Are you sure that's a good idea?" Penny asked. Ethan wasn't sure if she was referring to Kevin or taking over Ethan's books.

"Yes. Kevin will need accounts of his own, and I want someone I trust implicitly with Ethan's account," Robert said.

"How many of my accounts are you giving to Kevin?" Penny asked, warily.

Yes, something was going on with Kevin.

"Just a couple. I have every faith that you can handle Ethan and most of your other accounts. He's actually very easy to work with," Robert said, before leaning closer to Penny. "He pretty much just signs anything."

"Hey. Should I not trust what you are putting in front of me to sign?" Ethan grumbled, and Penny finally really smiled. He'd missed that smile. How her pale green eyes sparkled, her cheeks blushing a soft pink.

"You'll sign it if you know what's good for you," his uncle teased. "And, I do think this will be a good fit."

"If you're sure you want me to know how much money you make," Penny said, hedging.

"The whole world knows what I make. Just Google it," Ethan said, knowing there was a Wikipedia page with all of his stats on it—professional and personal. He wondered if she'd googled him already, and he cringed at what she might've found. The good—and the bad—was available for everyone to see. Being a professional hockey player had been his dream since he'd strapped on a pair skates, to play pond hockey with his friends in Lake Tahoe when he was eight. And it came with perks that he'd never imagined. Unfortunately, it also came with living under a microscope, where every misdeed was blasted for the world to see. And he'd had a few of them after Julie.

"Umm," she hesitated, and he knew she'd looked him up already.

"Don't believe everything you read, or see, for that matter." It was moments like these that he itched to be back in Italy, where they were just two consenting adults taking in the sights and each other.

"I won't," she said. He desperately wanted to believe her.

"Well, now that that's settled, you two should schedule a time to go over everything," Robert said.

"Yes, we should," Penny said. He couldn't ignore the tiny thrill that rocked through him at the thought of spending more time with her. He shouldn't crave that, but he did.

"Can I swing by after I take my former accountant out for lunch? Or we could leave Robert here and I'll take you to lunch." The words were out before he remembered they were still in Robert's office, under his watchful eye.

"Umm. You could swing by my office after lunch," Penny said, her thumb swiping over her tablet. He wondered how many lists she had on that thing and if he was in there. He'd put money on finding a pro and con list about him in there.

"See you then," Ethan said, rising when she did, and attempting to not watch her as she exited the office. "So, lunch?" he asked, slipping on his coat, his eyes still focused on his uncle.

"Is there something I should know about? Should I have kept your account?" Robert asked.

"Nope. You trust her, so it should be fine. I'm starved. We should go," he said, inching toward the door that had just closed behind Penny.

He would not rush through lunch just to get back to her. Definitely not.

CHAPTER 6

An hour later, Penny was still trying to figure out what had just happened. And why Robert had handed over Ethan's account. Yes, Robert was busy, and the firm was growing, but why her? Why now? Shit. Should she have fessed up to knowing Ethan? It was the right thing to do, but she couldn't bring herself to tell Robert the truth.

And she'd had ample opportunity to do just that. When he'd talked to her earlier this morning and initially asked if she would take Ethan's account. That would've been the perfect time. Or when he'd let Ethan know about the change. Another opportunity squandered because she'd gotten caught up on how gloriously his shoulders had filled out his gray knit sweater. She could've emailed him in between those two times, too, but her confession should've been face-to-face.

She'd made a list of all the times she could've clued Robert into her carnal knowledge of his nephew. Not that she planned to describe her week in Italy to her boss, but a quick mention of *oh, we've met before and maybe this isn't a good idea*, should've been easy. But, the few times she'd tried to tell Robert the truth when they'd initially spoken, he'd interrupted her with more details about Ethan's account, and she'd kept her secret. Hell, this was the definition of conflict of interest. But Ethan didn't seem to mind, so why should she?

She'd tried not to stare at her clock for the last hour, each minute ticking closer to her doom.

She snorted. A bit melodramatic, much? Her stomach was a big, ugly knot. Yes, she'd seen him a handful of times in the last few weeks, but just in passing. She hadn't actually had a conversation with him since the first day she'd seen him in Robert's office two weeks ago, when he'd accused her of knowing who he was and using it for her gain.

And while he no longer appeared pissed at her for bailing on him, they'd hadn't talked about it. She pulled out her tablet and scanned through her calendar, a grocery list she'd made this morning, and her weekend to-do list. A calmness settled over her with each swipe of her finger from one list to the next. Crap, she'd forgotten to add flour to her grocery list. She'd wanted to make cookies two nights ago and had been out of flour.

How the hell had that happened? She blamed Ethan. Her leg bounced, her shoe tapped on the floor protector under her desk. She was restless. And distracted. And forgetting things like flour. Basic staples that she always replenished on time.

She stood up and walked around her office, pinching the bridge of her nose. She had to get a grip.

Stop thinking about him. Or how he looked last night...

Ugh. She had to focus on work. Of course, telling herself not to think of him had the opposite effect. Now she was thinking about his sweaty abs on the jumbotron, and his grin when he'd spotted her through the glass.

A knock pulled her from her thoughts with a hard jerk. She spun, losing her footing for a minute, and grabbed the edge of her desk as Ethan's smile turned to one of concern. He rushed into her office, reaching for her, the door shutting with a soft slam behind him.

His hand gripped her elbow, pulling her into his body, and the air rushed out of her lungs, stealing her squeak.

"You okay?" he asked, a smile playing at the corners of his mouth. That damn crooked smile would be the death of her, if a slip and fall didn't do her in first.

She should pull back, but she didn't want to. She wanted him to wrap his arms around her, settle his hand at the small of her back, and tug her close. Jesus Christ. She needed to gain control and tell her stupid brain—and body—to shut up.

"I'm fine. Thanks," she said, pulling free and instantly missing his warmth. He was like a space heater, and her office was cold. She took a calming breath, her rationalizations bordering on insane.

"How's the knee?" He gestured to her leg.

"Better. Almost done with therapy, and I can walk faster than I did in all of those museums," she said with a soft laugh.

"Your pace was fine. And I should've asked that when I first saw you, but I was in shock. I should apologize for how I reacted in your office. I know you never expected to see me again—hell, I never expected to see you again…" he trailed off. She refused to hear wistfulness in his tone. She was imagining things.

Her laugh came out strained. She could handle angry Ethan, could brush him off, but sweet Ethan—he would break her.

"That's okay. It was a shock to me, too. And I want you to know, that I didn't ask to take over your account," she said, keeping her expression open, honest.

"Oh, Penny," he said, linking his hand with hers, his blue eyes piercing right through her, and she struggled to take in a breath.

"What?" she rushed out, schooling her body's instant response to him, willing her heart to stop pounding every time he touched her.

"I didn't think that for a minute."

She pulled free of his hand. "I should tell him about our history. About Italy."

"I don't think you need to do that. I'm fine with you handling my account," he said.

"But you don't even like me anymore." Why had she said that?

"That's not true," he said.

And then he touched her cheek. Oh look, the butterflies had returned and they'd taken some speed before showing up. She bit the inside of her cheek to resist the urge—no, the need—to wrap her arms around his neck and take what she wanted. What she couldn't—and shouldn't—want.

She swore she was going to get whiplash. Hadn't he hated her just last week? "I thought you hated me for what I did." she said, her voice low, not wanting the answer but unable to stop the question.

"I don't hate you, Penny. I hate how everything ended, but I understand it. Seeing you was a surprise, and my reaction was just that, surprise, confusion." He took her hand again. "But now that we are both here, aware of who the other person really is, what do you say to dinner?"

Again. Whiplash. She stared at him, her mouth gaping. "Seriously?"

"Why not? We had fun together. You know we never ran out of things to say during all our meals in Italy."

She felt a tug at her heart, remembering how easy everything was back then. The conversation, the sweet kisses, the constant touching as he guided her through museums and vineyards, and in bed. She fought back her shudder. He'd been amazing in bed. Especially their first night together. When she'd cried. God, it'd been embarrassing. Her knee wasn't up to bending, and she hadn't told him about her injury, but after she did, the tenderness he'd shown her. Well, the casual hook-up had turned into so much more.

And that had scared the hell out of her.

"What are you thinking about?"

Her skin heated, and she focused back on him. "Nothing."

"Not our nights in Italy?"

Dammit, how could he read her so well. Of course, the flush she must be sporting was probably a dead giveaway. But did he have to freaking point it out?

"Ethan, stop. We can't." She had to nip this in the bud immediately before her imaginings got the better of her common sense.

"Why not?"

"Because I work for your uncle."

"So, we can't be friends?"

"Umm." Was that all he wanted? Had she been reading into something that wasn't there?

"We can be friends, I guess."

"Or more?" he asked, that damn dimple peeking out. Why did he have to have a freaking dimple? She wanted to stick her tongue in it. She *had* stuck her tongue in it.

She internally shook her head. *Focus, Penny, focus.*

"Ethan, you can't say things like that."

"Why not? Are you dating someone?"

"Does it matter?"

"It's just a question between friends."

"No."

"No, you won't answer, or no you're not dating anyone?"

"No, I'm not dating anyone," she bit out.

"Good to know."

"Why? I won't go out with you."

"I don't recall asking." He grinned. "Just making friendly conversation among *friends*."

He was going to drive her to drink.

"But you thought it."

Why was she continuing this line of conversation? *Shut up.*

"Of course I thought it. I think about you a lot."

"Right. Sure you do." *Stop it, heart flutter.*

"Why do you assume I haven't?"

"It's been months. You're a big sports star. I assumed you'd found another girl as soon as I left. You always have a different girl in every picture I've seen." She wanted to punch herself when his eyes lit up. Fuck. She was revealing way too much.

"So you did Google me? I told you not to believe everything you see."

"Even the pictures?"

"Even the pictures. Which are all old by the way, because there hasn't been anyone else since you."

Holy hell. There she went again with her gaping mouth and wide eyes—yes, you can feel your own eyes widening. How was her heart not galloping out of her chest, and why did he have to say such sweet shit like that?

"But why? We were never supposed to see each other again. It was just a fling."

"Believe me, if I could explain it, I would." His harsh laugh made her chest hurt, but she couldn't ignore what he'd said. No one. No one since her. How was that even possible?

She had to end this conversation immediately before she did anything stupid, like jump into his arms and kiss the hell out of him. He really needed to stop staring at her.

Damn his bedroom eyes.

"This isn't going to work."

"What? Being friends or working together?"

"Maybe both."

He took her hand again. "We'll figure it out. My uncle raves about you, so if you're overseeing my books, I have the utmost faith in you."

"Are you sure you want me digging into your financials?"

"You can dig into whatever you want." He chuckled. "That sounded weird."

She couldn't stop her laugh. "I missed you," she said, wishing she could take it back as soon as his smile widened. Damn. She hadn't meant to let that slip.

"I missed you, too. But I have to get home for my pre-game nap," he said, giving her hand one last squeeze before he released her.

"Nap?"

"It's a requirement so I'm rested and ready to go for the game tonight."

"Oh. So you didn't want to go over your account?" She refused to be sad that he was about to walk out of her office.

"Nah. But we could discuss it over dinner or drinks Saturday night."

"That's probably not a good idea."

"Just think about it. And if I need to review any paperwork, you know how to find me."

"Yes. And good luck tonight," she said, trying to steer the conversation anywhere else.

"Thanks…if you ever want tickets to the game, just let me know."

Right. So she could stare at his abs on the jumbotron again.

"I'm not really a hockey fan."

He put his hand to his heart in mock horror. "Well, we'll have to fix that. Hockey is the best sport ever created. No, the best *thing* ever created."

She laughed. "Okay, okay. Don't you have a nap to get to?"

"You could join me," he said. There wasn't a smirk or wiggled eyebrow in sight.

"Just go, Ethan."

"We'll talk soon," he said, giving her one last smile before walking out of her office.

Shit. She was screwed.

"Just because you scored the shootout win last night doesn't mean you can slack at practice today," Siebs called out as Ethan skated up the ice, pissed that he'd missed that last shot. Fanned, actually. Siebs had every right to call him out.

"I meant to pass it to Cheesy," Ethan said, sliding onto the bench and grabbing the closest water bottle. They'd been working on power plays for the last twenty minutes. He and Cheesy were pretty in sync by this point in the season. It'd only taken about a month to get in line. Ethan knew that was one of the main reasons the Strikers wanted him. Cheesy hadn't had consistent linemates for the last three years, and they'd played well together for Team USA at World Championship last year.

"Pretty sure you fanned, Harty," Cheesy said, shooting him a grin as he ran his hand over his stick, checking for tears in the tape. That grin had taken a while, too. Cheesy was too serious. And on camera—forget it—he was a mess. Deer caught in head-lights mess. And as much as Ethan wasn't a fan of the spotlight, he hadn't shied away from it either. Talking to reporters was part of the job. He just wished they'd keep the questions focused on his game and not his personal life.

Not that he'd helped that focus. But he was working on it. One boring night at a time. Let someone else be the bad boy of the team. Ethan was tired of that title. Of course, he couldn't fault them since he'd contributed greatly to his image of play-boy. And the rumors that had trailed him from New York hadn't helped matters.

"You good?" Cheesy asked, nudging his shoulder hard enough to get his attention and get him to slide down the bench.

"Yeah," Ethan said, clearing his head. He had a practice to focus on. Two dozen extra suicide drills up and down the ice was Siebs's favorite form of torture for anyone who was slacking, and Ethan was determined to never make that list. He'd done enough of them at the start of practice and was in no mood to do anymore.

"You were on fire last night, and the night before," Cheesy said, focusing back on the ice as they waited for their shift.

"Team effort. I'm just glad the points are starting to swing our way," he said. They'd won their last four games. On top of that, last night had been the back end of a back to back. Odds were that streak would end soon, but not if he had anything to say about it. He'd prove his worth to the team one shift and one point at a time.

"Four goals and a shootout win in two games is more than just a team effort," Cheesy said.

He wouldn't claim that it was because of Penny, but he'd been lacking in the points department until she'd shown up at the game two nights ago. A hattie the first night and two goals the next night was rare. Extremely rare. Not that the second goal counted in his points, since it was the shootout win. He needed to get her to more games to see how much of a good luck charm she really was. Maybe he just had to see her for the magic to work. Hockey players were superstitious as hell, and he'd get her season tickets right next to the penalty box if his point streak continued.

Who was he kidding? He'd give her season tickets just to see her at every game. Her flushed cheeks when he banged into the boards in front of her, the soft gasp that reminded him of every soft gasp she'd let out as he'd kissed down her body in Italy. He shifted on the bench. Now was not the time to reminisce about Penny in bed. About what he wanted to do to her every time he saw her. He pushed her from his mind, and focused on practice.

"Just in the right place at the right time," he said.

"So humble. You finding humility in your old age, Harty?"

"I'm not that old," he grumbled. "I only have two years on you."

"That's at least a decade in hockey years," Cheesy said. "Hop to it, old man. Just try not to fan again."

Cheesy grinned as he jumped over the boards, Ethan right behind him. And when the puck hit Ethan's tape, he sent it sailing into the net, right over the blocker side of Gally, their starting goalie. Nothing but net.

* * *

"Great practice, boys," Cheesy said an hour later as they all filtered out of the locker room.

"Morning skate is optional tomorrow, but greatly encouraged," Siebs called out behind them.

They had a rare three nights off, and Ethan was looking forward to the mini break. Twelve games in twenty days was a lot, and he was pleased that they'd come out with nineteen points. Now if they could just keep that up for the rest of the season, he'd be happy. He knew that it would be a feat just to get past round two of the playoffs, but if they kept this up, the idea was no longer far-fetched.

"Hey, Hartless. You joining us at Byrne's for lunch?" Baz called out.

Man, he was tired of that name.

"No, he's having lunch with me."

Ethan spun on his heel, seeing his agent walking down the corridor. He didn't remember scheduling a meeting with Sam.

"Came down to discuss your contract and thought we'd grab lunch," Sam said, when he reached Ethan's side.

"Yeah, sure." Ethan tried to read his agent's expression, but Sam's face was blank. Ethan wasn't sure if that was a good sign. The man's poker face was one of the reasons Ethan had signed with him. He hadn't expected Sam to be discussing contracts yet, but hopefully he had good news for Ethan.

Ethan said goodbye to his teammates.

"There's a restaurant right up the street. Best steak in town. It literally melts in your mouth," Sam said as Ethan followed him out of the arena, unable to quell his chuckle. The man was always in search for the best steak.

"You know, I'm still surprised that you wanted to stay with the Strikers," Sam said once their lunch order was placed and the waiter left the table.

So was he. He'd been shocked by the trade announcement in July and had planned to bide his time before getting the hell out of the town he'd grown up in. The town—the family—he wanted nothing to do with.

"Yeah. Things change," Ethan said. "So how are negotiations going?"

"Your point streak is helping, but the numbers still aren't where I want them."

"I'm working on that. Just have to continue this streak."

"That will help. But they are hesitating to ink a big deal this early. Want to see how you gel with the team. You've been great with the media. No issues," Sam said.

"But they're waiting for me to fuck up." Not that he intended to go out and party his ass off or act inappropriately, but it chafed. He couldn't totally fault them on that. His track record wasn't stellar. But that was in the past. The General Manager was a stickler for presenting the best image. They were supposed to be role models. Embarrassments to the team were not tolerated, which was why Ethan had been surprised that the Strikers wanted him.

"You just have to give it some time. Give it another month. Keep your nose out of trouble, and we'll go back to negotiations. It probably sucks living like a monk, but it's working.

Then you can hook up with anyone you want. Let's just get the contract done first, before you go back to your old ways."

"Shouldn't be an issue." He didn't have any desire to party like he had before. To see his picture splashed on social media.

"You've been good since you got here. No random puck bunnies posting pics of you in bed."

He was still pissed about that. It'd only happened twice, and hadn't been more than his face and maybe a shoulder, but it could've turned into something more. He'd made sure to never fall asleep at another woman's place after that.

"Actually, you've been almost saint-like." Sam eyed him. "Is there something you aren't telling me?"

"No. I'm still settling in. I haven't gone out with anyone." He hesitated in admitting that. Sam had been with him since he'd moved up to the big leagues six years ago. He'd been playing the field since everything had blown up with Julie right before he left the minors. But he was tired of the games.

It had nothing to do with Penny. He bit back his snort. Even he knew that was a load of shit. While she might not be the sole reason for his newfound desire to steer clear of bunnies, he'd be an idiot not to realize that she had a lot to do with it. And now that she was his accountant, he had every excuse to see her. Maybe she'd be up for dinner tomorrow night.

"You disappear on me?" Sam asked, cutting through Ethan's thoughts.

"What? No. Just annoyed that they're holding back."

"You could always find a nice girl to settle down with. Bet management would love that." Sam bit out a harsh laugh. "Who am I kidding? Hartless settle down. That'll be the day."

He hated the idea of Sam learning about Penny. Not that he was settling down any time soon. But thinking about it no longer made him break out into hives. What was she doing to him? And why didn't he care to fight it?

CHAPTER 7

This day needed to end—desperately needed to end. Penny finally had her office to herself, and all she wanted to do was bang her head on her desk. Kevin had just vacated the chair next to her after another bout of training. *Bout* being the appropriate word since she felt like she'd just gone a few rounds against stupidity, and it was draining. She was also at her wit's end with Kevin, but at least she'd finished her work for the day before he'd popped his head in. She'd been doing that lately, rushing through her work in case he stopped by.

Accountants should never rush. If she missed something, and her clients were audited, they'd be livid with her, and she'd be out of a job. Which had led to her triple checking her work on the days that Kevin didn't show up in the afternoon. Not that she didn't at least double check everything to begin with, but it was irritating as hell.

Kevin refused to take notes, showed up late for their scheduled trainings, and never retained anything. Thus, the life of an over-privileged son. She didn't know why Alan was determined to make his son learn the business, but Kevin saw it as a meal ticket and pretended to care whenever his father stopped by. How could she tell her boss that his son was a complete waste of time?

So here she was. Stuck training someone who didn't care that there were other qualified candidates available to hire. Add the constant thoughts about Ethan, and she was beyond annoyed. And frustrated, since all she could think about was taking him up on his offer of a nap. Not that she had time to nap. But she missed snuggling up against his overly warm body.

She shook her head, the numbers on the screen dancing in front of her. Numbers didn't dance. They were placed in a logical straight line, sorted in perfect columns. She liked columns and lists and logic and...

"Ouch," she muttered as she spun in her chair and whacked her knee on her desk drawer. Why wasn't it shut? Oh right, because she was distracted as hell, and had been about to grab a file when her thoughts had turned to Ethan once again.

"Knock, knock."

Speak of the devil. Oh God, why was he here? She slammed the drawer shut and smoothed down her skirt before telling him to come in.

"Hi. What are you doing here?" she asked as he walked into her office and propped his ass on the edge of her desk next to her. What was wrong with the perfectly good chair across from her desk? The chair that wouldn't cause his pants to stretch tightly across his impressive thighs, only to be matched by his equally impressive ass. Not that it was on display right now, but she knew it was there.

"Thought I'd stop in to see how my books were doing."

"Really?" She held back her snort. No one stopped in to check up on their accountant. He was transparent, and in that moment, she was totally on board with that.

"I should take a more active interest in my accounting."

"So why are you really here?" She couldn't fight her smile. This would be so much easier if he wasn't so damn charming. Again, sweet Ethan was going to wreck her, but she was starting to not care.

"Just checking in. Is Kevin giving you grief?"

She paused. "Wait. How did you know about Kevin?"

"You mentioned him to Robert last week and looked annoyed."

And he'd caught on to that and followed up? Screwed. She was totally screwed.

"Just another frustrating day of training," she said, and then paused. "Please don't tell your uncle I said that."

"I wouldn't. Anything you tell me remains between us, I promise." His blue eyes shone with sincerity, and she wanted to believe him.

"I haven't had a chance to go through your file yet. Did you want to discuss anything in particular? And did you want to take a seat?" She gestured to the chair safely on the other side of her desk.

He shifted on her desk, his jeans lovingly encasing his strong thighs. What would they feel like beneath her as she straddled his hips? They hadn't been able to do that on account of her knee and its refusal to bend correctly after her injury. But she'd wanted to. Hell, she still wanted to. Heat rushed to every part of her body, zinging down to her toes. She resisted the urge to hide under her desk until her flaming cheeks settled down.

"What are you thinking about?" he asked, shifting again on her desk, and she refused to stare at his lap—or his face. She spun back to her computer, her fingers skimming over the keyboard much like they had over his abs all those months ago.

"Nothing. I should probably get back to work unless you needed something." She took in deep calming breaths, willing her pulse to chill the fuck out already.

"Does this bother you? Me sitting here?"

"It's very unprofessional," she replied.

"Then it's a good thing I don't work here." That damn crooked smile deepened. She wanted to run her hands along the stubble at his jaw. She remembered how it felt between her thighs. *Get a hold of yourself!* She shook her head before looking up. Today's deep blue shirt brought out his eyes. Why did he always have to look so scrumptious?

"Yes, it is," she mumbled before her cell phone started ringing the specific tone she'd set up for her mother. How much stress could be piled on her in one day? She ignored the call and turned back to Ethan.

"Join me for an early dinner. I don't have a game tonight, and it looks like you could use a break," he said.

"Ethan," she started, just as her office phone rang. This time she looked at the caller ID. She'd learned her lesson last week when Michael had called. It was her mother again.

"Just a friendly bite to eat, I promise," he continued.

"Okay."

"It's just dinner—wait, did you just agree?" His smile reached up to his eyes.

She nodded. She'd agreed before she could second guess herself and because she wanted to get out of her office before her phone rang again.

"Ah, where do you want to go?" he asked.

"I don't know. You invited me. Where did you plan on taking me?"

"To bed?"

"Why do you have to ruin the moment?" She tried to hide her smile.

He grinned. "Sorry, you caught me off guard. I didn't think you'd agree."

"I do have a lot of work to finish…"

"Nope, we're going out." He stood up and held out his hand.

A spark shot through her when their palms met. She let him

pull her from her seat and help her into her coat. A shiver rolled through her as he brushed her curls away from her coat collar. She gasped when she felt his lips at her nape.

"Did you just sniff me?" she asked, pulling away from him.

"Of course not," he scoffed, straightening his own coat.

"Umm, I'm pretty sure you did."

"Maybe I tripped and my nose hit your neck," he said, the corners of his mouth tilting up in a small smile.

"Tripped?"

"Yeah. Your clumsiness must be rubbing off on me," he said, his grin widening.

"I don't think it works that way." She smiled.

"Sorry, I love your neck."

"Don't make me regret this," she said as she walked out of her office.

"You won't," he promised.

Ethan couldn't believe she'd said yes to dinner as they walked down the block to a restaurant she'd mentioned. She must be stressed. He wanted to have a few words with Kevin. Or his uncle. But he'd promised not to say anything to Robert. It wasn't his place to step in, regardless of how much he wanted to.

"Why did you finally agree to dinner?" Ethan asked as soon as they sat down and the waiter had left with their drink order.

"Because I'm having a shit day and wanted to get out of the office. And because I miss you." The second statement was a whisper, and he couldn't believe she'd actually said it.

He reached across the table, running his thumb over the back of her hand. She pulled her hand away, gripping the menu.

"Ethan, we can't just pick up where we left off." Her eyes drew him in.

"You keep saying that, but you agreed to dinner, so I thought—"

"I still work for your uncle, and you are now my client. We can be friends," she said.

"Can we? After everything we did together, the time we spent together, you can just be friends?" He knew he was laying it on thick, but he was determined.

"Don't push me on this, Ethan. My job is extremely important to me, and I really should tell Robert about this," she said, waving her hand between them.

"We don't need to tell him just yet, and I promise that I'll try to be on my best behavior."

She gave him a soft smile. "Somehow, I doubt that, but thanks."

"Scout's Honor." He held up two fingers. That was the sign for a Scout, right?

She snorted. "Sure, like you were ever a Boy Scout."

"I'm really good at tying knots." He wiggled his eyebrows at her. Her musical laughter washed over him. This. This was what he'd missed for the last six months.

"Such a perv."

"But not a creepy one, right?"

She chuckled. Watching her shoulders shake with humor made him smile, and he remembered the first night he'd asked her to dinner after their vineyard tour all those months ago. He hadn't been ready to leave her, and he'd promised her he wasn't a creepy stalker. She'd continued to tease him about that comment for the rest of the trip. He'd missed the ease they had. He wanted that back—more than he should.

"So, tell me about the rest of your time in Italy. Did you go back to Siena for Il Palio?" She played with her straw, twirling it around in her glass. It was distracting as hell, watching her nails tap the top of the straw, reminding him of her nails skating down his chest.

Get a grip. He shifted in his seat as she eyed him questioningly. What were they talking about? Oh, right, the famous horse race.

"Yes, we went back for the second race in August. It was amazing. The same horse won both races. That never happens," he said. "And the horse's name was Penelope."

"You're lying," she scoffed.

"I'm serious. Look it up. I think it translated to Precious Penelope," he said, and she already had her phone out, her fingers flying over the screen.

"Holy crap. What are the odds? Preziosa Penelope won both races. It says that it's only happened like three times. Did you get any pictures of the horse crossing the finish line? I want to see my namesake."

He laughed. "Aside from all the pageantry before the race, most of my pictures from the actual event are chaotic and dusty."

"I bet."

"But I do have a few of them on my phone," he said, turning his phone on and thumbing through the pictures before holding it out for her. "Just swipe left."

She took it from him, her fingers brushing his. He would not focus on the need in his belly at her touch.

"Just left? What happens if I swipe right?" she asked, her finger poised over the screen.

"Swipe whichever way you want. It's mostly Italy pics. I told you there weren't any other women after you."

"I wasn't asking about that," she said, her voice low. "Oh," she gasped.

"What?" he asked, leaning across the table.

She turned the phone to face him. It was the last picture they had taken together—a selfie he'd demanded. She was laughing behind a glass of wine, while he pressed a kiss to her cheek and smiled at the camera. She was stunning. Her eyes bright, and cheeks flushed from the sun and the wine, and hopefully from him.

"Looks like you've been swiping right. That's a great picture of us," he said, something in his voice that he couldn't name.

"Yes. I look so—so happy," she dragged out, almost as if in wonder that she'd been that happy.

"And then in less than twelve hours you left me in your room." He wanted to take back the words instantly as her smile vanished. She looked down at the phone again.

"I'm so sorry about that, Ethan," she said. He tilted her head up to look at him.

"And I'm sorry I keep bringing it up. I can admit you bruised my pride—maybe my ego, too—but we are getting past it, and it's unfair for me to dredge it up again," he said, hoping she believed him, hoping that he'd get the fuck over it because he wanted to see where this was going, and bringing up what happened was not going to help him get what he wanted. And that was Penny back in his life—back in his bed.

"Then stop bringing it up," she said, a soft smile playing at the corner of her lips.

"I'm working on it," he said.

"Let me see those pictures, then."

He swiped the phone back on and handed it to her.

"These pictures are awesome. But so many people, and that is a lot of dust," she said.

He chuckled. "That's what you get for a ninety second horse race in the summer with a massive crowd. Jake wanted to be down in the action, so we spent most of the hours leading up to the race packed in like cattle in the square."

She wrinkled her nose. "Glad I missed that. Way too much chaos."

"It was a blast. I would've sheltered you from the craziness."

"Not sure that would've been possible. So, how did the rest of the trip go?"

"Not the same without you, but we had a lot of fun. Kayaking through Italy was an adventure. We just went wherever the water took us."

She grinned. "You're ridiculous. And, no thanks. I need a schedule."

"No kidding. Have you started flagging the guidebook for your next trip?"

"No plans yet. But I have those stickies ready to go," she said, laughing. "Don't poke fun at my awesome organizational skills," she said, taking a sip of her wine. "What about you?"

"Nothing planned yet. Once the season wraps up and I know where I'm heading next year, I'll have a better idea."

"Next year? So, you might not stay with the Strikers?"

He ignored the thrill that rocked through him at how disappointed she sounded at the thought of him leaving.

"It's a possibility. I only signed a one-year contract with the team, so next year is up in the air."

"Do you want to stay here?" she asked, and the thrill ramped up again.

"I would stay if they offered. I like the guys on the team. I've played with a few of them over the years."

"That's good. I take it you didn't request the trade?" she asked.

"No, I didn't," he stated, unable to mask the abruptness in his tone.

She sat up straighter. "Oh, I'm sorry to pry. I was just making conversation."

He hated the awkwardness that settled over them. "You

aren't prying. It just wasn't something I'd planned on. I liked playing in New York." But his options had been taken away due to a stupid misunderstanding. Not that the parties involved had misunderstood, but the gossip surrounding it, and his reputation—it'd just been easier to accept the trade and move to the other side of the country.

"That sucks. But you like your new team, so I hope you can stay. You know, because you like them." And with that—and the flush in her cheeks—his anger with everything that had happened vanished. This was why he needed to keep her around. She made him happier than he'd been in a long time, and not just superficially happy, that he let everyone see, but actually happy.

"Yes. And most of my family is here." Not that he'd seen them. He would—eventually. Ally was home for Christmas and he wouldn't have a choice.

"You never told me much about your family," she said.

"Not much to tell. My parents and my brother live here. My little sister is away at college. I don't see them often."

"They must be excited that you are home."

"I haven't seen them since I've been back," he said, unsure of why he was offering up information that he usually was tight-lipped on.

"Really? Why not?"

"Besides my uncle, and my younger sister who just got home for winter break two days ago, I'm not close to my family." Just the idea of sitting at his parents' dining room table in a few days irked him, but with the three-day break in his schedule, and the fact that he now lived on the same side of the country as his family, he no longer had an excuse to bail.

"What about yours?" he asked.

"Honestly, I've avoided them for the most part, but I'll have to make an appearance for Christmas dinner this weekend."

"Do you want to talk about it?" He didn't want to talk about Michael, but he had to ask.

"Oh look, our food is here," she said, her avoidance blatant as the waiter placed their dinner on the table.

"I'm here to listen if you want to talk. And I'm still available to kick Michael's ass if you want."

CHAPTER 8

Why did he have to say shit like that? Be so understanding and sweet? And why had she agreed to dinner? Nothing good could come from this, but she couldn't stop herself from saying, "Thanks. I'm here to listen, too." She was getting in deeper than she should, and the softening of his face at her comment made her want to know what happened with his family, but she wouldn't pry—yet. They were still on tentative ground.

"Everything's fine, and it's great to see my uncle on a regular basis. It's been years."

Dammit. She was itching to ask.

"So, are you coming to our game tomorrow?" he asked.

She tried not to get whiplash from the quick subject change. Family was definitely off the table.

"I didn't plan on it. That game the other night was my first, and I'm not really a sports fan," she said, wondering if she was imagining the brief flash of disappointment in his eyes. Why should he care if she liked hockey? Or showed up at a game? "Hockey's so fast, I didn't know what was going on."

"That we can fix. I can answer any questions you have. It

takes a few games, but you'll get it. Didn't you have fun at that last one?" he asked.

"It was okay, just a lot to take in, and I couldn't follow the puck," she said, refusing to admit how hot he'd been on the ice, and the excitement she witnessed with each goal, regardless of which of his teammates scored.

"Just okay?" His voice was incredulous as he leaned back, his hand pressed to his chest in horror.

"Oh, stop," she said, reaching out to swat his hand, then pulling back immediately as heat rushed through her at the brief contact. Why had she touched him? It never ended well when she did. That was a blatant lie. It always ended way too well when she touched him. She never wanted to stop touching him as soon as she started. She stifled a breath when he reached out, and grabbed her hand, linking his fingers with hers. She couldn't think when he touched her. Her mind and body instantly returned to Italy. They'd existed in a perfect bubble for that week. How she wished they could exist there permanently.

It was a ridiculous thought, but it didn't stop her from having it.

"What are you thinking about? I'm sure hockey didn't put that blush in your cheeks," he said. She cursed her open-book face.

"Nothing. Must be the wine," she said, fiddling with her glass, refusing to meet his gaze.

"Right. The wine. Don't you wish we could go back?" he asked, and she couldn't resist looking up at him. She bit back her indrawn breath at the sincerity in his eyes. She'd do anything to go back. To change how she'd left things. But they couldn't, and picking up where they left off also wasn't an option. There were too many variables.

"Maybe one day I'll return. It was a great vacation." She attempted to sound nonchalant but she wasn't fooling him, if his grin was anything to go by. "Now, tell me why I need to love hockey," she said, pulling her hand free and downing the rest of her wine. Not that getting tipsy around him was a good idea, but she needed to do something with her mouth before she reminisced further and pressed her lips to his to see if his kiss was just as magical as she remembered. Yeah, she should lay off the wine after this—maybe one more glass.

"Because I play it," he said, shooting her a grin, his clear blue eyes sparking the butterflies in her stomach to warp speed.

She smiled. "Any other reason? And why didn't you tell me you played hockey when we were in Italy?"

"Because you said you just wanted to have fun, no talk of jobs, last names, family..." he trailed off.

"Yeah, that last one definitely bit me in the ass," she said, shaking her head.

"And it was nice to have someone not know that I was a professional athlete. I was able to be normal. Have fun."

"Because being a star athlete is so awful?" she teased.

"Don't get me wrong, I love playing professionally. I'm living out a dream that I've had since I was a kid. But sometimes the attention is too much. It was nice to just be Ethan for once. Like a fresh start."

His tone was wistful, and her heart clenched. Something happened with that trade this summer, and she itched to pry, but resisted.

"I can't begin to understand that, but I do understand a fresh start. Now tell me more about this sport you love so much." Yes, hockey would distract her from wanting to reach across the table.

"I'd rather talk about Italy," he said, and heat shot through her body.

"I'm not sure that's a good idea." Italy wasn't a safe topic, it would lead to memories that she should forget. And while he no longer appeared mad at her for how they ended, she wasn't sure picking things back up again wouldn't bite her in the ass down the road.

"Don't overthink it. What is so wrong with *friends* reminiscing about a vacation? Next time we're in Italy, we are going to explore Lake Castiglione more. That was the day you finally ditched the guidebook." And there was that crooked smile again. God, she loved that damn smile.

"That's also the day you got us lost. And almost ran out of gas in the middle of the Italian countryside," she said, shaking her head. Trying not to remember the panic attack she'd had on the side of the road, or how he'd calmed her down, taking the time to reassure her instead of claiming she was overreacting as her ex had done every time she'd panicked. No. She didn't want to think about Michael anymore. She wanted to focus on how sweet Ethan had been that day. And then she'd left him the following morning. God, she was such a chicken. She was tired of being a chicken.

He grabbed her hand, and she was lost in his gaze. The mixture of concern, question, and hope held her captive, and she linked her fingers with his. His thumb brushed along her palm and she shivered.

"But I wasn't really lost. Just taking the scenic route." He'd said the same thing at the time, and she smiled.

"You're such a liar. We were totally lost. I swear you drove us around in circles for over an hour."

He grinned and shrugged. "You say lost, I say scenic."

"Still not funny. What if we'd really run out of gas and no one found us?" she asked.

"Where's your sense of adventure?"

"It's subdued and aided with a guidebook," she said, giving him a small smile.

"That guidebook," he said, shaking his head. "So many pink flags."

"But I visited them all and had a very successful and enjoyable trip," she said, trying not to huff when he made fun of her organizational skills.

"I hope that I had something to do with the enjoyable part. That it wasn't just museums and churches that did it for you." He wiggled his eyebrows at her, and she laughed.

"That's so wrong. And yes, you aided in the enjoyable part." Her cheeks were flaming at this point, and as he ran his thumb along her palm, the rest of her body flared to life, and her breath caught in her throat.

"Good to know. And it's mutual, Penny," he said, and she officially stopped breathing.

"Ethan, you should stop," she whispered as he leaned in. She should tug her hand from his, but she couldn't will her body to pull away. And when had he slipped into the seat next to her?

"But you don't want to and neither do I." There was no other word to describe it. His eyes smoldered, and she wanted to disappear into their deep blue depths. She wanted him to always look at her the way he had in Italy—the way he was looking at her now. She'd never felt more cherished—more wanted—than she did when he stared at her. And she was tired of resisting what was so blatantly obvious, so she leaned in, and let the magnetic pull do the rest.

His lips brushed hers softly, and she melted closer, the heat from his hand cupping her face, stole her breath and everything around her disappeared as her focus narrowed down to this one moment. Kissing him opened the floodgates to every memory she had of her time with him in Italy. Every soft caress she tried to ignore, the soft sounds of his groan against her mouth as he kissed her harder, taking the breath from her body.

She slid to the edge of the seat, wishing she could climb into his lap, and tilted her head, her tongue darting out to trace along the seam of his lips. His hand settled at the small of her back, his fingers dancing along her spine, and a shudder rolled through her. His lips pressed harder, and she opened her mouth, thrilling as his tongue surged inside, and they swallowed each other's moans. They fit together perfectly. And the months of separation faded away. She'd kiss him forever if she could.

"Ethan?" a woman's voice called out.

Ethan's body stiffened, and he broke the kiss. She didn't miss his sharply indrawn breath before he turned to face the intruder. "Julie. Darren." His tone was casual, but held a tense bite.

Julie? Wait. She knew that name. No. It wasn't possible. Penny looked up at the couple standing in front of their table. They were a gorgeous couple. The woman was tall, statuesque, with a willowy build. Her light blond hair fell in waves so perfect they rivaled a Pantene commercial. Even if her name wasn't Julie, Penny would've hated her. The man at her side was handsome. Dark hair cut short and eyes that perfectly matched Ethan's.

"It's been a long time," the man said. Penny thought Ethan had called him Darren.

"Yes, it has," was Ethan's clipped response.

"Will you be at Christmas dinner?"

"Not sure yet," Ethan said. The tension vibrated off of him.

"Don't you have a break in games at Christmas? Mom was hoping you'd come. Ally's already home, but I'm sure you knew that," Darren said.

Mom?! No. Not possible.

"I'll try to make it."

Penny nudged him, giving him a soft smile when Ethan turned to look at her. The light in his eyes had vanished, and she wanted to punch their intruders for that alone.

"Sorry, Penny, this is my brother, Darren, and his wife, Julie." The word *wife* came out as a sneer. *His brother?* This couldn't be the same Julie that Ethan had dated. Penny tried to keep her head still and her mouth closed, but all she wanted to do was gape. No wonder Ethan didn't want to discuss his family.

Although, they could both commiserate about their shitty relatives.

"It's nice to meet you," Penny replied, giving Julie and Darren a tight smile before focusing back on Ethan. He gripped her hand under the table, and she ran her thumb along his palm. The anger radiated off him, and she hated it. Their perfect moment had vanished.

Dammit. She'd finally kissed him again—and she wanted a repeat—but his brother and his *ex-girlfriend* were a major mood killer. Holy crap, it was like a daytime TV nightmare right in front of her. A slew of questions rolled through her brain, and she itched to blurt every one of them out, but she held it together. Explanations could come later.

Julie and Darren murmured their greetings, and Ethan just nodded and kept his focus on Penny. She tried not to fidget in her seat.

"We should let you get back to your meal," Darren said. "And we hope you'll make it to Christmas. Ally—and everyone else—will be heartbroken if you don't come."

Penny stared back at Darren. The sincerity in his voice appeared genuine, but the man had married his brother's girlfriend, so Penny took that sincerity with a large grain of salt.

"We'll see," Ethan muttered, and it was like he'd disappeared. Was he still hung up on his ex?

"Nice to meet you, Penny," Darren said with a final nod, before he led Julie away from the table.

Penny pulled her hand from Ethan's and looked him straight in the eye. "So, Julie? Please tell me your ex didn't marry your brother." She refused to let that elephant go unnoticed.

He hated the look in her eyes and let out a harsh laugh. He'd always kept this nightmare close to the vest, another reason why he'd avoided coming home, but there was no getting out of the conversation he never wanted to have.

"I think you already know the answer to that question."

"Wow. That's—that's something."

Questions swirled in her eyes. "It's something. Sorry about that. I haven't seen them in years. At least six years."

"So, your ex and your brother," she prodded.

"Yes. My ex and my brother. I'd love to tell you that they hooked up after Julie and I broke up, but that would be a lie." He hated how bitter he sounded, but it still pissed him off. His *goddamn* brother.

"Can we talk about it?" she asked.

"You sure you want all the gory details? It's worse than what happened with Michael."

"If you want to tell me." She held his gaze, and surprisingly all he saw was shock and anger. Pity was usually in the forefront when he started his tale—another reason he kept it to himself as much as possible. But he owed her an explanation after he'd shut down on her when Darren and Julie had arrived.

"Julie and I started dating in high school. After I was drafted, I continued to play with my juniors team and then moved to the AHL. I also moved around to a few different teams. Because of the uncertainty, Julie stayed here. She went to college, and we visited as much as we could. I knew my big break was coming. I'd been playing for New York's minor affiliate and had been called up a few times, and they were finally ready to keep me up. Sam, my agent, was finalizing my new contract, and I flew home to surprise Julie and give her the good news. She'd just finished her master's degree so I was hoping she'd move out to New York with me."

He paused and took a gulp of his beer. "I showed up at her apartment. I had a key, and I let myself in. And walked in on her and *my brother*. I lost it. Yelled and destroyed a few pieces of furniture." He shook his head, the image of Julie rolling around in bed with his brother was forever burned into his brain. "Not my finest moment."

She squeezed his hand. "I'm so sorry, Ethan."

"They'd been hooking up for months. Darren had just finished law school, and I was a hockey player that might never stay with the big leagues. She took the stable option."

"Don't you dare justify her actions. What she did—what he did—is reprehensible. Your own brother."

"Yes." He let out another harsh laugh. "But the joke was on her because the next week I signed a multi-year deal with New York and never looked back. Haven't seen either of them since right after I caught them. Needless to say, that was a wedding I skipped."

"Oh my God. How did your family react? I mean, they got married. Did they elope?"

"Nope. Had a traditional wedding, from what I was told. My little sister said it was rough for a while, but my parents supported the marriage. I've stayed away ever since." It still burned when he thought about it, but in the last few years, his anger and hurt rested solely with his brother and family. He didn't miss what he'd thought he'd had with Julie. He missed his family.

"That's awful. And it sucks that they didn't support you." From what she'd told him about her loving family, she knew a thing or two about that. It was never a subject he wanted to be able to commiserate with her on.

"My uncle was pissed at the entire situation, but he went to the wedding. Most of the family did."

She ran her thumb over his knuckles, and he linked their fingers, needing her touch. She held his gaze. "Please don't hate me for asking, but I have to. You shut down when you saw her. I know it's been years, but are you over her?"

"Yes. It sucks that it happened, but we weren't meant to work out. My family's reaction—basically losing a brother I'd looked up to—that is what angers me. Not her. My anger toward her faded a long time ago."

He hated the doubt in her eyes, but it—and their kiss—gave him hope, and he tugged her close.

"Talk to me. I can see the wheels spinning."

"It's just a lot to take in."

"Don't let them ruin our night."

"Sorry, still trying to process this. No wonder you were so angry when I told you about Michael."

"Of course, I was. Only an idiot would cheat on you."

"Same for you, too. She's an idiot. And your brother—I have no words." She grimaced. "Family shouldn't do shit like that."

"I know."

"What are you going to do about Christmas?" He'd successfully avoided Thanksgiving because of an away game, but the NHL shut down for the three days around Christmas so players could spend time with their families. Ethan was one of the few that didn't appreciate that gesture. Although Ally would be home and he missed his little sister.

"I'll show up and spend time with my sister and Robert. Ally graduates in the spring. I always flew her out to visit me in New York, but now that I'm home, I hope she'll stay close by. You'd love her. Her number love is strong. She's getting a degree in mathematics with a minor in statistics." He shot her a grin. While the thought of that degree gave him hives, he couldn't be prouder of his sister, and regardless of what happened with his family, he'd promised Ally that if the team didn't make the playoffs, he'd be there to cheer her on when she walked across that stage in May.

"Wow. That number game is stronger than mine. I'm just an accountant."

"But an amazing accountant. You haven't even made me look at any paperwork yet. That's my kind of accountant," he teased.

"Just you wait. It's the end of the year. The next few months—oh, the paperwork you'll sign."

She laughed as he shuddered.

"Just put those little flags you love where I have to sign. I trust you. Now, I'm done talking about our families and paperwork. They've rudely interrupted you finally kissing me."

"Pretty sure you kissed me first." Her false indignation was adorable, and he leaned in, pressing a kiss to her nose.

"Ethan. We really should call it a night," she said, but her actions belied her words as she continued to lean into him.

"Your place or mine?" he teased.

"Ethan. I'm still not sure this is a good idea." But her words held no weight as her lips met his and all thoughts of exes and families were pushed aside. He finally had her right where he wanted her.

***

"We're down by two with twenty minutes left. Get your shit together and win this. Colorado shouldn't be handing us our asses. They played a grinding game against LA last night, and we're rested. No excuses," Rob Malone, current Strikers coach, lovingly referred to as Bugsy, ordered the following night.

Bugsy might not have been looking directly at him, but Ethan felt the remarks aimed in his direction. Every shot of his had missed, and the one that had almost gone in had been on his own damn net. He'd been distracted since yesterday, and he knew it wasn't totally because of kissing Penny.

Not that he hadn't been thinking about kissing her again since he ran into her at Crash and Byrne last month. Okay, that was a lie, he'd been pissed that night, so kissing her hadn't been his first thought—probably his second. And after last night, he wanted a repeat. Multiple repeats. Kissing Penny was better than he remembered, and he was pissed that they'd been interrupted.

What were the fucking odds that Julie and Darren would show up at the same restaurant? He was just accepting the fact that he'd have to play nice at Christmas in two days, and to run into them when he wasn't ready—shit, what a nightmare.

And the doubt in Penny's eyes when she'd asked if he was over Julie—he still wasn't sure she'd believed him. Nor when he'd reiterated it as he'd helped her into a cab after she sternly refused to let them have a sleepover.

He bit back a grin. He was wearing her down. They were good together. He knew it. She knew it. She just wasn't ready to admit it yet.

CHAPTER 9

Penny walked up the front steps to her parents' house Sunday afternoon. Tasteful lights decorated the shrubs and front porch. Old-fashioned warm white lights, not those new ones that ended up looking blue. But no reindeer graced the yard, and no penguins marched up the front steps. Everything was subdued. One day she was going to have a house she could load up with lights. Her homeowner's association was very particular on what was allowed to be displayed, and large, light-up penguins weren't on the list. She appreciated how detailed their rules were and followed them to the letter, but one day a sleigh would sit in her front yard, maybe a reindeer or two beside it.

Yes, it was Christmas, and she should feel festive, but everything was still strained with her family, and she hated it. At least her mother was keeping it small this year, so it would only be the five of them. She straightened her Santa hat headband, and tightened her hold on the container of perfectly decorated cookies under her arm. She might not totally embrace the spirit this year, but her need to dress appropriately hadn't vanished. People called them ugly Christmas sweaters. She just called them sweaters. At least this one didn't light up. She bit back her smile and knocked on the door.

Her father opened the door and ushered her inside. He gave her a stiff hug, which she briefly returned. "Hi, Penny. I'm glad you could come." It was as close as her father would get to saying he'd missed her. Thanksgiving had been tense, and she'd managed to bail on the three dinners prior to that.

She wanted to say, *Of course I'm here, it's freaking Christmas.* But she resisted.

"Hi. Am I the first one here?" she asked.

"Yes. Jill called to say they would be a few minutes late."

Of course. Her sister never managed to be on time for anything. Punctuality was important. It was polite. Over the years, she'd resisted the urge to tell her sister they needed to be somewhere at least thirty minutes before the actual time.

Jill had called her last night to tell her that she better be at Christmas dinner because she had an announcement. Penny had an idea about what her sister was going to tell them. If Jill was pregnant, her parents would *ooh* and *ahh* about how excited they were that Jill was pregnant. And then they would look at her.

That sad look.

She'd seen that look before—when she'd called off her wedding.

That look sucked. It made her feel like she should be walking around with a baby bouncing on her hip, in her four-bedroom home, with a promotion. Oh, and the perfect husband who never would dream of cheating. Or at least have the illusion of a husband that never cheated. She'd started questioning her parents' perfect marriage after their blasé reaction to Michael's betrayal.

Penny bit back her laugh when she entered the kitchen. Her mother, wearing her now signature frilly apron, pulled a perfect turkey from the oven. How times had changed. After over thirty years in the financial field, her mother was now retired. No longer were meals made in a rush, which included defrosting chicken in the microwave.

She shuddered, remembering the rubber chicken of her youth.

Now her mom made meals from scratch. When she had time between her golf league and book club. It was like entering a parallel dimension when she came to visit. She'd seen *The Stepford Wives*, and it had freaked her out.

Her parents had met in college, completed their bachelor's degrees, were married, and then supported each other as they went for their master's degrees. Once college was completed, they bought a house, got a cat, and had two children. They'd been so career driven that sometimes she and Jill had wondered if their parents just had kids because it was next on the list.

List making must be genetic.

Her mother placed the turkey on the counter and turned. "Hello, Penny. We're so happy you could make it." Had her parents rehearsed that line?

"Hi, Mom." She moved to give her mother a hug, but stopped as her mother waved a hand around the curls on top of Penny's head.

"What's happening here?"

And here it comes.

Wait, how long had she been in the house? Three minutes…tops.

She wished that was a record, but sadly, the record of ninety seconds, when she'd come home from college with her nose pierced, still held up.

Granted, she had done it for shock value, so she couldn't really fault her father's outrage.

It'd hurt like a bitch—thank you low tolerance for pain.

"What's wrong with what?" Penny shot back.

"Your hair. It seems to be much curlier on the top and straighter on the bottom. It looks a little odd."

"Thanks, Mom," Penny replied as she tried to pull away from her mother, who had decided to grab her curls. "You really know how to make a girl feel good."

"Did you wash it today? Maybe you should go see my hairdresser."

"Yes, I showered, and no, I don't want to see your hairdresser," Penny grumbled. Self-esteem from sixty to zero in one point five seconds. Didn't know it could go in reverse.

"Don't be so grouchy, Penny. Frown lines will only get worse as you get older. Speaking of that, have you been using the moisturizer I gave you?"

"Yes, Mom." The anti-aging one. She was only twenty-eight. When had she gotten old enough to use that? By the time this conversation was over, she was going to need to start taking Prozac.

"Oh good, honey. I think you should get an eye cream, too. Might help with those dark circles." Her mother smiled at her.

Prozac and vodka. Were those on tonight's menu?

"We're here," Jill yelled from the living room.

"Oh, they're here," Penny's mom said, clapping her hands together in excitement. At least her mom's eyes lit up for one of her daughters. The perfect one, of course. Jill had started dating Brian three years ago. She'd then completed her master's degree at twenty-four. A year later she was married, and most likely she was here to tell everyone she was pregnant.

Right. On. Time.

God, she hated how bitter that sounded.

"Dinner's almost ready," her mother called out as Jill and Brian entered the kitchen.

"Mom, it smells great," Jill said as she tucked her shiny and straight blonde hair behind her ear.

Yep, straight—and not a hair out of place. Sometimes Penny

wondered if she was the milkman's kid, but supposedly her father had had curly hair, prior to it falling out.

"Thanks, honey. So what's this big news?" her mother asked, practically salivating.

"Oh, I couldn't wait to tell you, and I'm so happy everyone is here. You're going to be a grandma," Jill squealed as their mother swooped in to hug her.

"I just knew it. Finally, a little one to spoil. When are you due?" Penny's mother bent down to talk to Jill's non-existent belly.

"In about seven months. A summer baby," Jill replied.

"Congratulations, Jill," Penny said as she gave her sister a hug.

"Yes, congratulations." Their father came into the kitchen, shaking Brian's hand before hugging Jill. Penny shifted back into the corner as her mother raved about all the presents she would buy for her first grandchild.

"Penny, can you set the table?" her mother called out. "For six."

"Six? I don't think the baby needs a place setting yet. It's still inside Jill," Penny scoffed.

"No, there's someone else coming for dinner."

"Who? For Christmas? I thought this was a family dinner?" Penny asked.

"Yes. It is," her mother replied. The doorbell rang. "Penny, can you get that?"

Penny made her way to the front door. Who was coming for dinner? She opened the door and bit back a curse.

"You've got to be shitting me."

"Hi," Michael said. Michael. As in the cheating, douchebag ex, Michael. Family dinner, her ass. And on freaking Christmas? Who the hell had she pissed off?

"What are you doing here?" she demanded.

"I was invited for dinner," he replied, holding out a bottle of wine.

"Don't you have your own family?" she asked, refusing to take the bottle, and crossing her arms over her chest.

"Hello, Michael," Penny's mother said as she came down the hallway. "Penny, aren't you going to let him in?"

"Why is he here, Mother?" she gritted out.

"We thought you two should talk, and Michael said you won't return his phone calls," her mother continued.

She hated that she wasn't surprised by her mother's invitation to Michael. Where was the family loyalty?

"Maybe that's because I don't want to talk to him. I don't want to have anything to do with him. In case you forgot, he cheated on me."

"And I cannot apologize enough for that. I want to make this work, Penny. I love you," he pleaded.

"Penny, just listen to him," her father said as he came down the hall.

"You're all unbelievable. Was this all a ruse to get me here tonight? Is Jill even pregnant?"

Her mother gasped. "Of course she is. We had no idea she was pregnant until she just told all of us in the kitchen. Do you honestly believe we would stoop to that level?"

"I'm not sure, Mother. I'm just not sure." She shook her head, trying to hide her disbelief and pain. Not to sound melodramatic, but did they care about her feelings at all?

"Why don't we all go into the dining room and have a nice dinner," her mother said. She grabbed Penny's hand. "Let's not ruin Jill's special day."

"I'm pretty sure you did that when you invited Michael," she replied before spinning on her heel and stomping into the dining room. She was officially trapped. She would sit through one meal, and then she would leave. She had no desire to hear Michael out, but she wanted to support her sister. And it was Christmas, after all.

Michael took the seat next to her, and she scooted her chair away from him. He took her hand under the table and she wanted to vomit. She ripped her hand away from his grip. "Touch me again and I will punch you in the throat," she whispered harshly.

"Penny, please," he pleaded.

"No. I don't want to hear it. I'm going to have as nice a dinner as possible with my family because it's the holidays, and then we are going our separate ways, and I never want to see you again. I cannot believe you got them to invite you to dinner."

"How's work going, dear?" her mother asked. Penny turned to see her mother smiling at her. That brittle smile that never made it to her eyes. Appearances were everything to her family.

"It's fine." Short answers would get her through this meal.

Her mother kept up the conversation, asking Jill about work and Michael about his family. Her father talked about the office. All in all, it was typical dinner conversation, as if there wasn't a giant cheating bastard elephant in the room.

When Michael mentioned for the fourth time how much he'd missed everyone and how happy he was to be at a family dinner again, she resisted the urge to stab him with her fork, but couldn't take it anymore.

"I can't do this," she said as she shoved back from the table, her chair falling to the floor.

"Penny," her mother gasped.

"No. I need to go. I'm sorry to ruin Christmas." She rushed from the dining room and was in her car and down the street before she realized it. Luckily, it was a short drive home because the tears racing down her cheeks were disturbing her vision. She should've stood up for herself more, ordered Michael to leave, but she'd let him in. Let her family think that what they'd done was okay. Why did she let them walk all over her?

She pulled into the lot behind her building and made it into her townhouse without seeing anyone. She probably looked a fright. She stripped off her clothes and climbed into bed, pulling the covers over body, and curled up in a fetal position. She was moving past her cheating ex, but could she move past the fact that her family continued to support their reconciliation? Why was it so difficult for them to be on her side?

She itched to call Ethan. And say what? Come over? My family sucks. Your family sucks. Let's commiserate.

But he was probably dealing with his own holiday drama. While her situation was awful, it couldn't compare to what Ethan was going through tonight. She was still reeling from his confession about his brother. Who did that? And how could his family support Ethan's brother and ex? No wonder Ethan had stayed away.

And yet she wanted to be there for him today. Maybe squeeze his hand under the table in support. Maybe stake her claim.

She paused. She had no claim on Ethan. She wasn't supposed to *want* a claim on Ethan. But with each day, she did. And those kisses—she'd missed those kisses.

They'd been just as amazing as she'd remembered, but she was apprehensive. So many things could still go wrong, and her judgment had clearly proved faulty before. Could she trust herself now?

Ethan took in a deep breath and rang the doorbell. He'd grown up in this house, but he no longer felt welcome. Just a visitor wishing he'd come down with a stomach virus or something. How was that for holiday cheer? Ally had called him again this morning to make sure he wasn't going to bail. He wished Penny was standing next to him. She centered him, even when she was driving him crazy and running away. Hopefully, their kiss the other night had changed things, but he couldn't be sure.

"You're here," his little sister said, slipping through the open front door and slamming into him. He had to juggle the bottle of wine that threatened to crash on the front steps.

He chuckled, wrapping his arms around her and giving her a tight hug. She burrowed into his chest like she had when she had been a kid afraid of a storm. Even before the nightmare with his brother, Ethan had always been closer to Ally. She was eight years younger than him, a happy mistake in his parents' eyes, but for some reason, he'd always been able to relate so much more to her than to Darren, who was only two years older than him. Their personalities just meshed.

When everything had gone down six years ago, she'd only been sixteen. He'd hated not seeing her, but he couldn't bring himself to come home. But two years later, they'd picked up right where they'd left off. Visiting her at college, or flying her out to see him, had strengthened their bond even further over the last four years.

"Hey squirt, it's good to see you, too," he said, his laugh muffled in her hair.

"Don't call me squirt. I can't help it that you're a giant." She pulled back, grinning at him. "I'm so happy you didn't bail."

"I am feeling a little nauseated," he said, reaching up to tweak her nose.

"Seriously, how are you doing?" she asked, her smile soft.

"I'm fine. It's just dinner, and I have you to distract me," he said, trying to reassure her. Christmas dinner probably wasn't the best time for this little reunion, but he'd been away for Thanksgiving, and he'd had no desire to show up for a random family dinner.

"Well, I'm glad you're here. I haven't seen you in ages." She pouted, drawing out that last word. Sometimes he wondered if she should've gone into acting instead of mathematics. So dramatic.

"I've been home since September. You've just been too busy with school to come visit. All those numbers taking up your time." He grinned, and his thoughts turned to Penny and her obsession with numbers and lists. He wondered how she was doing tonight. He itched to text her, but resisted.

"What's that look for?" Ally asked, cutting through his thoughts.

"Nothing. Are you coming to the game on Tuesday?" he asked, hoping to steer her away from more questions. Not that Ally wouldn't love Penny, and hopefully vice versa. He just wasn't ready to talk about her with Ally.

"Of course. Right next to the penalty box, please. I like seeing those hot guys all riled up," she said, grinning. "Especially Dominic. He's yummy. And single, right?"

That mischievous twinkle in her blue eyes, that perfectly matched his, set him on edge. "Absolutely not. No hockey players for you. We're all horrible. And I'll get you seats in the upper bowl. A bird's-eye view of the game is the best way to watch it."

"No, it's not, and you're not all horrible. But I bet Dom is," she said with a grin.

"I retract my offer. No games for you," he said, tucking her under his arm.

"So not fair. What good is having a hockey player brother if he's not going to introduce me to his hot teammates?" she said.

"When do you go back to school again?"

"You know I'm teasing. And it's good to see you smiling again. Should we go in and polish off a bottle of what I'm assuming is ridiculously expensive wine?"

"Might as well." Or they could just stay out on the front

stairs. It wasn't that cold out. Especially compared to the East Coast winters he'd gotten used to.

"And you can tell me all about your new girlfriend," she said, and then turned and walked into the house.

He was stunned for a moment. "Wait. What are you talking about?"

"Darren said he ran into you looking cozy with a puck bunny," she replied.

"What the fuck? She's not a puck bunny," he growled. He knew by her giggle that he'd been caught.

"Ooh, sounds serious. Darren just said he ran into you on a date. I added the puck bunny part."

He shook his head. He'd fallen right into that. "You scare me sometimes."

"Only sometimes? Guess I have to up my game."

He laughed, following her into the house, feeling relaxed for the first time since he'd woken up this morning.

"I haven't heard that laugh in so long." His mother's hushed words cut his chuckle, and he stared back at the woman he hadn't seen in six years. Her small smile was a twist to his gut, and he knew how selfish it'd been to stay away for so long, and yet he'd still done it.

"Hi, Mom," he said. She rushed toward him, wrapping her arms around his waist, squeezing him as tightly as she could.

"I can't believe we finally got you home. I've missed you so much," she whispered against his chest.

He tried to hold back his shock as he held her. Yes, he'd had his reasons, but in this moment, he realized he'd been a complete ass. He'd stayed away for too long. Maybe not from his brother and Julie. But from his mom. From everyone else. He might tower over his petite mother, but in that moment he felt about three inches tall.

"I missed you, too, Mom," he said, his voice gruff. He pressed a kiss to the top of her head.

She pulled back, her emotions clear on her face. "It shouldn't have taken you this long to come home, but I understand. And your father and I are sorry for everything that happened." The last sentence was whispered, and he stared down at her. Had they not truly supported what Darren and Julie had done?

Ethan was determined to move past this. It was time. "I'm sorry for staying away, but I'm here now."

"Yes, you are. And I expect you to come to dinner without Ally forcing your hand."

"I will," he promised.

"Good. Now, it's almost time to eat, so let's go," she said, giving him a pat on his back before spinning on her heel and heading down the hall to the kitchen.

"See. That wasn't painful," Ally said, a soft smile playing at the edge of her lips. "Now, can we talk about my hockey seats?"

He pulled her in tight, and chuckled. "Nosebleeds for you, kid." As he followed in his mother's wake, with Ally at his side, he hoped the rest of the night would go just as smoothly.

"You made it," Robert called out. He came over to relieve Ethan of his bottle of wine, and gave his shoulder a squeeze.

His father walked over, giving him a stiff hug. "Ethan, it's good to see you. It's been a while."

"Yes, it has," Ethan said, returning the hug. This was going much better than he'd anticipated.

"Can I get you anything?" his father asked, as if no time or separation had occurred. That was his father's way.

"Dinner's ready," his mother called out, bringing one last dish with her. "Ethan, you can sit next to Ally."

"I finally graduated from the kid's table," Ally said, steering him toward his mother's end of the table. He muttered greetings to a few cousins, another uncle, and his aunt, and took a seat.

"That's because you were the last kid left," Ethan said, reaching up to tweak her ear.

"Hey, knock it off," Ally exclaimed in fake annoyance.

"One day we'll have more kids in the family." Ethan didn't miss the wistful tone in his mother's voice.

"Yes, you will," Julie called out. Ethan bit back the pure irritation coursing through him. He'd managed to not acknowledge them at all, spotting them at the other end of the table right before he'd sat down. He'd kept his expression neutral, still hating the fact that she was here. That they still hadn't apologized for what they'd done behind his back.

He swore he was over her, and he was. But his brother, that was another story.

"Did you have something to tell us, dear?" his mother asked.

"Not yet. But, we are planning on kids, hopefully in the near future," she said, her smile bordering on smug. Why hadn't he seen her constant need for attention when they'd been together? Of course, they'd both been so young, and thinking back, he'd overlooked a lot of things because he'd thought he was in love with her. But the lust-clouded glasses had broken long ago. Not that he was grateful for what had happened, but he was happy that they hadn't ended up together. If only the guy she'd ended up with hadn't been his brother, then Ethan would have no issues.

"Julie. Now isn't the time," Darren bit out, his hand gripping his wine glass tight enough that Ethan feared for the stem.

"What? It's the holidays, and we're all family," she said before taking a sip from her glass.

Ethan turned back to his mother and Ally, focusing on the conversation around him, answering questions about the team and if he missed New York. He tuned out his brother and Julie. They'd hash it out eventually. Even he knew they couldn't avoid it. But for now, he was happy to be back with his family. Sure, it would never be the same as before, and he probably wouldn't show up for dinner once a week, but it was a start. That's all he could ask for.

CHAPTER 10

"You ready?"

Penny jerked her head up at Lexi's voice. Shit. Was it noon already? She'd made lunch plans with Lexi this morning. Penny glanced at the clock on her computer. Twelve on the dot. Crap, she was so behind today. It was the first day back after the extended holiday weekend. She had a surprise training session with Kevin, where he'd refused to take notes again, and now she was behind. But she needed to get out of the office before she drove herself insane. She saved the file she was working on and pushed away from her desk.

"I am now," she said, standing up and grabbing her phone.

"Can't wait to escape already?" Lexi teased. Penny leaned over her desk and clicked save one last time for good measure before slipping on her coat.

"End of year craziness, but we scheduled lunch, so I'm ready." And now that she thought about it, she was hungry.

"We can skip if you want," Lexi said just as her stomach growled.

Penny laughed. "Your stomach disagrees."

"I thought those Christmas cookies I had for breakfast

would hold me over, but I was wrong," Lexi said, and Penny chuckled.

"Christmas cookies for breakfast? Did Abby get cookies, too?" Penny asked. Not that she would mind cookies for breakfast. Especially the Italian treats that Grant's mother had no doubt provided. Damn. Now she wanted cookies.

"Of course not. She had a well-balanced breakfast of cereal. And not a sugary kind, thank you very much. I wasn't in the mood to make anything for myself, so cookies it was," Lexi said, and then grinned. "The usual?"

"Sure," Penny replied. They headed out of the office, and to the café down the street.

"So, bad day?" Lexi asked after the waitress had dropped off their drinks and taken their lunch orders.

"Just the usual. Kevin is driving me insane. We all know he only has his job because of his father. He's not even applying himself, or taking any notes. Robert assigned him a small, standard account. A married couple with regular jobs, a primary home, and no kids. I mean, it's basic tax preparing 101, and he still asked where to list the mortgage interest." She shook her head. "Did he even go to school for this? Yes, we aren't doing actual live returns right now. We are at least a month out, but come on. How is he going to keep pace over the next few months when we are slammed and I can't correct every file?" She huffed in irritation. She'd never had this much trouble training someone, and it rankled.

"Yikes. I think even I could prepare that return."

"If he can't handle a basic tax return, how is he going to handle our clients with multiple properties and multiple businesses?" Penny grimaced. He was not going to ruin her perfect record of trainees, dammit.

"Why don't you talk to Alan, or even Robert, about it?" Lexi asked.

"It's a dicey situation since he's Alan's son. How am I supposed to tell him that basic calculations stump his son?"

"It completely sucks, but you'll whip him into shape," Lexi said.

"This one might be a lost cause. And what will that say to Robert and Alan? Why would they promote me if I can't bring Kevin up to snuff?" She hated how whiny she sounded, but it freaking irritated the hell out of her that Kevin's lack of giving a shit would reflect poorly in how the company owners viewed her ability to train efficient staff. Robert hadn't brought up the possible promotion recently, but she had to believe it was still on the table.

"You'll figure it out. Now, enough about the clueless one, tell me all about Christmas."

"What?" Penny sputtered, almost knocking over her glass at Lexi's abrupt change of topic.

"Christmas. You know that holiday we had a few days ago? Presents? Crazy family drama? How did it go?" Lexi asked. She smiled as she took a sip of her soda.

Lexi got right to the heart of it, but Penny didn't want to talk about running out on her family. It still hurt. She ducked her head, taking a long sip of her soda, mumbling, "It was fine. Yours?"

Lexi sat up straighter, her eyes locking with Penny's. "Oh no, what the hell happened?"

"Just a standard family holiday dinner. Jill is pregnant. Mom commented on my hair. And Michael was invited."

Lexi visibly recoiled. "What the actual fuck?"

"Oh look, here's lunch," Penny said, heat staining her cheeks. The waitress had definitely heard Lexi's outburst.

"Sorry for that," Lexi said. She gave Penny a pained smile. "Are you serious? Good thing Amanda isn't here. She would've been a lot louder."

Penny half-grimaced, half-smiled, and let out a small huff of laughter. "You think? I will be relaying this info to her via text."

"I'm half-tempted to tell her to get over here now."

"Please don't. I'll work up to telling her. She's going to lose it. More than you just did. You're the more rational one of the group," Penny said, hating the hitch in her voice. She would not lose it at lunch. Over the last day and a half, she cried tears she didn't even know she still had.

Lexi reached out and squeezed Penny's hand. "Whatever bodily harm you want me to inflict on him, just let me know. Or I can send Grant over. He can be scary if you need him."

Penny barked out a strained laugh. "Good to know. And I don't believe that about Grant."

"Believe it. He keeps his temper under wraps. I've only seen it a few times. Remember that douche you set me up with that Grant ended up punching? Not that the ass didn't deserve what he had coming to him."

"I'm still so sorry about that. Michael said he was a nice guy. Of course, coming from Michael, that's not saying much," Penny grumbled. She'd been so freaking pissed when Lexi had told her about the set-up that had gone horribly wrong. Michael had recommended one of his friends and co-workers for Lexi to meet, and Penny hadn't vetted him. She hadn't even asked her father about the guy.

The guy had tried to get Lexi drunk and had gotten super handsy. Luckily, Grant had swooped in and rescued her—a task he excelled at—and punched the guy in the process. It'd been well-deserved from what Lexi had told her. Penny had been furious with Michael, but he had just shrugged it off, saying his friend had too much to drink and wasn't usually like that.

His blasé response should've been another red flag, but Penny overlooked it. She'd overlooked a lot.

"Don't worry about it. It's kind of hot when Grant gets caveman-y." Lexi grinned, pulling Penny back from her thoughts.

"Now. Stop distracting me and tell me about dinner," Lexi continued.

"Okay. My mother asked me to answer the door, and there he was, bottle of wine in hand, smug smile in place. I mean, how could they?"

"Seriously, what the hell is wrong with them? I mean, I get that Michael works for your father, but blood should take precedence over business. And it was freaking Christmas dinner."

Penny continued to rehash the events of Christmas dinner, and Lexi's anger grew. "You really should've stabbed him with that fork," Lexi said.

"I know, but instead I bolted. I'm trying to put everything behind me and fix my relationship with my parents but they are not helping. Then I cried myself to sleep and wished I could call Ethan." Penny's hand shot up, covering her mouth. Dammit. She hadn't meant to bring him up.

"Oh, Penny. I hate that you are going through this, but you've been holding out on me." She *tsked* and shot Penny a grin. "So, what's going on with Ethan, and why couldn't you call him?"

"It's nothing. It's not like we spend a lot of time talking on the phone, or hang out, or anything like that," she said, and then took a bite of her sandwich. Maybe if her mouth was full, she'd stop offering up info she wasn't ready to share. If she didn't talk about Ethan, then she wasn't putting herself out there with him and risking her heart again. She internally shook her head. Did she want to put herself out there with him?

A shouted *yes, you idiot* rang through her head. Not that she hadn't already figured that out. She just wasn't in the mood to admit it yet.

"What's going on in there?" Lexi asked with a wave of her hand, her sandwich forgotten as her grin widened.

"Nothing. We had dinner last week, and he kissed me, and

then we ran into his ex." And there she went again, offering up unsolicited information.

"You kissed him?" Lexi asked. Penny didn't think her friend's grin could get any wider.

"No. I said he kissed me." And then she'd kissed him, and he'd returned the favor multiple times. God. She wanted to see him again. Stupid away games. But he said he'd be home this weekend. Not that they'd made plans or anything.

"Oh. And I'm sure you didn't climb into his lap and kiss him right back."

"I did not. We were in a restaurant."

Lexi laughed. "Wait. Is that so wrong? You should try it sometime."

Penny rolled her eyes. That's exactly what Lexi had done on her first non-date with Grant. She'd never known her friend had it in her. Amanda, definitely. But never Lexi. And after everything Lexi had been through, with her husband leaving her to raise their infant daughter alone five years ago, Penny was grateful that Grant had stumbled into her friend's life.

Hell, she wanted that. The love, and the ease of being with someone she could count on—could trust. But could she have that with Ethan? Was he ready? Was she?

Her thoughts instantly went back to that dinner. That amazing kiss that was rudely interrupted by his ex. He swore he was over her, but the following night he'd played horribly. She was still trying to figure out the game, but his distraction on the ice had been clear, even to her.

She wanted to trust him. She just wasn't sure she could trust herself.

Ethan refused to acknowledge the spark that rolled through him as he walked down the hall to Penny's office. He hadn't seen her in a week, since that kiss. Christmas and mismatched schedules had halted any follow up kisses. She'd hinted about not having plans tonight, and he didn't have a game, so here he was, trying to avoid bumping into his uncle and the questions that would follow.

He rapped sharply on her door and ducked his head in when she called out to enter.

"I'm here for that nooner you mentioned last week," he said. He shot her a grin and walked into her office, shutting the door behind him.

Her cheeks flushed a brilliant red. "Seriously, you can't say shit like that out loud. People—your uncle—could've heard you."

"I didn't shout it. I promise no one heard anything. The hallway was blissfully empty."

"That's because it's almost six. A little late for a nooner."

He loved how flushed her cheeks were as she whispered that last word.

"But now you're thinking about one," he said.

"I am not, and I don't recall mentioning a nooner anyway."

"Are you accusing me of making that up?" he said, his grin widening as she rolled her eyes and tucked a blonde curl behind her delectable ear. He planned to taste that skin in the very near future.

"Ethan, what are you doing here? What if someone saw you? Like Robert?"

He caught the panic in her voice and felt like an ass. He'd convinced her that not telling his uncle right now would be okay, and then he'd busted into her office after hours.

"I'm sorry, Penny. I know that you are taking a risk, but I did peek down the hallway before heading toward your office, and no one was coming. Plus, I'm a client, so this could totally be work related."

"That is a weak excuse, at best," she said. "So, what are you doing here?"

"You mentioned that you didn't have plans tonight, so I'm here to convince you that you should have dinner and drinks with me instead of washing your hair."

She laughed. "Washing my hair? Really? You've turned me into a cliché."

"I mean, if you need to wash your hair, I'm happy to help. You know, to conserve water," he said, wiggling his eyebrows at her, loving her bold laugh. He'd make it his goal to only make her laugh that way from now on.

"You have a one-track mind," she said as she ran her fingers over her keyboard and stacked the paperwork on her desk. Clear signs that it wouldn't take much to convince her to join him tonight.

"And you've missed it," he shot back with a grin. "Now pack up your stuff. I'm busting you out of here. You're probably starving."

"I'm fine," she said, but he heard the hesitation in her voice, so he pressed on, propping his ass onto the edge of her desk.

"Come on. Have dinner with me." He reached out, trailing his finger down her soft cheek, relishing in the hitch in her breath and the shudder that rolled through her.

"I don't know if that's a good idea."

"You know you want to, and I bet you're hungry," he said.

She nodded, her eyes darkening, and he knew she was interested in more than just food. "Maybe," she said.

"Me too," he whispered. He lowered his head, pressing his lips tentatively to hers. At her sharp breath and moan, he cupped her cheek and deepened the kiss. His belly churned with need, and he itched to spread her out on the desk and do what he'd wanted to do since he'd seen her last month.

He ended the kiss and reached down, pulling her from her chair and turning to place her on the edge of her desk.

"Ethan," she gasped, her hands immediately linking behind his neck, a shiver rolling through him as her nails brushed against his skin.

"I was getting a crick in my neck," he said by way of explanation. sealing their lips again, and devouring her mouth. She groaned against him, her fingers curling into his hair, scraping against his scalp. He tilted his head for the perfect angle, and she opened her mouth to his questing tongue. She tasted just as amazing as he'd remembered.

He swallowed her moan as their tongues tangled, and she pressed flush against his chest. He broke away and trailed kisses down her throat before finding that spot behind her ear that drove her insane. Her hands tightened in his hair as he nibbled along her collarbone, bathing her skin in kisses, thrilling at every gasp, every indrawn breath, and every soft moan of his name.

"Ethan, we should stop," she panted as he continued his torment, his body tight with need. His thigh pressed between her legs, heat radiating off her body. How much damage would they do if he just swept the contents of her desk to the floor? The computer could stay. The rest was in the way.

"You started it," he mumbled against her throat.

"No I did not," she pushed back from him in outrage.

He chuckled, pressing his lips to her throat. "Okay, maybe not, but I can't resist you. Now, shut everything down so we can grab dinner before I send everything on your desk to the floor and kiss you how I really want to."

She scrambled away from him, saving a file on her computer and tucking file folders into her desk drawer.

"I'm not sure if you really want to get out of here, or if you're worried I'll mess up your organized system by knocking everything to the floor." He shook his head at her glare, but she didn't disagree with him.

"You are not ravishing me on my desk. My files are perfectly organized and stacked for review. And someone could walk in."

"I'm not sure what concerns you the most, but I locked the door," he said, leaning down to nibble on her lips.

She broke the kiss, glancing at the door.

"You don't believe me? I have no desire for anyone to interrupt us. It's another reason why I showed up after five on a Friday. Most people have already bailed for happy hours and to start their weekends."

"That's very considerate of you," she said, her desk finally clear of paperwork.

"Isn't it? So how about I ravish you on the desk now," he said, grinning and moving toward her. She held him off with a hand.

"Nope. I'm starved—for food. Let's go."

"You are a tease," he said, helping her into her coat, using that as an excuse to brush his fingers under her collar. He felt the shudder rock through her. He resisted the urge to pull her against his body.

She spun in his arms and pressed a hard kiss to his lips, stealing his breath. "So are you," she said as she flooded her office in darkness and opened the door.

"Oh, Penny. I didn't realize you were still here," a woman said, heading down the hall toward them.

Ethan felt Penny stiffen, and then she stepped away from him with a muttered *dammit*.

"Hi, Jessica. I thought you'd headed out with everyone for drinks."

"Not yet. Just finishing up one last account, and then I'm leaving." Jessica focused on him. "You look familiar. Have we met?"

"I don't believe so." He held out his hand. "Ethan, nice to meet you."

"Ethan. Oh right, you're Mr. Knight's nephew. I've seen you in the office."

"Yes. Robert assigned Ethan's account to me, so we were just finishing up some paperwork," Penny chimed in a little too brightly. Ethan caught the slow smile on Jessica's face.

"Well, have a good weekend. Nice to officially meet you, Ethan," Jessica said.

"Shit. This is what I didn't want," Penny bit out after Jessica was out of sight.

"What's wrong?" he asked, keeping pace with her as she briskly walked down the hall toward the lobby. He grabbed her hand as soon as the building door shut behind them.

"She's the biggest gossip in the office, and she just caught you, the boss's nephew, walking out of my office after hours."

"Don't worry about it. I'm your client, so going over paperwork at six isn't a huge deal," he said.

"Don't say that you're a client. That makes it even worse."

"Even if we haven't actually gone over anything yet because the new year just started? Don't stress. And who cares what she thinks?"

"I do," she muttered.

"Well, stop." He linked his hand with hers, pulling her outside into the crisp night air. It stole his breath for a moment. "If there's gossip, don't listen to it. I know you're concerned about how this looks, you working for my uncle and working on my account, but we aren't doing anything wrong. Let's just wait and see if anyone says anything, okay?" He tried to reassure her, tugging her close and brushing a kiss across her brow when they were out of sight of the office. He hoped she'd come to terms with what they were. It was only a matter of time before everything came out. Hopefully not the part about Italy, but everything always came out eventually. They'd done nothing wrong, and he would prove that to her, no matter what happened.

"Now, no more freaking out. I'm starving."

She laughed when his stomach rumbled. "Far be it for me to let you starve."

He tucked her into his side as they walked down the street, attempting to shield her from the bracing wind and anything else she wanted to be protected from. He was determined to make this work.

CHAPTER 11

Penny pulled her hand from Ethan's, grabbing the martini the waitress had dropped off and took a healthy sip. Anything to make him stop touching her. He was driving her crazy and doing it on purpose. She hadn't been able to stop herself from agreeing to dinner when he'd ambushed her in her office a few hours ago.

This was her last drink and then she was going home. *Maybe.*

"So where are we going on our next date?" he asked.

"This isn't a date," she replied.

"It's Friday night, and we are out having drinks, just the two of us. And we had nachos. And burgers. That's an appetizer and an entrée. This is a date." He flashed her that crooked smile that made her want to agree to anything he said.

"This is friends getting a bite to eat."

His thumb traced over her palm and desire shot down to her toes. The stress of the week, of running into the office gossip after he'd kissed the hell out of her in her office, vanished as she took another sip of her martini and tried to blame the warmth in her belly on the booze.

"Whatever. This is a date."

She laughed. "So, if I were to agree to an actual date, what would you suggest?"

He grinned, probably thinking he had her. Hell. He did. "Dinner and then skeeball?"

"Skeeball?"

"Apparently, there's a bar crawl and a bunch of bars have skeeball machines and hold tournaments. Competition and booze. Could be fun," he said.

She laughed. "I secretly love arcade games. Haven't played in years, but I excelled at skeeball."

He chuckled. "See, I knew it was the perfect date idea."

"Even if I beat you?"

"If it gets you to agree to a date, then I'm in. But, I'm very coordinated and excel at all forms of competition, so you can try…" he trailed off, his eyes twinkling under the low light.

Twinkling? Seriously?

"Cocky bastard," she said, shaking her head. She'd show him. "And I could totally win. I'm coordinated, too."

"Really? I think your knee disagrees. How's it doing, by the way?"

"I almost have my full range of motion back. I did have a little setback a few months ago when I slipped in the shower. Took the curtain right down with me, so at least the floor didn't get wet." She shook her head, cringing.

"Oh, man. And yes, it's a good thing you managed to keep the floor dry in your fall." He shook his head. "You are definitely not coordinated. Penny, what are we going to do with you?"

She refused to think about how loaded that question was as he smiled at her, desire-filled promises in his eyes that she wanted to explore.

"Don't make fun of me. I can't help being clumsy. You know, I never crawled as a baby. They say that babies who never crawl and just go straight to walking end up being clumsy adults. So it's not my fault," she huffed.

He linked his hand with hers. "I'm just teasing you. I'm glad the knee is healing. Maybe we should go to a museum instead. Walk slow, take in the exhibits. Just like in Italy. And then we can go to this gelateria up in North Beach that you'll love. I've heard great things about their stracciatella. Wasn't that your favorite?"

Dammit. He was getting her with the memories, and now the gelato.

"Maybe." She'd give in to him. She was tired of being stronger because of work and whatever reasoning she could drum up to not see him.

"Maybe isn't no," he said.

"Ethan, we probably shouldn't." But she wanted to. Oh, how she wanted to.

"We can go as friends," he said.

"Can we?" She tilted her head in question.

He chuckled. "Okay. Maybe not, but I'm trying here."

"I know. I'm sorry for being difficult."

"You're worth it," he murmured as he squeezed her hand. She stopped breathing. His touch. Those words. They wreaked havoc on her self-control, as did the kisses she couldn't resist.

She knocked back the rest of her martini to keep from leaning across the table and kissing her self-control goodbye—and him. "I really should get going." She felt that warm buzzy feeling run through her body and knew that chugging that last drink hadn't been a good idea.

"Please don't rush off," he said as he took another long drink of his beer. She watched his throat muscles move as he swallowed, his strong jaw covered in the stubble that she wanted to run her hands over. She shook her head, trying to clear her fuzzy brain.

"Another round?"

Penny's head jerked to see the waitress standing next to her. *Jesus!* She hadn't even heard her approach. And there the waitress was, smiling at Ethan, not even attempting to hide her perusal of him. Penny looked over to see Ethan looking at her, and not the waitress. It was on the tip of her tongue to ask for the tab.

"Sure, I'll have another." Who said that? It sounded like her voice, but she hadn't planned on having another drink.

His eyebrow quirked in question, but he said nothing. She shrugged and played with the napkin her empty martini glass had been on, before looking up at him.

"Guess I'm not ready to go after all," she said with a shrug.

His grin widened. "I'll take another one, too." The waitress spun on her heel, leaving them alone again.

"I watched your game last night."

"Really? What did you think? I played much better than I did before the Christmas break," he said.

"Do you want to talk about Christmas?" she asked, stupidly needing to be reminded of his baggage. Like that would change how she felt about him and how much she wanted this night to continue.

"It wasn't as awful as I anticipated. My parents missed me, and my little sister kept me entertained for the night. I didn't speak to my brother, but it's probably better that way."

The frustration was clear in his voice, as was the happiness when he mentioned his parents and sister.

"I'm glad it went well, for the most part. I'm sorry you have to deal with them."

"It's fine. It's not a problem for me anymore."

God, how she wanted to believe him, but she saw how he'd played the night after they'd run into his ex and his brother. It still affected him, even if he didn't want to believe it. And it was still there, hanging over whatever was happening between them, but for now, she'd let it go.

"What about you?" he asked.

"Fine. My sister is pregnant, and everyone is happy about it.

It was small this year. Just my parents and my sister and brother-in-law." She left out Michael, having no desire to have that conversation and hating herself for bringing up the sticky subject to begin with. "I'm just glad the holidays are over."

"Me too. I just wish I was here for New Year's Eve. You would be required to accompany me on a date."

She didn't balk at his quick change of topic since she had no desire to talk about her family either. "Really? Required? New Year's is only two days from now. A little presumptuous to assume I don't have plans," she huffed.

"I just would've invited myself along," he said with complete seriousness, and she couldn't fight her smile.

"So I take it you have an away game?"

"Yes. It would be our second date, but I have an away game. Leaving early tomorrow and we're gone for most of the week. Eastern road trip. Three games in five days."

"That's a lot."

"Yes, but we are playing both New York teams and Philly, so it's not that much travel once we're out there."

"This will be the first time you play in your old arena, right?"

"Yeah. It'll be bittersweet. I called that arena home for over five years."

"Is it weird to play against your old teammates?"

"It is, but we do it all the time in international competitions. You're adversaries on the ice, but once you're off, you're back to being friends."

"That's so strange," she said, fascinated by the very idea of supporting your teammates at the international level that you'd just tried to take down at the national level. How did you quickly switch who you were competing against?

"Nature of the game. And at some point, you've played on a team with almost everyone, between juniors and the pros."

"Maybe I could come to another game some time," she said.

"Just let me know ahead of time, and I'll have tickets waiting for you. But you have to promise to be decked out in my jersey."

"I'll think about it. Twenty-two isn't really my number."

He laughed, then leaned across the table, and pressed a hard kiss to her lips.

"What was that for?"

"Because I felt like it. Do I really need a reason?"

"No," she whispered, kissing him back.

* * *

Before she knew it, three hours had passed and the drinks and conversation had continued at a steady pace. They'd moved on from discussing his away trip to the game in general, and on to all the possible dates he'd come up with, including the Exploratorium. She'd thought it was just a kid's science museum. But, apparently, it was adults only on Thursday nights. She refused to acknowledge her flushed cheeks when she thought about sneaking into dark alcoves with him. She'd even offered to take him to her favorite spot in the city. It must have been the alcohol talking at that point.

He knew most of the places since he'd grown up here and had gone to school in the area. She wondered if they'd ever crossed paths when they both lived in the city over the years.

She was definitely feeling fuzzier than she'd planned, but she could honestly say that she didn't regret her decision to stay. Again, that was probably the alcohol talking. The same alcohol that had her sitting closer and closer to Ethan by the hour.

They were facing each other. Drinks forgotten on the table as Ethan told her about getting lost with his cousin during a tour of Alcatraz when they were kids.

His eyes sparkled with humor, and she leaned in closer, shifting her body.

And then her butt started to slide off the stool, and her eyes widened. Her mind moved in slow motion, and before she could utter *oh shit*, Ethan had hopped out of his seat and caught her against his chest.

"Oomph." She found herself plastered against him. *Plastered*, now that was a funny word, and at this point, could have two meanings. No, she wasn't completely plastered. It wasn't as if she was about to pass out from the booze.

Although, he was doing a number on her senses just by holding her, so passing out was still an option.

"Weren't we talking about your coordination skills earlier? Are you okay?" he asked, still not releasing her.

His breath washed over her face. It should smell. Why didn't it smell? Hours of beer and bar food should make his breath unpleasant. Had he popped a mint when she wasn't looking? His hands were on her waist, holding her steady. She tried to step back, but he held her firm.

"I'm okay." Wow, did her voice sound as breathy to him as it had to her?

"Are you sure?" he asked.

"Yeah," she said as she tried to straighten. Her traitorous feet wobbled beneath her.

She laughed. "I just haven't stood up in a while." She sounded loud. "I'm going to go to the restroom and I'll be right back," she continued.

"Okay."

He backed away slightly, still holding her hand as she steadied herself on her feet.

She made her way to the bathroom, weaving between the high top tables and concentrating on putting one foot in front of the other. She knew he was watching her, and the last thing she wanted was to faceplant onto the floor.

It would be sticky and gross. And not to mention, mortifying. No thanks.

After entering the surprisingly empty women's restroom,

she quickly finished and made her way slowly back to Ethan. One foot in front of the other.

She glanced up to see him watching her, and her cheeks heated.

It wasn't him, it was the alcohol.

Who was she kidding? It was totally not the alcohol.

He looked so hot. His shirt molded to his chest. Not super tight so that he looked ridiculous, but fitted enough to hint at the pecs she wanted to nip with her teeth. His hair was mussed and her fingers were itching to run through it again. It should be a crime to have hair that soft.

He stood as she got closer to him.

"What?" she asked as she got within speaking range of him.

"Just wanted to be ready in case you wobbled again." He smiled at her. A small smile that made her heart flip over in her chest.

"Very funny," she said, moving to take her seat.

Before she knew what was happening, he'd lifted her up and plopped her onto the barstool.

"Whoa." She reached out, putting her hand on his shoulder to steady herself. His muscles bunched under her grip. There was something so unbelievably sexy about having him lift her with ease. "You didn't have to do that," she said, trying to steady her breath, her heart still racing.

"Yes, I did," he said, standing in front of her, invading her personal space, his intent clear.

His hands hadn't left her waist, and they burned through the fabric of her skirt like a brand.

"I'm fine, thank you," she said, but he moved in closer.

His lips were a breath away from hers. "You know that blush is quite adorable on you."

"Ethan, we shouldn't," she whispered.

"Yes, we should."

His lips grazed over hers like a silken caress, and her attempt to gather her wits failed horribly. He caused all rational thought to flee from her brain whenever their mouths met. It was a problem. But not one she wanted to dwell on now, or ever, as long as he kept kissing her.

He nipped at her lower lip, and she tilted her head. Her hands settled around his waist, her fingertips running along the base of his spine. A shudder rolled through his body, and she thrilled at her power over him, hoping it was just as strong as his power over her.

With one last nip, he broke the kiss, resting his forehead against hers.

"I wish we were alone," he said.

She kept her eyes closed, not wanting the moment to end.

"Let's get the check," he muttered, pulling back from her.

"Okay." Her voice was breathy and husky at the same time.

"Stay here,' he said, straightening.

He took a few deep breaths before he turned and made his way to the bar, and she smiled.

She pulled out her wallet as he came back to the table.

"It's all set."

"What? Is she bringing the bill?"

"No. It's all set. I paid," he replied.

"What? How much do I owe you?" she asked.

"I never make a lady pay on a date," he grinned.

"This wasn't a date," she huffed.

"Stop arguing with me, and let's go." He pulled her from the barstool, his fingers intertwining with hers.

It was dark when they exited the bar. How long had she been in there?

"I don't see any cabs," she said. She didn't trust herself on public transportation after all that alcohol.

"We don't need one," he said.

"Well, you might not. But I need to get home," she said.

"You've had too much to drink. I live just a few blocks over.

We can walk to my place and I'll have a car service take you home in the morning if you aren't up by the time I have to leave."

"Are you sure? This is a bad idea," she said.

He put his jacket on her shoulders, and she turned her head into the lapel. It smelled like him. Spicy and male and—ugh, he really wasn't playing fair.

His fingers brushed the curls from her face. "I'll sleep on the couch. You'll be perfectly safe."

"I still think this is a bad idea," she muttered, but even she could hear that there was no feeling behind it.

"Trust me," he said as he started off down the sidewalk, her hand firmly clutched in his.

Trust him.

At that moment, she wasn't even sure if she could trust herself.

A short walk later, Ethan led her up the stairs into his townhouse. He couldn't believe that he was finally getting her into his home, and then he'd stupidly agreed to sleep on the couch. How he was going to sleep with her only a few feet away from him, wrapped up in his sheets, he had no idea.

"Wow, it's a lot more spacious than I would have thought," she said as she turned about the living room.

"I just bought it. The realtor said the previous owner did some extensive renovations."

"You actually bought a house. So, you're really planning to stay?" Was that hope in her eyes? Or were they fuzzy from the alcohol?

"Yeah. I'm going to stay. If they want to keep me, that is. Still working on a new contract, but my agent is hopeful." Sam had called him the other day, more hints about his image. Ethan had been squeaky clean since he'd left New York, and he wanted management to take notice.

The fact that an act he'd had no control over had been the final straw in his trade and was affecting a possible new contract grated on his damn nerves, but there was nothing he could do aside from showing the Strikers that he was not the party boy they signed six months ago. His focus was hockey and making his new team proud.

Her smile grew. "Oh, that's nice."

"Do you want anything to drink?" he asked.

"I think I've had enough alcohol for the evening. Maybe just some water," she said as she followed him into the kitchen.

"Sure."

"Nice kitchen. Do you cook?"

"Not really. I can get by, but I can't make meals like the ones we had in Italy."

"That food was amazing," she said wistfully.

He handed her a glass of water, and they made their way back into the living room.

She set her glass on the coffee table. "Where is the bathroom?" she asked. He pointed down the hall.

"Thanks," she said as she made her way down the hall.

Ethan sat down on the couch. Then he stood up. Should he turn some music on? Maybe the TV? Should he light some candles?

Candles? She'd had a lot to drink. Now wasn't the time to seduce her.

He turned on the lamps on each end table to give the room some light, but kept the overhead light off. He sat back down on the couch and waited for her to return.

Her sweet smell surrounded him when she walked back into

the room and plopped down next to him, desire pooling low in his belly.

She kicked off her shoes, sinking her toes into the carpet, and sighed.

Shit. He was completely turned on. One little sigh was all it took. He groaned.

"Sorry, I promise my feet don't smell, I just hate shoes," she said, and smiled softly.

"Let me give you a foot massage," he said. He put a pillow in his lap, to hide his obvious need, and pulled her feet onto his lap.

"Are you trying to seduce me?" she asked.

"Of course not," he replied, and grinned. His thumbs pressed into the arch of her right foot and she jerked back.

"Oh my God, that tickles," she laughed.

"Sorry. Let's try again." He grabbed her foot and brought it back to his lap. He slowly massaged her heel and the side of her foot, and she didn't pull away.

"Ooh, that feels good," she moaned.

He worked his way up to the ball of her foot. He felt her tense, and he looked over at her.

She was biting her lip, her white teeth nibbling on the full pink flesh of her lower lip. Her eyes sparkled in the low light. She still had his jacket on, and he loved how it enveloped her. Her skirt was riding up her thighs, and he could see a small strip of lace on her upper thigh.

Ah hell! She was wearing thigh highs. *For the love of...* His good intentions would not survive, and at this point she might be able to feel his arousal through the pillow.

"It still tickles," she whispered.

He lost all common sense with those whispered words.

He tossed the pillow aside and pulled her into his lap, still careful of her knee. She fell against his chest with a laugh.

"Ethan, you aren't supposed to be seducing me." She playfully swatted his chest.

"Honey, at this point, you're seducing me," he said as his lips met hers. He swallowed her gasp and dove in.

He pulled his and her jackets off and tossed them across the room. His hands skated up her spine, and she trembled.

His tongue traced the warm recesses of her mouth as she clutched his shirt, her fingers curling into his chest.

Her thin blouse hid nothing, and he groaned, her nipples pebbled points under her shirt.

She shifted in his lap, her skirt riding up. He swore he could feel the heat from her core through his pants.

Sweet Jesus. What was he doing? She had too much to drink, and he was taking advantage of her.

He pulled away from the kiss.

"I'm sorry, Penny," he said.

"Why did you stop?" She sounded as breathless as he did.

"You've had too much to drink. I'm not going to take advantage of you in this state," he said as he pushed her away from him.

"I'm not drunk, Ethan. I know what I'm doing," she replied. Her green eyes were still darkened with desire.

"No you don't, Penny. I saw how much you had tonight." He hated being the good guy when she looked at him like that.

"I know what I'm doing, Ethan. And I want you." She sat up in his lap, running her hands down the buttons on his shirt.

"You're going to regret this in the morning," he continued.

"No," she said as she opened the top button on his shirt.

"I'm." Button number two popped open.

"Not." And then the third was released.

He kissed her quickly on the nose and set her on the couch next to him. Clearly, he was auditioning for sainthood.

"I want you, Ethan," she murmured against his throat as she

trailed her lips up and down his flesh. "I've missed you," she whispered.

"I've missed you, too. More than you know," he said.

He looked down, waiting for her to say something else. She let out a puff of air, her eyes closed. She'd passed out next to him, a small smile tugging at her lips. He wondered if she'd heard his last comment. And he wondered if he would be able to will his painful arousal away as he carried her into his bedroom. To sleep.

CHAPTER 12

Whoever was tap dancing on her skull needed to knock that shit off. Penny reached up, shoving away the curls matted to the side of her face. Hell. Her hair hurt. She groaned and cracked her eyes open, wincing at the offending sunlight streaming in through her bedroom window. No, not her bedroom. She lifted her head—instantly regretted it—and glanced around the unknown room.

Light gray walls, overly large windows with the curtains pulled back. She glared at the evil sunlight, the cause of her pounding head. She snorted. It hurt. The sunlight had nothing to do with the current state of her head, it didn't help, but it was an enabler. The multiple martinis she'd consumed last night were to blame.

As she looked around the room, last night's events filtered back in.

Ethan. Conversation that never waned. Martinis. Lots of martinis. At least there hadn't been any shots.

Kissing. His perfect lips against hers. That damn grin she couldn't resist.

But she didn't remember making it to his bed. She groaned.

She hadn't been this hungover since her bachelorette party, which was the last time she'd woken up in a bed that wasn't hers. It'd been Amanda's, and the rest of the day had been a combination of visiting the ER, followed by a painful confession, and copious amounts of chocolate and grease to soak up the booze.

She shook her head, not wanting to think about that night or the pain of her called off wedding. She took in the rest of the room. A large TV took up space over a dresser covered in clutter. Spare change, socks, and various other items were tossed haphazardly across the wood surface. She resisted the itch to organize because sitting up was still not something she was looking forward to.

The house was silent, but she smelled coffee. It called to her, but her headache pounded, mocking her desire to swallow a vat of caffeine and become human again. She buried her face in the rumpled sheets, hugging the pillow next to her head. Ethan's warm scent lingered, and she wanted to wrap herself in it. Something crinkled against her nose, and she pulled the offending sheet of paper away.

Good morning, beautiful,

Heat fluttered in her chest. She'd missed his endearments. Every morning in Italy he'd greeted her differently, and she'd wondered how many words he had in his endearment arsenal.

She focused back on the note.

Had to make my early flight and didn't want to wake you. Mostly because I can only imagine what your head must feel like right now. Maybe a few less martinis next time? Take the meds and water next to you and the coffee should be done at eleven. Don't worry about checkout, you can stay as long as you want.

See what I did there?

He followed it up with a winking face and heart, most likely soften the dig. She bit back her snort before chasing down the ibuprofen with the glass of water he left on the end table. Did he really have to bring that up? Of course, putting the check-out time at the end of her note to him in Italy had been a little douchey, but she hadn't been thinking clearly when she'd left him in that room and escaped back home.

Sorry. Couldn't resist. And really, stay as long as you want.

Another winking face.

Call the car service for a ride home. They have a tab for me.
I wish I could start the new year with you, but I'll be back on Thursday. Come to the game on Friday. I'll leave two tickets at will call for you. It starts at seven, but get there early so you can watch warm-ups. We are going to make you a hockey fan. Best sport there is.
If you need me.

And he'd included his cell phone, email address, social media accounts, and even his home address—for the home that she was currently in. The note she'd left him all those months ago had given him no way of contacting her. She'd thought that was what he wanted, but with each day they spent together recently, she was beginning to think he'd wanted to be able to find her when he came back to the States.

How the hell was she supposed to have known that? Had there been signs?

Maybe.

She dropped her head, her hangover had started to abate—ibuprofen for the win—and finished reading the note.

> Or you can take a vacation day and come over Friday afternoon for my pregame nap. You make a great snuggle buddy.
> Happy New Year and I better see you on Friday,
> Ethan

Oh crap, the rest of the night came back. Making out on his couch. Him telling her they should sleep off the booze. Her resisting, trying to strip him, and him setting her next to him. She'd snuggled into his side and—and then nothing. Shit. Had she passed out on him? Goddammit. That was embarrassing as hell. Had she drooled on him? Had he tried to wake her up and take her home?

The rapid-fire questions rocketing through her brain were causing her headache to return. Fuck. She had to get out of there. Her feet hit the floor, and she stopped, bracing her hands on the edge of the bed, the soft sheets bunched in her grip. She wanted to stay. She ached to stay.

She could tell herself whatever she wanted, but she'd be at the game on Friday. Seeing him on the ice all hot and happy wasn't something she was going to pass up, but she'd need reinforcements. Someone who would tell her if she was crazy. Not that Amanda was known for her level head, but she could trust Amanda's judgment—for the most part.

She would sleep off the hangover and head home. She'd get Amanda's opinion tomorrow night while they were celebrating the new year. Penny planned to stick to water tomorrow. Her belly rolled just thinking about any more booze.

* * *

"Oh, don't you look adorable with his name and number plastered all over you," Amanda teased as they headed to their seats Friday night.

"You know, I could've invited anyone else. And it's not like you can see it," Penny said, finding their row and sitting down. They were a little early, so the ice was still empty. She'd wanted plenty of time to browse the pro shop. Not ready to drop a ton of money on a jersey, she'd finally settled on a t-shirt with his name and number on the back, that she'd covered with a zip-up hoodie because it was cold—and winter.

"You should take off your jacket when they come out for warm-ups and plaster yourself against the glass so he can see you."

"Absolutely not happening," Penny muttered, again questioning why she hadn't asked Lexi to join her.

"Did you talk to him at all since your make out-slash-pass out moment last weekend? I still can't believe you passed out on him." Amanda's eyes sparkled with barely suppressed laughter.

"Don't remind me. I feel awful about that. And we haven't really talked. A few text conversations, but he was on a road trip." He had called her at midnight on New Year's Eve and made kissing noises through the phone, claiming he'd get his New Year's kiss in person the next time he saw her. It was frighteningly adorable and she couldn't wait.

Today's text conversation had consisted of him asking her to join him and some of the other guys for drinks at Crash and Byrne. She'd said she'd think about it, but who was she kidding? Of course she was going. But she was sticking to water. Okay, maybe one drink. A little liquid courage calmed her nerves.

The music changed, and in a rush, the players skated out onto the ice. She refused to acknowledge how her heart raced when she spotted number twenty-two. Ethan, along with a few of the other guys, didn't wear a helmet during warm-ups. She'd contemplated how risky that was, asking him what percentage of guys got injured during warm-ups because they didn't have helmets on. He'd reassured her that it was minimal, but as an easily avoidable issue, she didn't understand why he wouldn't just wear the damn helmet, as the pucks flew through the air, banging against the glass.

"There he is. Pretty hot, too," Amanda said as Ethan skated by. He was looking in their direction, but she doubted he saw her.

Until he waved and mouthed, "Hi." And the butterflies in her stomach jumped to warp speed.

"Looks like he's happy to see you. Guess you didn't drool on him that much," Amanda teased.

Penny groaned. "How about you not remind me of that?"

"Fine. Can we talk about why I've never watched hockey? Jesus, they're hot. It's like gorgeous lumberjacks on skates."

Penny let out a bark of laughter. "I guess it is. But it's also fun to watch. They're so fast, and it's freaking impressive. I've tried ice skating a total of four times, and I sprained my ankle every time."

"You're a little clumsy, my friend. And we went skating when we were in college. You were fine."

"Uh, no. I hung on to the railing around the rink for dear life while you skated around like you were training for the Olympics. Then I spent the next few days with a taped-up ankle."

Amanda's shoulders shook with laughter. "Guess I'd forgotten that. Maybe you could get your new boyfriend to teach you."

"He's not my boyfriend."

"Sure he's not."

"Don't you think it's moving too fast? I mean, it hasn't even been two months since we reconnected, and for that first month, I avoided him at all costs."

"Technically, you've known him for months, you just tried to forget about him for a good chunk of it. Stop questioning everything and go for it. You were different when you came back from Italy. There was a lightness I haven't seen in years. If he's the one who put it there, you need to grab on and enjoy it. Now, tell me about these other players. So many hot men in one room. Good thing I have the ice to cool me down. Think they'd frown upon me marching out there and lying down on the ice?"

Penny laughed, and focused on warm-ups. "Probably not a good idea."

As the players exited the ice, Ethan skated by one last time and shot her a wink.

Damn butterflies kicked up speed again. But Amanda was right. He made her feel again. Things she hadn't felt in so long—if ever. Why should she keep fighting that? She'd never thrown caution to the wind before, but a high percentage of people survived it, and so could she.

CHAPTER 13

"What's up with you?" Cheesy asked as they prepared to head back out onto the ice to start the game.

"Nothing. Just ready to win. We need the points," Ethan said, trying to turn his focus to the task at hand and not to the woman in the stands that his eyes were constantly drawn to. She had on a black Strikers shirt, and the inner caveman in him hoped that his name and number were plastered along the back of it.

Now he just had to convince her to come out with him tonight. He'd missed her, more than he wanted to admit, and had felt like a total moron kissing her through the phone on New Year's, but her laughter had made it worth it. He'd just been grateful that she hadn't been offended by his note. It'd been a little ballsy to write it, but he hadn't been able to resist.

"Sure it doesn't have anything to do with the girl you were winking at in the stands?" Cheesy said. Ethan couldn't read his tone. Cheesy wasn't known for teasing the guys. He was always focused on winning. Ethan got the drive to focus on playing, but Cheesy was never "off." The guy needed to relax.

"You should come out with us tonight," Ethan said, steering the conversation away from Penny.

"We'll see. Just make sure you aren't distracted by her. Chicago isn't an easy team to beat, and in our last game, they handed us our asses. I'd rather not have a repeat."

"Then it's a good thing that I win when she's in the stands."

"If that's the case, you better get her season tickets." A hint of a smile graced the captain's face. Maybe Cheesy was teasing. The guy needed to work on his delivery.

"If you guys are done chit-chatting, how about we get out there and win," Baz called out, breaking into a grin that showed just how many teeth the guy was missing. No player ever wore their good teeth during a game. Ethan was lucky he still had all of his.

"Let's do this," Ethan repeated, bumping gloves with Baz before following the large defenseman toward the ice.

The crowd roared as the players hit the ice again. And the euphoria of playing the game he loved shot through him. He knew it was going to be a rough, physical game, and Ethan wouldn't have it any other way.

* * *

"You have a hot date or something?" Sully asked. They immediately headed toward the bar as soon as they entered Crash and Byrne.

"What are you talking about?" Ethan asked, scanning the room and hoping that she hadn't decided to go home. Seeing her at the game tonight had energized him. They'd beat Chicago four to three, and he'd scored two of those goals and an assist. She was definitely a good luck charm. Aside from playing like shit in that game before Christmas, he was averaging just over a point a game for the last month.

He'd texted her that he'd be at Crash and Byrne once they

wrapped all the post-game media. She responded by telling him how amazing he'd played. Surely that meant she wouldn't stand him up.

"You rushed through your interviews and shower. Thought you'd leave without us," Sully said before nodding a hello to Adam, the owner, and Sully's former AHL teammate.

And then he spotted her. She offered him a quick smile and wave, sitting up straighter.

"That's the good luck charm, right?" Cheesy asked, with a head tilt toward Penny's table.

"Good luck charm?" Sully asked.

"Yeah, she was at the game tonight. Harty claims that when she shows up, we win," Cheesy said. "And since we beat the number one team in the standings tonight, you better give her season tickets."

"She looks familiar. Wait, isn't that the girl who ran out on you at the grand opening of Adam's new bar?" Sully asked, laughter in his eyes.

"Uh, yeah. We got over that."

"I think I need to hear this story," Cheesy said.

"Maybe another time. You boys are welcome to join us." He offered for purely selfish reasons. Sully and Cheesy could flirt with Penny's friend and then Ethan could keep Penny to himself. It was an asshole move, but he missed her, and she'd finally agreed to meeting him out on her own. Their last dinner had been a result of him dragging her from her office, so it didn't count.

"Hi there," he said when he reached her table. He ducked down, pressing a soft kiss to her lips, swallowing her light gasp before she could object. He was done with pretenses.

"Umm, hi," she said after he pulled back, her cheeks a bright red, her eyes dark.

"Hi, I'm Amanda," her friend said, holding out her hand.

"Nice to meet you," he said, and then introduced them to Cheesy and Sully.

"Cheesy, Sully, Harty. Do all of your nicknames end in *Y*?" Amanda asked.

"Most, but not all," Cheesy stated, his serious face back. Ethan held in his chuckle. For such a goofy nickname, the man was way too serious.

"First round's on me because of the win," Penny said, before gesturing for them to sit down.

"I like this girl. Good luck charm *and* she buys a round," Sully said, taking the high back chair between Penny and Amanda.

"Good luck charm?" Amanda asked.

"We win when she comes to the games," Cheesy said, and then turned his stern expression on Penny. "You are now required to come to all our home games. Maybe you could fly out to a few away games."

Penny laughed. It rolled over Ethan in waves, and his gut clenched with the overwhelming desire to always make her laugh.

"I'll keep that in mind, and I've only attended two games."

"And we've won both, so let's not question it," Ethan said, pressing a kiss behind her ear. "Nice shirt, by the way," Ethan said, loving his last name stretched across her shoulders.

"This thing? I just asked for the least popular player. It's so sad that they gave me this one. I thought people liked you," she teased.

"You're asking for it," he growled close to her ear, thrilling when she shifted on her seat.

The waitress popped up next to Sully and asked, "You guys want your regular?"

"Of course. Burgers with the works. Do you ladies want anything?" Sully asked.

"No thanks. We ate during the game. I'm surprised the kitchen is still open," Penny said.

"Sully used to play in the AHL with Adam, the bar owner. On game nights, Adam keeps the kitchen open for us since we're usually starved by the time we get out of the arena," Ethan said.

"Yes, and Sara makes the best burgers. Make sure you tell her I said that," Sully chimed in as the waitress jotted down the order and then left.

"She's going to spit in your food," Ethan said with a laugh.

"She loves our mutual flirtation," Sully said.

"Sure, sure," Ethan said.

"So…congrats on your goals. Almost a hattie," Penny said.

"You know those aren't common, right?" Ethan said, sliding his chair closer to her before dropping down onto it and resting his arm along the back of hers.

"I know. Sully got a hat trick," she said.

"Uh, no I didn't," Sully said.

"Yes. A Gordie Howe one. A goal, an assist, and a fight. I read about it online. I've been studying up," she stated proudly. He couldn't wait to give her the gift he had in his car. Her fact loving brain would love it.

"Very true," Sully said.

"Amanda, are you a hockey fan?" Cheesy asked.

"Not really. That was my first game. It's definitely hard to follow because you guys are so fast. And it's so hard to see how attractive you all are under those helmets. I know it's for safety reasons, but you should all at least warm up without them on."

Ethan tried not to laugh as Cheesy blustered at Amanda's blatant flirting. Poor guy.

"Interesting theory, but I'd rather not get a puck to my unprotected face during warm-ups," Cheesy replied.

"Just a suggestion," she said, holding his gaze intently.

"So, when's the next game, since I apparently have to show up," Penny asked.

"We have tomorrow off, but we expect to see you there on Sunday," Sully said.

As the discussion turned to the next game, Ethan loved hearing Penny's input and answering her questions. She was taking an avid interest in his career, in what he cared about. He'd never had that before, and as he leaned in and pressed a kiss to her cheek, he decided that he wasn't going to let her run again.

Penny sipped her second drink almost two hours later. The guys had stuffed themselves with mouth-watering burgers and traded stories about hockey, pranks on the road, and how they'd gotten to the Strikers. She was fascinated by their different routes to the big leagues. Hockey players didn't make it to the pros without pure grit and determination.

Ethan and Cheesy had remained with them for the rest of the night. Sully was at the bar flirting with the cook, Sara. The man was trying too hard in his flirtation attempts.

Penny was a bundle of energy, and she couldn't blame the alcohol since she'd only consumed two martinis and the handful of fries she'd snagged from Ethan's plate to offset some of the booze. She just loved spending time with him. When they were together, it was like no time had passed since Italy.

Tonight's conversation had flowed, and he'd kept her laughing. But on the flip side, all his attention had left her nerves frayed. His hand brushed against the back of her neck, or he linked his hand with hers, pressing a soft kiss to her cheek. One more touch, casual or otherwise from him, and she would burst into flames.

"How about one last round?" Ethan asked, nodding to Penny's empty glass.

"One more and then I should call a cab," she said, hoping she was at least slightly subtle, but knew she'd failed when he grinned.

"I'll take you home," he said.

"How presumptuous of you."

"I wasn't inviting myself over for a sleepover, but the offer is always open," he whispered against her ear.

A shudder rocked through her, and she took a steadying breath. "One more drink and we'll see." Not that she didn't know exactly what they were leading up to.

His eyes twinkled as he grinned at her. He took everyone else's order and turned toward the bar.

"I'll go with you," Cheesy called out, following behind Ethan.

Penny pulled at her turtleneck under her Strikers shirt.

"A little hot under the collar?" Amanda whispered next to her, her gray eyes laughing.

"I'm wearing a damn turtleneck, what do you think? And I'm surprised you noticed." Penny nodded toward Cheesy.

"He's hot, right?"

"Mmm, I guess."

"You guess? Right, because you've only looked at Ethan all night."

Penny stammered. "No, I haven't." She needed to find less observant friends.

"Of course not." Amanda grinned.

"I know, and I'm so screwed." Penny rested her head on Amanda's shoulder.

"You're not drunk, are you?" Amanda asked.

Penny raised her head. "Nope. Barely buzzy. And second guessing everything."

"Stop fighting it. You both want each other, he invited you

here tonight and never left your side. He's funny, attentive, and cute. Stop over-analyzing it and go for it."

"But—"

"No. Don't pass this up just because of work or whatever hang-ups you have about him. He's one of the good ones," Amanda said.

"I know," Penny whispered.

"Here you go." Ethan returned, handing her a martini. Their fingers brushed and little bolts of sensation shot through her body.

"Thanks," she mumbled. She ran her fingertips along the glass and couldn't help but notice that Ethan watched her hands as well. She grasped the glass and took a sip.

"You okay?" he asked.

"Yes. I should've asked for a water, too."

"It's on the way. Ran out of hands," he said sheepishly. Dammit, why did he have to be so adorably sweet? He reached out, his finger twirling around one of her curls and tugged. She felt the pull down to her toes, and her stomach clenched.

She leaned into his touch as his finger caressed her cheek. "Maybe we could have a sleepover," she replied.

"I thought you'd never ask," he murmured as he shifted closer to her.

She ran her finger over his hand on the table, her eyes half hooded as she looked up at him. His eyes darkened as he watched her, and when he leaned in to kiss her, she didn't stop him.

His lips brushed across hers, the softest of touches, and she melted against him, her head tilted back as his lips pressed harder against hers. Her hand gripped his shirt, curling into his chest as she pulled him closer, their heads slanting for a better angle. He deepened the kiss before pulling back, resting his forehead against hers.

"Sorry. I've wanted to do that all night," he said, his voice rough.

"Me too," she whispered.

Amanda cleared her throat, and Penny pulled back, her cheeks hot.

"Get a room," Amanda teased.

"Maybe we will," Penny shot back, laughing when Amanda just nodded.

"I'm probably going to head out soon, anyway," Amanda said. "I'll grab a cab home."

"Did you drive?" Ethan asked Penny.

"We took BART to the game. There's a stop just up the street from here. Didn't want to have to deal with a car if I had too much to drink. I'm only a few blocks from here, so I figured I'd walk home," she said with a shrug.

"Really? By yourself?" His brow quirked up. Sure, her sleepover sounded premeditated when he questioned her like that.

"I probably would've grabbed a cab," she said, trying to play off her intentions. Not that she'd had intentions. Wait. Had she?

"I'll drive you home. Amanda, do you want a ride?" he asked.

"I'll drive her home," Cheesy piped in. Penny's gaze darted between Cheesy and Amanda. It seemed so random since he hadn't returned most of Amanda's flirtations. But Penny had been so focused on Ethan so she might've missed it. And now she felt like a crappy friend.

"Sounds like a plan, Cheese," Amanda said, draping her arm around his waist. She was a foot shorter than the guy so that was the best she could do.

"It's Ben," he said stiffly.

"Suits you better than Cheesy," she teased. "So, Ben here will give me a ride home and you two kids can go get a room."

Penny held back her snort. Subtly, thy name is not Amanda.

"You had to go there, didn't you?" Penny muttered, and covertly elbowed her friend.

Amanda grinned, pulling her in for a hug and whispering in

her ear. "Have fun. And I want to hear all about it—in the morning."

"I hate you," Penny grumbled.

"No, you don't. Now don't keep that hot man waiting. You ready, Cheese?" she asked.

Ben glared at her, but dropped some money on the table to cover half the tab. "Yep."

"Let's go," Amanda said, bidding them good night and following Ben out of the bar.

"That's interesting," Ethan said with a chuckle.

"Yes. I'm not sure what just happened," she said, shaking her head.

"I'll just settle the tab and then we can go," Ethan said. Her nerves started as he walked away. Was she making a mistake?

"Stop over-thinking it," he said when he returned.

"Sorry," she said.

"Whenever you're ready." It was a loaded statement.

She tucked a curl behind her ear. "I'm ready." She drained her water and hopped off her barstool quickly. Her ankle wobbled.

Damn shoes. Yes, blame it on the shoes because that's what's messing with her equilibrium. Not the alcohol, or the fact that she was now pressed against his body, or the fact that she was about to take him home with her. His arms locked around her waist.

"Are you okay?"

"Umm, yes. Totally mortified, but yes." She tried to step away from him, but her limbs didn't want to move. His heartbeat raced under her hand on his chest.

"Are you sure your knee is okay? Not that I mind having you in my arms."

"My knee is fine. It's really my feet."

"I'm excellent at giving foot massages. Don't you remember?" he asked as he kept her flush against him.

"Maybe," she whispered. But she remembered. He'd given her a foot massage right before she'd thrown herself at him and then promptly passed out. Not one of her better moments, and she wished he wouldn't remind her.

"Come on, let's go," he said as he pulled her toward the door, his fingers laced with hers.

The cool night air hit her as they walked outside, wiping away some of her buzz, and she shivered.

He tucked her arm into the crook of his elbow, pulling her close. "Better?"

His warmth seeped through her side, and she could only nod. He led her to his car. A luxury sedan, but not the sports car she'd assumed.

"Which way?" he asked.

"It's just three blocks up and then take a left."

"I had fun tonight," he said as they set off.

"Me too," she whispered. He linked his fingers with hers, squeezing her hand as he drove. She'd missed him. Missed this. Sure, they'd only had a week in Italy, but there'd been an ease between them.

"Turn left here, right?"

"What?" She shook her head.

"Left here?"

She looked away from him. They were already on her street. "Ahh, yes it's this street. Number 145." They managed to find street parking, and he was out of the car and opening her door before she could grab her purse.

He pulled her from the car, and reached behind her to grab his bag.

"Now who's presumptuous," she teased.

"Would you rather I go home?" he asked, that crooked smile in place. She'd trace it with her tongue tonight.

"Definitely not," she said, wanting there to be no more questions between them.

CHAPTER 14

Ethan's arms tightened around her waist as Penny pressed him against the door. Her hands sunk into his hair, clutching and tightening, and a groan rumbled in his throat. The pull on his scalp, the perfect combination of pleasure and pain. He tilted his head, and deepened the kiss. He traced his tongue along the seam of her lips and gained entrance on her gasp, her tongue reaching out to meet his.

He released her waist, trailing his hands down her spine, and she arched against him, her tongue dueling with his.

"Oh, Ethan," she moaned against his mouth, and he pulled back to nibble at the corner of her lips.

"I can't get enough of you," he murmured against her heated flesh, nipping kisses along her jaw before sealing his lips with hers again. Her heartbeat raced under his touch, and a shiver rolled through her.

She broke the kiss. "It's freezing out here." Her voice came out in shallow pants.

He chuckled. "You couldn't keep your hands off me long enough to open the door."

"Shut up," she said, opening the front door, and pushing him against it as it shut behind them. He widened his stance, and she molded herself to his body. There were too many layers between them. She ran her hands up his chest, her eyes glittering in the low light, and his stomach clenched under her touch. He wanted—no, needed—her more than his next breath.

She pushed his coat from his shoulders, and he let it drop to the floor as her hands trailed back down his chest, and it was his turn to shudder.

"Before we go any further, I want you to be sure." The last words escaped on a groan as her fingers traced down the center of his belly, stopping at the button on his jeans.

She let out a frustrated sigh and looked up at him under hooded eyes. "Stop questioning this. I've never been surer of anything in my life. I want you, Ethan." She ran her hand along his stubbled chin and flattened her body against him. "Don't you want me?"

He groaned. "You have no idea how much."

"Then stop talking and kiss me," she whispered before her lips met his. Her hands sunk into his hair as she kissed him, deepening the kiss as her tongue surged into his mouth. She was so eager to take control, and he loved it. All the tension and desire that had been building up tonight, and over the last few weeks, was poured into this kiss.

He pulled back, his lips trailing down her throat, peppering her with little nips and soothing each bite with a kiss. Her pulse beat erratically under his tongue, and her fingers gripped his hair. He pulled her tight against his body, his cock straining with need as she rubbed against him.

He kissed along her jaw, before brushing her hair aside and sucking on her earlobe. She moaned again, her body rocking into his, as if she was trying to get closer to him, to mold herself to him. His tongue darted out to trace the shell of her ear, before latching back onto the lobe.

"Oh God," she gasped as her fingers clutched his shoulders. "Bedroom. Now."

"Are you sure?" he asked, praying she was.

"Yes." She sounded exasperated that he kept asking, but he didn't want her to regret this in the morning.

They were both reasonably sober, but he had to be sure. "Then what are we waiting for?" he said as he walked her backward down the hallway and toward her bedroom.

Her eyes were filled with desire and humor as she grinned at him. "You keep stalling with your stupid questions."

"Says the woman who never runs out of questions. Open lines of communication are important," he teased.

"You're ridiculous." She laughed, and trailed her hand down his chest, slipping her fingers under the hem of his shirt, and traced along his waistband. He sucked in a breath as one finger ran down the length of his zipper. He wanted to rip his clothes off and remove all barriers between them.

He pulled her hand away. "If you keep touching me like that, I won't last," he gritted out.

Her eyes darkened. "There's always round two." His chuckle was pained as she pulled free of his grasp and ran her fingers over his chest. She pushed him backwards until his legs hit the edge of the bed.

A sliver of moonlight coming in from the window washed her in shadow, and he wanted to see her. "Turn on a light," he whispered against her skin.

She flipped on the bedside lamp before moving back in front of him. She nibbled on her lower lip as she watched him, her pupils fully dilated.

"So beautiful," he murmured, sinking his hands into her curls and tilting her head up for another kiss. He wanted to devour her. To consume her and never let her go. Her taste, her smell. He wanted everything. She gasped against his mouth as their tongues met and dueled. She sucked on his tongue, and he ached to feel her mouth on his cock.

He finally pulled back, spreading kisses down her throat as she writhed against him. He sat down on the bed, pulling her between his thighs. His hands skimmed down her curves to the nip of her waist before inching underneath her shirt. He trailed his fingers up her belly, along the edge of her bra, and her stomach muscles clenched under his palm.

She yanked her shirt over her head, her lace-covered breasts at mouth level.

He smiled. "Impatient, are we?"

She swatted his chest. "Shut up or I'll put it back on."

He grinned, grabbing her shirt from her grasp and tossed it across the room, far out of reach.

Her pale pink nipples were visible through the thin lace, and he leaned in, pulling her right breast into his mouth. Her hands sank into his hair, holding his face to her chest as he continued his torment, pulling her deep into his mouth before releasing and tracing his tongue around her lace-covered nipple.

He reached behind her back, popping the clasp of her bra, and nudged the cups down. She released her grip on his hair, and the straps fell down her arms, the slip of fabric falling to the floor, her heated flesh bared before him.

Her nipples pebbled to hard points with each shuddering breath, the flush spreading down her chest. Fuck, she was stunning.

He tugged her close again, his arms locked around her waist as he leaned in and feasted. His tongue tracing along her breast, not touching her nipples, pulling every tormented moan from her lips as she urged him to take her into his mouth.

He gave in, pulling her breast into his mouth, and her hands clutched at his scalp, her nails digging in, holding him to her body. His cock strained against his pants, his stomach clenched with every soft groan, every whispered plea. How had they waited this long? He would never get enough of her.

"Oh God, Ethan," Penny moaned as he treated her other breast to the same torment and heat shot down to her toes. She rubbed her thighs together, trying to assuage the need building in her body. She was going to burst into flames.

He released her breast, and spread kisses down the center of her chest, across her belly. Anywhere he could reach. She needed him now. Stripped. Naked. Hers for the taking. Now.

"You are overdressed," she said. His fingers skated over her sensitive nipples. She bit back a moan at his touch.

He pulled his shirt off over his head with one hand, mussing his hair in the process, and her fingers itched to explore those strands again. The electric blue of his eyes, now only a thin circle around his large pupils, stared back at her as heat raced through her body.

She ran her hands over his shoulders, tracing the muscles along his arms before trailing her nails down his chest. His stomach muscles clenched under her touch, and he groaned when she scraped her thumbs over his nipples.

He stood up, removing the rest of his clothes, along with hers. He turned to pull back the bedding. The muscles shifted along his back as he pushed back the comforter. His high and tight ass made her salivate, and she touched her lips. And he called *her* beautiful.

He turned, and her eyes froze on his hard erection. She reached for him, her finger tracing over the smooth head. A shudder rolled through his body as she gripped him. He pumped in and out of her hand in shallow thrusts, and she tightened her hold. She relished in his strength and in their equal need for each other.

He ducked his head into the crook of her neck, his lips trailing over her shoulder, his scruff scraping over her flesh and sending bolts of pleasure through her body. His hands gripped her ass, squeezing her as she continued to stroke him.

"Fuck, Penny," he moaned against her throat before he pulled back to stare at her.

"We're getting there. So demanding," she teased, her harsh breaths belying her calm.

He chuckled. "God, I've missed you. This. You're even more beautiful than I remember," he said as he pulled her down onto the bed, rolling her toward him so they were pressed from chest to hip. His cock dug into her belly, and she rubbed against him. His fingers moved down her body, along the dip of her waist, before he squeezed her hip.

He rolled her to her back, and shifted on top of her. He moved down her body, spreading kisses along every inch of her sensitive flesh. She moaned, her head arching back, as he tortured her nipples with his tongue, pulling each one into his mouth again.

One hand skated down her body, and she spread her legs, letting him settle between her thighs. His finger traced through her curls, slipping through her wet folds, finding her clit. His thumb rubbed in small circles, and she gasped against his mouth as her body tightened.

"You're so ready for me," he groaned, his finger slipping inside. Her inner muscles clamped down around him.

"Oh Ethan," she moaned, writhing in his continued torment, a second finger joining the first as his thumb moved in small quick circles against her clit. She clenched the sheets in her grip, and her neck arched, her breath coming in shallow pants, as he kissed down her body.

Her thighs shook, and her stomach tensed as he continued to devour her, his teeth scraping against the sensitive bundle of nerves before he sucked her into his mouth. Her need narrowed down into one point before she exploded around him, her scream of release echoing through the almost silent room. Her limbs stretched out in pure boneless bliss. She wasn't sure if she could move, even when he started kissing his way up her body, and she felt sparks of need flow through her again.

"I need you inside me," she whispered against his lips. She pushed up on her elbows watching as he gripped himself and rolled a condom on. He shot her that crooked smile she loved, then he settled on top of her, his strength a welcome weight covering her body. His chest hair rasped against her tightened nipples, his scruff-covered jaw rubbed against the crook of her neck, making her toes curl.

"Is your knee okay to do this?" he whispered before nibbling on her earlobe. She couldn't believe that in his passion filled haze, he still thought to ask her. She'd hadn't tried to have sex with anyone since Ethan, so she had no idea if her leg would cooperate.

"I hope so," she whispered. He leaned down and brushed a kiss across her lips.

"You know that we will figure it out, just like we did in Italy."

Tears pricked the backs of her eyelids at his sweet words, remembering how gentle he'd been. How he'd kissed away her tears when her frustration had gotten the better of her because her knee just wouldn't work. Wouldn't bend the way it should. He'd taken the time to make it work. She'd lost a part of her heart to him that night.

She lifted her left leg and wrapped it around his hips as his erection nudged against her core. She hesitated, fearing pain, but her knee almost completely hooked around his hip and she let out a sigh of relief.

"Any pain?" he asked.

She might look a little awkward, but she wasn't in pain. She shook her head. "I'm okay."

He dropped one more kiss on her nose before he slowly slid into her body to the hilt. They groaned together as he settled inside her. His head dropped to hers, their foreheads pressed together as he languorously withdrew completely from her body before surging back in.

"God, I've missed you," he groaned against her lips. She felt his smile against her mouth.

He drew back, plunging in and out of her body as she ran her fingers up and down his chest, scraping her nails against his nipples. His eyes never left hers as they moved together. His thrusts sped up, and she arched against him.

"Yes, Ethan," she moaned. He ducked his head, his lips meeting hers and he slowed, rocking in and out of her body. His pelvis rubbing against hers. The tension built up as they moved together. He broke the kiss, nibbling on her neck, as he picked up his pace. Her nails trailed over his back, his muscles shifting under her palms. She ran her hands down his spine and grabbed his ass as he pumped in and out of her body.

He pulled back from her neck, spreading kisses along her collar bone. She arched her hips, holding him close, meeting him thrust for thrust.

"Oh yes, Ethan," she moaned, her body tensing. Her fingers found his chest again, scraping against his nipples as her neck arched, and she shouted her release.

He pumped in and out of her a few times before he shuddered and came with a long groan. He collapsed on top of her. His weight a solid warmth that she would happily stay buried under as long as possible. Her arms tightened around him, hugging him to her chest as their quickened breaths began to slow back down to normal.

He lifted his head, kissing her lightly. She ran one hand through his hair, brushing his sweat dampened strands away from his face. His blue eyes sparkled, and that crooked smile was back in place. She would never get enough of that smile.

"Don't move," he said, before he pulled away from her and rose from the bed to dispose of the condom.

"I don't think I can," she murmured, enjoying the view. His ass was spectacular.

He turned back and caught her staring. "If you keep that look up you will not get any sleep tonight."

She grinned. "Don't tempt me."

He returned from the bathroom and climbed back into bed, settling her against his chest so they were face to face. His fingers brushed her curls from her face, tucking the strands behind her ears. The feather light touch shot sparks of desire and need through her again. She was insatiable around him.

"How soon before we can do it again?" She placed her head against his chest, feeling his laughter. "I can't believe I just said that out loud," she mumbled.

He chuckled and tilted her chin up to look at him. "You can blurt out anything you want to me. And I was thinking the same thing. Just give me a few minutes."

She trailed her hands up his chest before flattening her palm against his heart. It beat strong and sure under her hand.

"So, the knee is okay?" he asked.

"So far so good." Thank God for that. Maybe they could try some different positions in the near future. The future. It didn't sound as crazy to her as it had before. He ran his hands up and down her spine, and she pressed herself into his chest.

She lifted her head, meeting his lips. He groaned against her mouth, and she'd put money on not getting any sleep tonight. Not that she could bring herself to care about sleep when she was wrapped up in Ethan's arms.

CHAPTER 15

Ethan groaned as he opened his eyes to the sunlight streaming across the room. Why hadn't he shut the damn curtains last night? The soft flesh of a woman's ass was tucked snug against his rapidly awakening lower body. The events of last night flooded back, and he instinctively tightened his hold on Penny.

She was finally in his bed again. Well, her bed. Her curls tickled his nose and he tucked the strands behind her ear. Would she regret that they'd slept together, all three times?

She let out a sleepy moan and wiggled her ass against his cock. It probably wasn't comfortable having something that hard sticking her in the back, but she'd put him in this state. His hands moved down her body, trailing over her warm flesh. She shifted against him, turning to face him.

"Good morning," she whispered, her green eyes still sleepy, showing no signs of panic or disappointment, so that was good.

"Good morning." He fused her lips with his, deepening the kiss as her arms linked behind his neck, her nails trailing through the base of his hairline. A shudder rolled through him at her touch.

Her breasts rubbed against his chest as their tongues tangled, and he wanted to slip inside her. He nipped at her lower lip before soothing each bite with his tongue. "I could get used to this."

"Me too," she murmured against his mouth. "But I don't know if that's a good idea."

He pulled back from her, locking his eyes with hers. "We are going to take this slow, and we are going to make this work."

"But—"

"No. This is just about us. We will deal with everything else later."

She settled against him, tucking her head into his shoulder. "I'm just nervous."

"Don't be. You can trust me. I would never do anything to jeopardize your job, or your happiness."

"Doesn't it seem rushed?" she asked.

"Maybe. But are you willing to let this go?"

She pulled back to look at him. He knew that trusting men was an issue for her, and he couldn't blame her. After what her douche ex did to her…well, he could relate.

"I've been where you are. It takes a while, but eventually you'll learn to trust again and I hope that you know that you can trust me." But why should she listen to him? He hadn't tried to trust anyone since Julie. Well, not before Penny. Without a shred of doubt, he knew he could trust her.

"Thanks," she whispered as she hugged him tighter.

"No more sad talk. What do you want to do today?" he asked.

"Umm."

"It's Saturday, and you're not working, and I don't have a game or practice today. We could be tourists in the city or go wine tasting in Napa. If we can't go back to Italy, we'll bring Italy to us."

"Isn't it too cold for that?" she said.

"Guess you'll just have to snuggle into me to stay warm."

"Or we could do indoor stuff," she said.

"Like right here? We could spend it in bed, but you'd probably wear me out." He grinned as she swatted his arm.

"I'm so sorry that my insatiableness is a burden to you." He caught the glint of humor in her eyes as she tried to look offended.

"It's definitely not a burden," he said as he rolled her beneath him to show her just how much he didn't mind her need for him.

Her laughter quickly turned into moans of pleasure as he gave her a proper wake-up call.

* * *

An hour later, Ethan slid an omelet onto Penny's plate.

"I didn't know you could cook," she said.

"I can't, really. Just breakfast."

"For all your sleepovers?"

"There hasn't been anyone else since before Italy," he said, taking her hand.

"I wasn't trying to pry," she started. "There's been no one else for me, either."

"Is it wrong to be happy about that?" he asked.

"No," she replied, and then took a bite of her omelet. "Wow, this is good."

"It's just ham and cheese, since you wouldn't let me put in any veggies. Not that there were many in your fridge." He laughed as she wrinkled her nose in disgust.

"Veggies mixed with cheesy, salty goodness is just wrong." She grimaced.

"You don't know what you're missing," he replied before digging into his omelet stuffed with the veggies he'd managed to find.

"I think you have some spinach in your teeth," she said as he advanced toward her.

"I'm surprised you actually had spinach."

"I thought I was buying baby lettuce. The packaging looks the same," she said, ignoring his spinach grin as he wrapped his arms around her. He ignored her protests and planted a big sloppy kiss on her lips. "Ugh, you are so gross."

He chuckled as he pulled away and took the seat next to her. She had the eating habits of a toddler.

"So, you have me for the entire day. What should we do?" he asked, knowing full well what he wanted, and knowing that at some point they should leave the house—be a real couple out sharing a lazy weekend together. Not that he would mind keeping her occupied in the bedroom until they were too tired to move.

"I don't know."

"I find it hard to believe that you don't have a plan for this weekend. A list of what you wanted to do?" he asked.

"Maybe all it said was you."

The air left his chest, and his body tightened with need. "If you say shit like that, I'll never let you leave here again."

"Promises, promises," she taunted.

His fork clattered against the plate, and he stood, stalking around the table. Her eyes widened, her chest rising and falling rapidly under her thin robe. God. Would his need for her ever stabilize? He hoped not. Especially since her need equally matched his.

He leaned in, pulling her against his chest. He nibbled her earlobe, her harsh breaths fanning his face, and pressed a hard kiss to her lips. Her hands sank into his hair, holding him close, her moan mixed with his.

"Oh Ethan," she whispered when he broke the kiss.

"I guess we could stay in," he said, hoisting her up on the kitchen island.

She linked her good leg around him, holding him tight, her fingers trailing across his chest.

"Nope. We are going out. I want to show you my favorite place in the city," she said.

"You mean, it isn't your bedroom?"

She laughed. "No. That's your favorite place." Her cheeks turned a brilliant shade of red at her statement. He pressed a quick kiss to her nose. Damn. She was adorable when she blushed.

"Absolutely." He helped her off the counter, his cock hardening as she rubbed against him. "I think we should shower together," he wiggled his eyebrows at her. "You know, to conserve water."

"How eco-friendly of you," she said around her laughter.

"Our environment is important," he said, grabbing her hand and starting down the hallway, loving her soft laugh. "Oh, I forgot. I have something for you," he said, guiding her into the living room, and dropping down to rifle through his bag.

"A present?" she asked.

"Now you'll be properly attired for the games," he said, pulling out a jersey with his name and number on the back. "And everyone will know who your favorite player is."

"You didn't have to do that," she said, holding the jersey to her chest.

"I wanted to. You're taking a real effort to learn about hockey, and since you're my good luck charm and need to come to all the games, you'll need a jersey."

"Thank you," she said, leaning in and kissing him.

"I also have something else," he said after he broke the kiss. He turned back to his bag, and grabbed the book.

When he looked at her again, his gut clenched. She'd dropped her robe and had slipped on his jersey. She was naked underneath.

"What do you think?" She held out her arms, mischief in her eyes, and then spotted the book.

"Ooh, look at all those flags." She reached out, and he dropped the book to the floor, pulling her close.

"I've never been so turned on by a jersey," he growled against her neck, and she shivered under his touch.

"Aren't you going to tell me about the book?" she asked in between kisses.

"Maybe later," he said, his hands under her ass, lifting her to rub against him.

She shoved him back and leaned over, picking the book up off the floor, the jersey riding up, giving him a tempting view of her perfect ass, and he groaned. His cock hardened to the point of pain, his boxer briefs stretched tight.

He spun her, pressing her back to his chest, his hand on her belly, holding her close, and he nuzzled her neck. She tilted her head, giving him even more access to her warm skin.

"Hockey made easy," she said.

"Basic hockey knowledge. I put a flag for every term and you can remove them when you learn about them at the game or from me."

"Oh, Ethan," her tone was almost wistful as she thanked him.

"Now, about that jersey," he said, sweeping her up into his arms.

She gasped, linking her hands around his neck. "Do you like it?"

He growled his approval and headed down the hall, her laughter turning to moans when he slipped the jersey from her body and worshipped her with his mouth.

The shower could wait.

"Too cold?" he asked hours later as they walked along the path around Spreckel Lake in Golden Gate Park. She shivered next to his side, but the temperature wasn't as cold as originally predicted. When he offered to go somewhere that they could stay indoors, she'd just tucked herself closer and kept walking. It was an excuse to snuggle into him, to keep his arm, a heavy weight, around her.

Just the memory of their morning was enough to fight back the chill. She planned to wear that jersey, with nothing else, again. The heat in his gaze when she'd slipped it on—her mind blanked for a minute. Holy hell, it was hot.

And that book. She didn't have a chance to look through it since he'd carted her off to the bedroom and wiped all coherent thought from her brain with his tongue. She shivered, and it had nothing to do with the cold.

But that book. He got her. He understood her need for knowledge. He didn't make fun of her for it, he encouraged it. How one little gesture could make her belly flutter, her heart race. She was too scared to put a name to what was going on between them, but she never wanted it to end.

"Are you too cold?" he asked, pulling her from her thoughts.

"Maybe a little." She huffed out a laugh. "The wind chill is brutal this time of year."

"We can go in. Check out one of the museums? I hear the Legion of Honor Museum has an amazing ceiling."

She laughed. She'd shared her ceiling love with him in Italy. Some of the most stunning parts of cathedrals and museums weren't what was on the walls, but above your head. The work that went into them was awe-inspiring.

"Maybe later, but I'm not going to lie on the floor with you, so don't even try it," she scolded him. He'd attempted to pull her down behind the altar at St. Catherine's in Siena on their first day of exploring the city together, but she refused. She was perfectly capable of tilting her head back and looking up.

"It was for your own safety that I made that suggestion. For someone so accident prone, walking around with your head back so you can stare at the ceiling is just asking for injury," he said.

"But I survived, and it would've been highly inappropriate to lie on the floor with you in a church," she said, her cheeks heating even in the brisk wind.

"What are you thinking about right now?" he asked, grin in place.

"Nothing. So, did you know that the buffalo in the park used to be named after Shakespearean characters?" she asked, switching the subject to something safe.

He let out a bark of laughter. "Your love of random facts is strong. And no, I didn't know that."

"Random facts make life interesting. King Lear and his daughters roamed the bison enclosure for some time."

"So, you're a Shakespeare fan?"

"Oh yes, I love him. I minored in British literature in college. Really, it was just an excuse to read the classics I loved, and to convince my parents that studying abroad in London was a requirement."

"I wished I'd studied abroad, but I only went to college for one year. Too busy playing hockey. Guess that's why I try to travel as much as possible during the off-season."

"What's been your favorite place so far?"

"This vineyard in Tuscany. It was amazing. Great food. Amazing wine. Even better company. I met this amazing girl there."

Calm down, heart. Just calm the hell down already.

"Really? Is this the best time to talk about another woman in front of me?" she teased, trying to get control over her swirling thoughts. He was a world traveler, and his best time was with her?

He chuckled, tweaking her nose. "Of course it was meeting you. Maybe in the off-season we can pick a spot on your bucket list. I know you have one."

She bit back her laugh. "Maybe."

"So where would you like to go? I'll buy you a guidebook now so you can fill it with flags."

From anyone else, that comment would be a dig. But from Ethan...from Ethan, he was serious.

"I'll have to consult my list," she said, playing along.

"Some place warm," he said.

"Definitely warm. I do wish I could travel more. I'm always working."

"Do you want me to talk to your slave driver boss? I kind of have an in with him." He winked at her. She didn't want to think about his *in*.

She was going to need to tell Robert at some point. Working on Ethan's account was a clear conflict of interest. She knew better, but she still held back, as if putting a name to whatever this was would end it, or bring up too many questions. Questions she wasn't ready to answer. It was ridiculous, but she couldn't help but wait for the other shoe to drop.

"Ethan," she scolded.

"I'm kidding." He pulled her against him, brushing a kiss across her brow. "But we do have to tell him at some point. I don't want you to get in trouble with the boss."

She sank into his arms. "I know. And I will. I'm just nervous about people finding out. My co-workers, to be specific."

"We'll figure it out, I promise."

"I hope so."

"Have dinner with me tonight?" he asked.

"You aren't tired of me yet?" she asked.

"Never," he whispered against her hair. He turned her to face him. "I can't remember a day when I had this much fun. Except maybe when I was in Italy with you."

"You say the sweetest things," she replied, then lifted her chin to brush her lips against his.

* * *

"Oh my God, this might be better than sex," Penny moaned a few hours later as she took a bite of the triple chocolate cake in front of her.

"I take offense to that," Ethan grumbled next to her. "And I'm jealous of a piece of cake."

She laughed. "Okay, maybe not as good as sex with you. Does that make you feel better?" She patted his arm.

"Don't placate me." She giggled as he attempted to glare at her, but his gaze was locked on her mouth. Heat rushed to all points of her body at his stare.

Today had been amazing. They'd ended up getting out of the cold and touring the Legion of Honor Museum. The stunning buildings and courtyard reminded her of museums in Italy as they walked around large pillars. The ceiling was amazing, and she'd resisted the urge to sprawl out on the floor and stare up.

She wanted more than anything to go back to Italy. To explore other parts of that country. With him.

"Taste it," she said, spearing another piece of cake and shoving the fork in his mouth.

"Mmm. That is good. But not as tasty as you, and definitely not better than sex." He leaned over and sealed his lips with hers. His tongue darted out, tracing along her lips, and she groaned again, allowing him entrance to her mouth. Their tongues tangled, and for a moment she forgot where she was.

CHAPTER 16

"So, where to next?" Ethan asked, tucking her into his side as they left the restaurant. He wanted to take her home and prove to her that he was better than cake, but he'd promised her a day of exploring, and he hadn't walked around the city in years.

"Some place that's inside," she said, burrowing into his chest. "It's so freaking windy." Her voice was muffled against him.

"It's San Francisco in the winter. And you wanted to go out. We could've stayed in your nice, warm bed and had takeout delivered." He pulled her tighter, pressing a kiss to her curls. He pretended that the shiver that rolled through her was because of his kiss, and not because the wind managed to cut through all their layers.

"I'm regretting my decision, but the cake made it worth it." She tilted her head back, grinning up at him, and he brushed a kiss across her lips. At her soft moan, he sealed his mouth to hers, giving in to his constant need to have her, to kiss her. He would never get over the feelings that rocked through him with just a small kiss.

"You and that damn cake," he growled against her lips, and then deepened the kiss again.

Her arms wrapped around his waist, her body pressed flush against his, and it was his turn to groan as she skimmed her fingers along his lower back.

After an endless moment, she broke the kiss, her breath just as labored as his. "Ethan, we should stop. Go someplace private. Someplace warm."

He grinned. "Your place or mine?"

"Maybe your place."

"Penny?" a voice called out, and she visibly stiffened.

"We should've stayed in," she muttered. "I'm sorry, please don't hit him."

"Hit him?" he asked. He turned to look at the guy who jogged across the street toward them.

"Penny. I thought that was you," the man said when he was finally at her side.

"Yep, it's me. What do you want?" she asked.

The smile on the man's face slipped, and Ethan immediately went on edge. Who the hell was this guy? Ethan tightened his grip on her waist, and glided his fingers along the small of her back, trying to give her whatever comfort she needed.

"Penny?" Ethan asked.

"Yes, Penny. You should introduce me to your friend," the man said, his smile tight and overly bright.

"Ethan, this is Michael," she drew out, her eyes imploring him not to do anything as his hand clenched at the base of her spine when she said that asshole's name.

"Michael, huh," Ethan said, gritting his teeth and tamping down the urge to flatten the douchebag with one punch. Anger radiated off of him, and Michael took a faltering step back. Ethan wanted to tell him to keep moving.

"Yes. And Michael, this is my boyfriend, Ethan."

A thrill rolled through him at her statement. Sure, they

hadn't put labels on anything yet, but he'd gladly take that one. He couldn't remember the last time he'd actually been in a relationship, but he wanted it with her. He wanted everything to work with her.

Ethan bit back his chuckle as the veneer dropped from Michael.

"Boyfriend? Really? How long have you known each other?" Michael demanded. Ethan itched to punch the guy.

"A few months," she said, pulling herself up straight and asserting herself.

"Months? Really?" Michael asked.

"Yes, months," Ethan repeated. "Is that a problem?"

"You didn't mention a boyfriend at Christmas," Michael said.

Christmas? What the hell?

"I was too busy resisting the urge to stab you with my fork," she bit out, pulling Ethan from his racing thoughts. In the two weeks since the holiday, she hadn't mentioned seeing Michael, let alone that he'd been at her Christmas dinner. He didn't want to jump to any assumptions, but what the hell was he supposed to think? What else wasn't she saying?

"Why do you fight this, Penny? We are so good together," the asshole whined, and Ethan's ability to resist punching the guy dwindled by the second. Was he for real?

"Pretty sure you cheating on me proves we weren't good together. Now, please leave. We have nothing to say to each other. It's over. I'm done rehashing. And stop bringing my parents into this mess you created," she said, her exasperation clear, for which Ethan was grateful. And then he felt like an ass for thinking about himself when she was still dealing with her ex.

"Come on, Penny. We have history. I've been a part of your family for so many years. You would really throw it all away? For what? This guy?" Michael said.

Ethan bit back a growl. What had she ever seen in this slimy bastard? "That's enough. You threw it away. You cheated on this amazing woman, and she's moved on. Now, she asked you politely to leave. I will not be as polite if you don't back up and disappear."

"So you've moved on with a caveman? Your father must be so proud," Michael sneered.

"Buddy, you have no idea what you are asking for right now," Ethan said, keeping his temper in check, his hand still clenched at the small of her back.

"Just go, Michael. It's done. We're done. And if you keep this up, I will talk to my father about how you're harassing me," she said. Ethan wanted to high-five her, but resisted. He still had a shit ton of questions when the asshole finally left.

"Are you threatening me?" Michael asked.

"Nope. Just a promise. Now, go away," she said, turning into Ethan, and gripping his hand. She tugged him down the sidewalk, never looking back to see if Michael had left. Ethan itched to look over his shoulder at Michael, but resisted, and kept pace with Penny as she walked briskly up the street.

When they reached the corner, he pulled her to a stop. "Are you okay?" he asked, his finger under her jaw, tilting her head up to look at him. The unshed tears undid him. He pulled her into a nearby alcove, away from the pounding wind and prying eyes.

"Talk to me," he said, running his thumb along her cheek, the need to soothe her overtaking every question and concern he had.

"I'm sorry about that. He makes me so freaking insane. My parents had invited him to Christmas dinner because they thought we should talk, and I had no idea he was going to be there. I did threaten to stab him with my fork when he tried to grab my hand under the table," she blurted out, furiously wiping the tears from her eyes before they could fall.

Pure hatred roiled inside him. "I'm regretting not punching

him right now," he said. She took the hand that wasn't caressing her cheek and squeezed his fingers with hers.

"It's not worth it. It just sucks that my parents are pushing this. I was so upset that I bolted from dinner and went home early. It sucked," she muttered. She shot him a small smile. "I even missed the best part of the meal—dessert."

He matched her smile. "That's enough of a reason to punch him as anything." He paused, running his thumb over her palm. "You could've called me."

"I figured you had your own drama to deal with. And I didn't want to talk about it." She tried to duck her head down again, but he refused to let her.

"Don't ever think you can't talk to me. You might have to hold me back from inflicting bodily harm on your family, but I'll still listen."

Her smile widened, and he leaned down, pressing a kiss to her nose. "Next time stab him with the fork."

Her soft laugh brushed over him. "I'll keep that in mind, but there better not be a next time. I'm not sure how much clearer I can get."

"I'm still having trouble believing your parents are encouraging him," he said, shaking his head.

"Me too."

He hated the pain in her voice. "You need to stand up for yourself. They are your family, not his. Stand your ground and walk away when you need to. They'll realize they are just pushing you away, and if they truly care, they'll back off."

"I know. I can yell at Michael all day, but my family…I guess I just expected more from them and every time I hope for the best, they destroy that," she said and it broke his heart.

"I'm so sorry you have to deal with this bullshit, but you're a strong and amazing woman. And they are going to realize what they are doing is wrong." Much like he truly believed his family had. Well, maybe not his brother, but the rest of them. He could kick himself for not seeing it sooner, but he didn't want to focus on his family right now. Penny needed his support and he had the perfect strong shoulder for her to lean on.

"Do you want to tell me what exactly happened?" he asked.

"Yes, but not here. Can we go back to your place?"

"Absolutely. I have some hot chocolate and warm sheets with your name on them," he teased.

"You do know the way to a girl's heart," she said, tucking herself back into his side.

Thirty minutes later, when he had her settled in his bed, the sheets pooling around them as she snuggled into his chest, and she told him about Christmas dinner, he was ready to commit murder. How the hell could her parents be so callous?

"Kevin, you can't write off one hundred percent of this new machinery. It has to be listed as depreciation. And here, you wrote this off twice. Unless he purchased two of them. Do we have the receipts to confirm?"

They'd been in her office for two hours going over one account for a small business client. Kevin wanted to write off every little thing. And sometimes twice. *Deep breaths. Calming breaths.* She was going to strangle him if he huffed at her in irritation one more time. She'd show him irritation.

"The IRS won't notice. What are the chances they would audit these specific clients?" He pushed his glasses up the bridge of his nose and scoffed at her. It was more of a sneer, and she wanted to wipe that expression off his face with a perfectly timed throat punch.

"With an attitude like that, those clients probably will get audited, and since my name is on the returns, I'm telling you to change them. You need to be logical here and err on the side of caution. Write-offs that are clearly high and not probable will get you into trouble. They will get this company into trouble," she said.

"My father would take care of it. You shouldn't concern yourself with this since they are going to be my accounts," he replied. Her hand itched to hit him. And if he brought up his father one more time—stupid nepotism. Part of her wanted to hand the accounts over to him and hope he learned his lesson, but since she was supposed to oversee his work, she knew it would come back to bite her.

"Why would you want to bring a possible audit or lawsuit against your father? Against this company?"

He shrugged. "Are we almost done here? I'm supposed to meet my dad for lunch in fifteen minutes." He glanced down at his watch, tapping the face. His expensive Movado watch. She only knew the name because he wouldn't shut up about it and how his father, *her boss*—a fact Kevin always had to reiterate—had given it to him on his first day at the company so he would always be on time. Not that it made him punctual whenever he was supposed to meet with her.

"Yes, I'll just wrap this up and then we're done," she said as she shuffled the paperwork back in the file. Hopefully she wouldn't have to see him for the rest of the day. Until he had another question, of course. She was tempted to call in sick for the rest of the week, but she was swamped, and it would just mean more work when she got back.

"Good. This is so boring," he complained.

"If you hate it so much, why do you work here?"

"Because one day my father is going to give the company to me, and it's a cash cow. I'd be an idiot to not take it." Awesome. She loved training this ungrateful little shit.

"Okay, I think we are done here," she said as she handed the file back to him. "Enjoy your lunch." She refused to suck up to him, but it wouldn't do her any favors to be a bitch to his face. Behind his back was different.

"Great. So, what are your plans?" he asked as he headed for the door. "Lunch with Ethan?"

What. The. Fuck!

"Excuse me?"

"You're dating Mr. Knight's nephew, right?"

"My personal life is off limits," she replied. Keep eye contact with him. Don't let him think he's got you. *Fucking gossip.* Office politics were like high school.

He smirked as he opened the door. "It's so obvious." The door shut behind him, and she wanted to throw something. She knew this would happen. And how long would it be before Robert said something to her? Or the entire office started believing that she was sleeping her way to the top?

She banged her head on her desk. She wished that Ethan was here to take her out to lunch, but the impromptu visits had to stop or the gossip never would. She hadn't really spoken to him since they'd run into Michael last weekend. A few random texts, but nothing more. She thought she'd reassured him that she was over Michael, but what if he was avoiding her because he didn't think she was over her ex?

She grabbed her phone to text him, refusing the wait for him to reach out first, and it dinged in her hand.

Ethan: *Hey gorgeous, how's your day?*

She smiled at the text. She was getting used to the pet name. And gorgeous was much better than sweetie pie or something embarrassing.

Penny: *Hi. I was just thinking about you.*
Ethan: *Hopefully dirty thoughts?*

Penny: Always a perv. You, I mean. Not me.
Ethan: Sure, sure. So, what's up? Thinking about a nooner?
Penny: Again, one track mind over there.

Not that she wasn't thinking the same thing. It'd only been two days, but she missed him.

Penny: You started this convo. Did you need something?
Ethan: Not really. I just wanted to tell you I miss you. When am I going to see you again?
Penny: I'm thinking about the game on Friday. I've been reading through my book and I think I have offsides figured out.
Ethan: Well I'm not planning on showing it to you during the game.
Penny: Of course not. But it always happens at some point.
Ethan: We try to avoid them, but it's common.
Penny: So can I get a ticket for the game?
Ethan: Of course. It'll be at will call again.
Ethan: You could always come to the game tonight, too. You know, since you miss me and all.

She grinned. She wanted to see him again, but her to-do list was insanely long.

Penny: I wish I could. Too much work to do. Too many corrections to make on Kevin's stuff.

She probably shouldn't bitch about another employee to the boss's nephew, but Ethan swore he'd never say anything to Robert, and she believed him.

Ethan: That sucks. I'm sorry you have to deal with the spoiled kid.
Penny: Yes, but I'll see you on Friday.

Ethan: *Maybe I'll swing by the office for a visit. Take you up on that nooner you keep suggesting.*

Penny: *To be clear, YOU keep suggesting it. But this week is crazy, so maybe no visits?*

Ethan: *Fine. But if you end up with some free time before Friday, I better be the first person you call.*

Penny: *I promise. And good luck tonight.*

Ethan: *Thanks. One day I'll get a hattie for you.*

Penny: *I hope I'm in the arena when it happens. I'll watch tonight.*

Ethan: *I can't wait to see how many flags are missing from that book on Friday.*

Penny: *Don't make fun of me. Soon it will be cleared of stickies and I'll be an expert!*

Ethan: *I'm holding you to that. Good night, hot stuff.*

Her grin split her cheeks as she texted him good night. He did things to her insides that she'd only read about in books. Was this what she'd been missing all these years?

She turned back to her list, wishing she didn't have piles of stuff to go through or Kevin's work to review. Her frustration grew every time he came into her office. What had she done to deserve dealing with this nightmare? Recently she'd been questioning why she stayed more times than she wanted to admit.

She had the savings to go out on her own, but the risk was massive, and she wasn't sure she was ready to take it on. But she also wasn't sure she could deal with Kevin much longer or continue to wait for the promotion that had been dangled like a carrot in front of her for far too long.

CHAPTER 17

"You guys played amazing last night," Sam said after they'd settled down for lunch at Sam's favorite steak restaurant.

"Yeah. The team was on fire. Just need Calgary to lose a few games so we can slip into the top three. I think we have a good chance at making a run in the playoffs. I'm itching to hoist Stanley," Ethan said. The team was flowing, and he was racking up points, almost even with goals and assists.

Sam chuckled. "Aren't you all?"

"Of course. I just feel like I'm starting over with the Strikers. I made a few finals in New York, but this team hasn't been to a final in decades," Ethan said. The trade had felt like a demotion. Sure, his behavior had encouraged New York's hand, but the final nail in the coffin had been a misunderstanding at best. Something he hadn't instigated in the slightest. Just the last excuse to boot him across the country, even if everyone on the team knew the truth.

"You'll get there. Your numbers are up from last year. You're gelling with your linemates. You've been on fire since early November," Sam said.

"I feel good about the team and where we're headed, but the trade still stings. Six years with those guys and a misunderstanding with the trainer's wife and I'm out," he grumbled.

"You were caught in the trainer's office kissing his wife," Sam said. Ethan bit back his grimace.

"She kissed me out of nowhere. I wasn't even touching her." He'd always liked Ivan. The man's wife, not so much. Ivan had been the team trainer since before Ethan had joined the team. And he'd married Melody before the start of the last season. The woman had thrown advances Ethan's way for months, but he'd shrugged her off. Until the afternoon she'd planted one on him. He shuddered at the memory. Ivan had caught them and lost his mind. Not that Ethan could blame the guy.

Melody had quickly placed the blame on Ethan, and even after the truth had come out, the damage had been done. A few well-placed rumors, that Ethan knew she'd started, combined with his partying ways, and management finally had an excuse for the trade. He'd played like shit last year, so that hadn't helped his case.

"I know. And everyone who matters knows the truth. New York was looking for a trade. Cap space was getting tight, so you were an easy decision," Sam said.

Ethan bristled. New York had a young star forward who was moving from his entry level contract, so they'd needed the space to keep him and give him the salary he deserved. It was part of the business of signing top talent. Ethan just wished he hadn't been the one left behind.

But he was proving his worth to his new team. With every point and every hit, he was showing New York that he still had it. Now he just had to get the Strikers on board for the long haul.

"Last I heard, Ivan had ditched the social climber and already found someone else. And he never truly believed her to begin with," Sam said.

"Still pisses me off." Sure, the list of women he'd dated—and he used the term loosely—might be a little long, but he only hooked up with single women. Why deal with the drama when there were plenty of unattached women around him?

"Put it behind you. It happened. It's done. And you've moved on. If you keep this up, this could be your highest scoring season in the last three years. Which leads me to why we're here," Sam said, swiping his phone on.

"Wait. We aren't here just to hang out and for me to buy you a ridiculously expensive steak?" Ethan said.

"I'll buy."

"And put it on my bill," Ethan said, and Sam chuckled.

"It's a business lunch."

"Anyway, so I'm hoping you're going to tell me you have a massive deal for me to sign." He wanted everything settled before they went into the All-Star break later this month.

"I have a preliminary contract. I'm not happy with it, but you are getting up there."

"What the hell, man? I just turned thirty."

"Which is like sixty in hockey years," Sam shot back, and Ethan knew it, but he was healthy and playing at the top of his game so he'd hoped for a big deal.

"So what is it?"

"Three years, ten million."

"Definitely wanted more. My playing this season should get me more."

"I don't disagree. You're playing great. I'm going to counter. Just wanted to tell you where we are right now. Your numbers are up, and you *were* acting like a monk since the trade."

Sam's emphasis on "were" stopped Ethan. "What is that supposed to mean? I haven't been out partying. My sole focus has been on practice, games, and getting to know the guys." And spending time with Penny, but he wasn't bringing her up to

Sam. He was enjoying the bubble he currently existed in with her. It almost reminded him of being with her in Italy.

"Quite a few pictures have popped up on social media with you and the same girl recently. Not a ton, and they don't have her name yet, but is it serious?"

Shit. He'd known this would happen eventually. Usually he was able to spot the amateur photographers, but Penny kept him distracted when they were together.

"What pictures? And how many?"

"Just a few so far. Why do you care? Not that you stick around with the same girl more than a few times," Sam trailed off. Ethan knew his M.O. He didn't need the reminder from Sam.

"I'm not sure what it is just yet." That was total bullshit. He knew exactly what they were, and when she'd referred to him as her boyfriend in front of her ex, a thrill had shot through him.

"Would she really care? Most of the women you *dated* wanted their pictures out there, some of them posted the pics themselves. A benefit of dating an elite athlete," Sam said as he cut into the steak the waiter had just dropped off.

Ethan bit back his growl of irritation. "She's not like that."

Sam looked up. "Holy shit, you care."

"Leave it alone."

"No. This could be good. How serious is it? She's hot, but also looks like a normal woman. Not your usual type. And she isn't an attention seeker. Where'd you meet her?"

Ethan took a bite of his lunch, not wanting to get into this with Sam. He wanted to stay in his protective bubble with Penny. He wasn't ready to be hounded again.

"This could work for us."

"This isn't a game anymore."

"Shit. You really do like her. Not going to tell me how you met?" Sam asked.

"She works for my uncle." The truth was better than another lie.

Sam chuckled. "Really? As what? Doesn't he run an accounting firm?"

"She's one of the senior accountants."

"Wow. So she's smart, too. Yeah, this could really work. How serious is it? And can you—"

"Wait. What the hell are you talking about?"

"Make it official. Put it out there that you're in a serious relationship with an accountant. I mean, an accountant, really? Star NHL forward falls for the tax lady." Sam continued to chuckle. "It's perfect. You're settling down. Your numbers are up. Your game is on fire. This could definitely work in our favor."

Ethan's fork clattered against his plate, his meal forgotten. He truly hated Sam at some moments, and this was up there at the damn top. "Absolutely not. I'm not going to exploit my relationship with Penny. Not to mention that she works for my uncle. Who doesn't know about us. I'm not doing that." She meant something to him, and Sam had turned it into a fucking promotional stunt.

"Her name is Penny. Good to know."

He glared at his agent. Sam hadn't listened to a word Ethan had said aside from Penny's name. "And you are going to forget every bullshit idea that just ran through your head, along with her name."

"Don't you want more money, more years? This could do it. And it's not like I'm asking you to keep dating someone you don't like. You like this girl, right?"

"Yes. But for pure and honest reasons. I'm not going to make this into a game. And if she thought for one second that I was playing her, she'd bolt." He knew that for a fact. She'd already been through a lot in the last year, and she'd perfected her running. He refused to give her another reason to leave.

"Just think about it. And don't get pissed at me. This is what you pay me for," Sam said.

"I pay you to get me the good deals because you're a shark, and I deserve the best contract. You shouldn't have to exploit people I care about to get me that," he shot back.

"Fine. We'll play it your way for now. Just keep it in the back of your mind and focus on your playing."

"That's all that should matter," Ethan muttered.

"You're right, but we all know it's more than just skill. You have an image that desperately needs repair. You're working in the right direction."

Ethan nodded and turned back to his meal. The food no longer held any appeal, and they finished lunch talking about his upcoming game. Comments about his contract and Penny were off the table for now. He refused to drag Penny into fixing his image. He'd kept the real reason for his trade from her, wanting to put the entire incident behind him. But how long could they go before she heard the gossip and the truth came out? And how long before their protective bubble popped a hole?

"So, do you always watch the games from here?" Penny asked Klara as the woman rocked her youngest daughter, Elin, against her chest. Klara was married to Johan Svedberg, known to the team as Sveddy, a forward who'd been on the team for a decade.

Klara looked over at her two other children playing with the rest of the kids, and nodded. "It's much easier than wrangling up the group to sit closer to the ice. And she'll be out by the second period." Klara motioned toward Elin.

"Awake, Mamma. I awake," the toddler stated, her pale blue eyes bright with mischief.

Klara rubbed her daughter's back, and Elin snuggled deep.

"Second period," Klara mouthed with a smile, and Penny chuckled softly.

This was Penny's first time in the WAGs room. Ethan had brought her up here before the game and introduced her around. Guess that made them official. She was trying not to freak out about that. Was she really ready for this?

She was officially dating a client. Had been sleeping with her client for a full week. It was a clear conflict of interest, and they needed to tell Robert. She needed to give his account back. Ethan told her not to worry, and she went along with it because confessing to Robert made it real and she was still waiting for something to go wrong.

And then she felt guilty. They'd been going along just fine. Not putting a name to anything, until they'd run into Michael. She'd staked her claim on Ethan, introducing him as her boyfriend.

She was still pissed about how delusional Michael was. How did he not understand that they were over? And when were her parents going to back off? It frustrated the hell out of her. The pure panic that had rushed over her when Michael had mentioned Christmas in front of Ethan. At least Ethan's anger had been directed toward Michael and not her for keeping that secret.

Stop.

They were in a good place now. And she was going to tell Robert on Monday. No more hiding behind what-ifs. Hopefully it wouldn't blow up in her face, but moving forward in her relationship with Ethan was something she wanted more than she'd thought possible. And the feelings appeared to be mutual.

So, here she was, in the wives' and girlfriends' room

surrounded by people who probably knew a lot more about hockey than she did.

She pulled her book from her purse.

"*Hockey Made Easy?*" Klara asked, leaning over her daughter, a grin on her lips.

"Umm. I don't really know that much about hockey, so I'm trying to learn," she said.

"Just show up to games. You eventually pick it all up. I've been watching since I was a kid. Johan and I grew up together in a small town in Sweden that everyone calls O-vik. When he came here to play, I followed him."

"Wow. He's always been a Striker, right?" Penny had done some research on the team. If she was going to be a fixture here—and, oh how she wanted to be—then she wanted to know about his teammates.

"Yes. In the National League for ten years. He played in the Swedish Hockey League for a few years prior to that," Klara said, slipping the pink noise cancelling headphones over Elin's ears as the music kicked up and the players hit the ice.

"Anytime you have questions, just ask me. Hockey has been my life longer than I can remember. We're a family here, and I wouldn't have it any other way," Klara said, giving Penny a smile.

"Thank you."

"Looks like your Ethan is in the first shift tonight. He had a rocky start at the beginning of the season, but he's been on fire recently. How long did you say you guys had been dating?"

Penny's cheeks heated. "About a month, I guess. Probably more. He says I'm his good luck charm."

Klara laughed. "These guys and their superstitions. The stories I could tell you about them. But if that's what he needs to win games, then I expect to see you at every home game. I want to see them in a Stanley Cup Final."

"Me too. And I'm not planning on going anywhere," Penny

said, staring down at the ice. She swore Ethan looked over at her and grinned. She held up her book and blew him a kiss.

After the anthem was sung and the ceremonial puck drop was complete, Ethan headed to the center dot and won the face-off. Hopefully they'd grab another win tonight. She liked being his good luck charm. And that he wanted her here, fully immersing herself in his life, in his hockey family.

* * *

"Who let you back here?" Ethan asked, the grin splitting his face doing all sorts of things to her belly. She clutched her book in front of her to avoid lunging at him after the game.

"Some guy I made out with. He was pretty hot," she teased as he approached.

He pressed a light kiss to her lips. She resisted the urge to wrap her arms around him, knowing that there were reporters nearby, and she wasn't ready for her picture to be splashed up anywhere. She wasn't sure she'd ever be ready for that.

"You were amazing. Two goals. Almost a hat trick. Just missed that empty net."

"Yeah. Hit the damn pipe," he said, shaking his head.

She pulled her book open, and flipped to the empty net page. "But I have a question. I mean, I understand the whole empty net thing, but I've also heard of a lot of empty net goals. It seems like a waste of time to pull your goalie if your team is down, just to get an extra player on the ice, since so many empty net goals are scored by the team already winning. What do you think the percentage is of empty net goals for the team that's already winning versus goals scored by the other team gaining an extra player? I bet it's not favorable to the team that's down. So why bother pulling your goalie?" she asked, pointing to her book. She'd already removed the flag since the explanation of empty nets had been obvious.

"Have I mentioned how cute you are?" he asked, pressing a kiss to her nose.

"It's a real question," she said between kisses. How she was forming actual sentences right now was beyond her, but she wanted to know.

He wrapped his arms around her, pulling her close into his body. The heat from his recent shower seeped through her clothes.

"Because at that point, what does the losing team have to lose? Might as well try to tie it up, even if it backfires."

"I guess, that does make sense," she said, pressing a hard kiss to his lips. Reporters be damned.

"So what other questions do you have? I see that book still has flags in it."

"I've only had it for a week. I need to go to a lot more games before I know everything."

"Well, that's perfect because I want you at every game. Was everyone nice to you upstairs? They seem like a nice bunch, but I've never brought someone in to infiltrate their ranks," he said with a smirk.

"Yes. Very nice. I spent most of the game with Klara and her kids, but she did introduce me around." And they had been friendly for the most part. A few had eyed her, probably wondering how she'd landed Ethan since she wasn't part of their model ranks, but she brushed them off and stuck with Klara and a few others. Hopefully the cliquey girls were temporary.

"Great. Now, what do you say to getting out of here? The things I want to do to you might be frowned upon in public."

His eyes darkened, and heat bloomed in her body at his words.

"I thought you'd never ask," she said, stifling a laugh as he spun on his heel, wrapped his arm around her waist, and power walked her out of the arena.

CHAPTER 18

"I've missed you," he murmured against her lips as her front door shut behind them. He'd made it back to her place in record time, and she was not complaining. She wanted him just as desperately as he wanted her. She wrapped her arms around his neck, holding him close as he consumed her mouth.

"Oh, Ethan. I've missed you, too," she moaned against his mouth, his touch robbing her brain of all coherent thoughts.

His tongue traced the seam of her mouth before plunging in and tangling with hers. He deepened the kiss and pressed her against the wall, her body flush against his, his cock digging into her belly as she grinded against him.

Her hands snaked up into his hair, locking on to the soft strands as she rose up on her tip toes to get closer. God, he felt good. She was almost positive that her knee was fully healed, and she wanted to jump up, wrap her legs around his waist, and climb him like a tree. But if it wasn't, then writhing in pain on the floor would definitely ruin the mood.

He continued to devour her mouth, groaning against her as she tightened her grip on his hair. He tormented her with his lips, his teeth, and his tongue. She couldn't get enough of him.

His hands trailed down her spine before slipping under her jersey. His blunt nails scraped against her skin, and a tremble rolled through her body as heat pooled in her core. He broke the kiss long enough to whip her shirt and jersey off over her head, tossing them aside. He kissed along her collar bone, nipping her flesh with his teeth before soothing each bite with a sweep of his tongue. Her head fell back, hitting the wall, her eyes closing in bliss as his lips moved down her chest.

"So beautiful," he murmured against her heated skin, pressing kisses along the edge of her bra. She released her grip on his hair so she could reach back and unclasp her bra, letting it fall from her body. She gasped, his lips closing around her right breast, pulling it into the hot cavern of his mouth and sucking deeply. She arched against him, trying to melt into his body as he continued to torment one breast and then the next.

He released her nipple, and dropped to his knees, kissing down her stomach, his hands reaching her waistband. He deftly popped the button open and pulled down the zipper, then shoved her jeans and panties down over her hips to the floor. He sat back, pulling her legs free until she stood before him completely naked.

"Why are you still clothed?" she asked as he stared at her. His chest rose and fell in rapid beats similar to her currently racing heart.

He leaned back in, pressing a kiss to her lower belly as his fingers moved through her curls. He didn't say a word before his lips moved lower, his tongue finding her clit.

"Oh yes," she gasped, pressing her core to his face. No longer caring that she was completely bare and vulnerable while he remained clothed. There was something unbelievably hot in standing naked in front of him while he wore his game day suit, his arms stretching the cotton button down, his suit pants unable to hide his need as he worshiped her body.

His tongue traced a lazy figure eight over her clit, and her fingers sank into his hair, holding his mouth to her pulsating body. Holy fuck he was good at that. Her breaths came out in pants as her stomach clenched. She arched her body, her head hitting the wall again as he plunged a finger inside of her.

"Ethan," she moaned as another finger joined the first, moving in and out of her tight heat. He latched onto her clit, his mouth sucking. Her body tensed. Her breathing stopped. And then with a crook of his finger, she exploded around him, shudders racked through her and she slumped against the wall. When she lifted her head to look down at him, that crooked smile she loved was in place. He held her hips and rose to his feet.

"Penny," he murmured as his lips met hers. Her arms wrapped around him as she pressed her trembling body to his and deepened the kiss. She tasted herself on his tongue and her need ratcheted up another notch. She needed him with a desperation she'd never felt before.

"Bedroom," she gasped between kisses.

He broke away from her mouth with a strangled *yes* and she tugged him down the hall.

She stifled a shocked gasp as he scooped her up into his arms. His long, purposeful strides had them in her room in seconds.

"Impatient, are we?" she said as he lowered her to the bed.

"Maybe." He grinned at her as he quickly removed his dress shirt and then pulled his undershirt over his head with one hand. If she'd tried that with her own shirt, she'd probably end up with tangled arms, and faceplanting onto the floor.

His biceps flexed as he moved. She nibbled on her lower lip, willing herself to not attack his defined chest. She wanted to trace his abs with her tongue, continuing down to his hip dip that drove her insane.

"See something you like?" he asked with a grin.

"Mmhmm," she murmured, not caring about his smug

expression. He was hot. She wanted him, and she wasn't embarrassed about that.

He quickly stripped off his pants and boxer briefs, and stood in front of her in all his naked glory. She licked her lips, focusing on his rock hard cock. She sat up, scooting to the end of the bed, and gripped him. He pulsed in her hand as she gave him a light tug.

"Penny," he groaned, his eyes drifting shut.

She lowered her head, running her tongue along the tip, tasting his salty arousal. His fingers sunk into her curls, tightening as she ran her tongue down the underside of his cock and back up to the tip, and then she sucked him into her mouth. She took in as much of him as she could, hollowing out her cheeks and swallowing when he hit the back of her throat.

"Oh, yes," he moaned as she continued to move up and down his shaft.

She wished she could look up at him. See if he was staring at her or if his eyes were closed tight. From this angle, it was impossible, but he was enjoying himself, if the moans and his tight grip on her hair were any indication.

Good God, she was good at this. Her murmur vibrated against his cock, and he almost gave in.

"I don't want to come in your mouth. I need to be inside you," he panted as he gently pulled back. Her mouth drove him crazy. They would have to try this again, but right now he needed to plunge inside her. And not in her mouth.

She released him with a pop as she tilted her head back to look at him. Her dilated pupils told him she'd enjoyed that almost as much as he had. How he was able to walk around with her and not attack her every minute of the day was beyond him, but he was not passing that up now.

She scooted back across the bed, settling against way too many pillows. What was it with women and more than two pillows?

Her breasts pointed up toward him, her pale pink nipples begging for his mouth. Her curls spread out around her face, a golden halo plumped up by said pillows. It put her on display for him. *So that's what they're there for. Okay, maybe not completely useless.*

"I think we can get rid of about ten of these," he said as he pulled a few pillows away, tossing them to the floor.

She grinned as she tossed the rest of them to the side, and waited for him to join her.

He moved up the bed, his knees resting between her spread thighs as he gazed down at her. He felt like he was home in her arms.

"What are you thinking about?" she asked, lifting her arms and running her fingers down his chest and abs. She traced the lines at his hips, and his stomach muscles clenched under her hands.

"Just that I can't get enough of you. Every time I want you more than I did before," he whispered before dropping his head and sealing his lips with hers. And it wasn't just the physical. He thought about her constantly, but he was afraid to confess that right now. She'd finally stopped running. He didn't want to freak her out and give her a reason to bolt.

She broke the kiss. "Stop stealing my thoughts."

And before he could say anything, she pressed her lips back to his, and his tongue plunged in, swallowing her gasp and twisting with hers. He rubbed against her, her arousal coating his cock as he bumped against her clit.

He blindly reached for the condom he'd placed on her night

stand, wishing he'd brought an entire box. He broke the kiss and leaned back, quickly rolling the condom on before settling between her thighs.

"We could've skip that," she murmured.

"What?"

"The condom. I'm on the pill and I'm clean."

He dropped his forehead to hers. "Now you tell me," he groaned before brushing a kiss across her nose. "Next time. I'm clean, too."

"Mmm, next time," she whispered. Her hand snaked down between their bodies, gripping him, and guiding him inside her. Her tight heat wrapped around him and he settled to the hilt.

"God, you're perfect," he moaned as he slowly began to plunge in and out of her, her muscles gripping him, holding him tight.

"Oh, Ethan," she whispered as her left leg wrapped around his hips.

"Is your knee okay?" he panted. She definitely had more range of motion than she'd had before, but he wished she could wrap both legs around his hips and squeeze him.

"Yes," she replied as she loosely settled it under his ass. He groaned as she pressed herself against him.

Her fingers clutched the hair at the base of his skull, and he lowered his head to trail kisses across her lips before settling his mouth in the crook of her shoulder.

Her hot breath wafted across his ear before her teeth pulled on his earlobe, sucking the sensitive skin into her mouth, causing his body to shudder.

Her hands moved across his shoulders, her nails digging into his skin as he plunged in and out of her body. Their gasps intermingling with each breath as he grinded against her, trying to rub against her clit while moving inside of her.

She arched her back, her hands raking across his shoulders. "Yes, Ethan. I'm so close," she panted, her voice strained with a need that matched his. He leaned in, nibbling on her earlobe and whispering how incredible she felt pulsing around him. He rocked against her, and her moans increased. He braced himself on one arm, and trailed his other hand down her sweat dampened body to where they were joined. He plunged in and out of her, his thumb rubbing her clit. Her legs tightened around his hips, her eyes locked with his. Her lips parted with her rapid breathing, and she threw her head back and exploded.

Her inner walls clamped down around his cock as he continued to move, and she continued to ride out her orgasm. And then with a few plunges, he came with a shout, before collapsing down on her body. He burrowed his face in her neck, pressing light kisses against her skin as her arms locked around his back, holding him in place.

"I don't think I can move," he mumbled against her. His face pressed to her throat.

She let out a half-hearted giggle and trailed her fingernails up and down his spine. He should be dead to the world, but he wanted her again. Once he could move. So maybe five minutes.

"I'm crushing you," he mumbled, but she just tightened her hold.

"I like you smothering me," she replied, her hands wandering down and gripping his ass, squeezing. "Mmm," she murmured. "You have the best ass."

He grinned against her. "Yours is better."

Finally, he pushed off of her. "Be right back," he said, and walked to the bathroom. Knowing that her eyes were following his ass, he did an exaggerated hip swivel. Her laughter trailed behind him, and he was back in a flash, slipping between the sheets. He pulled her up against his chest, that perfect ass of hers nestled against him.

She squirmed, rubbing against his hardening cock. "Stop moving unless you're ready for round two," he growled in her ear.

She laughed. "Already?"

"What can I say? I always want you."

"The feeling is mutual," she said, rocking her hips. He squeezed her waist before rolling her to face him.

"Keep that up and there will be no sleep for you," he said, pressing a hard kiss to her lips. They both pulled away, their breathing harsh. He'd keep it physical for now, but she had to see where they were headed. It was so much more for him.

"Sleep is overrated." She wrapped her arms around his neck and tugged him down for another kiss.

Who was he to complain?

CHAPTER 19

Her phone dinged again Monday morning, but a quick glance showed her it was a text from her mother. Since Penny was in the middle of a difficult tax return, with multiple types of businesses and a handful of properties, she set the phone to silent and scanned through the next section of the return.

Even though the documents her client provided were a jumbled mess, she loved sorting everything out and putting it in its proper place and on the correct line of the tax return. And she'd just gotten word that Kevin had called in sick. The day was looking up.

She was just finishing up, and starting to debate what she wanted for lunch, when there was a knock on her open door, and Lexi leaned against the frame.

"Hey. It's a little early for lunch, isn't it?" Penny asked, glancing at the clock on her computer.

Lexi walked in, shutting the door behind her and taking a seat, her expression unreadable.

"What's with the face? Is everything okay? Is something wrong with Abby?" Penny asked, sitting up straighter.

"I wanted to tell you before anyone else did. There are some rumors going around," Lexi started, and panic bloomed in Penny's chest.

"What rumors?"

"It's out there, Penny. It's just gossip right now, but they somehow found out about you and Ethan. And Italy."

Lexi's eyes filled with concern. Most likely a reflection of whatever was happening on Penny's face. And it wasn't good. Shit.

"How? Who?" she sputtered.

"I'm not sure. But the story is that you met Ethan in Italy and pretended not to know who he was. That you knew he was a rich athlete and Robert's nephew. That you are using him to move up in the company." Lexi's last statement was whispered, and Penny's stomach plummeted to her feet.

"But that's not true. I would never do that."

"I know," Lexi said, reaching for Penny's hand. "They're stupid rumors, but half of it is the truth. And it's going to get to Robert. To Alan. You need to tell them before someone else does. If they haven't already."

"Fuck. I knew this was a terrible idea."

"What was? Dating Ethan? Falling for him?"

Penny nodded.

"No. Keeping it from your boss after he handed you Ethan's account, that was probably not the best idea. But falling for Ethan. No. That was perfect. He brought you back to life. Made you smile again. He's good for you, Penny. Don't let stupid gossip ruin what you have. There's a way to fix this," Lexi said. She was so calm. Penny wanted to be calm, but her racing thoughts and sweaty palms nixed any chance of tranquility.

"What am I going to do?"

"It's going to be fine."

"I still don't know how anyone found out. I mean, was it

Kevin? But he didn't know about Italy. He's not a big fan of me, and the feeling is mutual, but who else would do this?"

"I don't know. And, umm, there's also pictures popping up on social media with you kissing Ethan after a game. And near some bakery downtown," Lexi said.

"What?"

"They aren't bad. They're just out there."

Penny unlocked her phone, but she had no clue where to even look. No one had tagged her on Facebook. Maybe they didn't know her name yet. "How do I find them?"

"Give it," Lexi said, holding her hand out, and Penny dropped the phone into Lexi's palm. Lexi scrolled through and then held it up to Penny.

"See. They're not bad. Just some kissing. Totally normal," Lexi said.

Except she was pressed up against Ethan like she was trying to seep into his skin, and Ethan's hands gripped her ass. Fuck. This was online for anyone to see. Robert. Her mother. Her co-workers.

She didn't want to look at the comments, but she couldn't stop herself.

Hartless's newest fling. We'll see how long that lasts.
Not his typical fare.
The player strikes again.

She flipped the phone face down on her desk and dropped her head. Everyone knew you should never read the comments, but they highlighted how mismatched she and Ethan were and she let her insecurities take over. "What if Robert fires me for lying?"

"You didn't lie. You just omitted," Lexi said. "It will be fine. Robert likes his nephew, and he likes you. Who knows, he could walk in here and welcome you to the family."

"You are insane. I have to talk to him now," she said, rolling back her shoulders and taking in a deep breath before she pushed her chair back from the desk.

"It's going to be fine."

Penny's computer dinged, and she glanced at her internal messenger app.

Robert: *Can I see you in my office as soon as possible?*

"Oh shit. I think I'm too late," Penny said, shaking her head.

Lexi leaned over, peaking at Penny's monitor. "It will be fine. Just go up there and tell him the truth. He's not going to fire you."

"You can't know that."

"No, I can't. But I think your job is safe. And then you are going to stop by my office and we will take an early lunch. Maybe Amanda can join us."

She sent a message back to Robert that she was on her way. "This is going to be a disaster, isn't it?" She stood up, and ran her hands down her skirt, willing her heart to stop racing and her brain to stop its downward spiral into unemployment.

"It will be fine. Just explain it rationally and then swing by my office," Lexi said, standing up and holding the door open.

"Oh, hi Penny," Jessica, salacious office gossip said, as soon as Penny walked into the hallway. The woman had a smirk on her face that told Penny all she needed to know. Had Jessica spread the rumors? No. She wouldn't have known about Italy, either.

"Hi, Jessica. Did you need something?" Her voice sounded calm in her ears. That was promising.

"Nope. Just walking by. Hope everything is going well." And there was that smirk again.

Penny nodded. "Yep. Just heading into a meeting." She headed for the stairwell before Jessica could say anything else. She heard Lexi ask Jessica a question, purely to stall the woman.

When she reached Robert's office, she took another calming breath—or four—and knocked.

"Come in," his voice called out.

"Hi, Robert. You wanted to see me?"

"Yes. Please take a seat."

He didn't sound hostile. That was a plus.

"I've heard a few things this morning, and I typically don't buy into rumors, but when it involves family, I have to ask."

She was going to throw up. Her belly churned, and she bit back the urge to revisit her breakfast.

"I'm sorry, Robert. I know what you are talking about, and, yes, I am dating Ethan. We did meet in Italy, and I had no idea he was your nephew until he walked into your office last month. I'm not proud of my decision not to tell you. And we did not start spending time together again until after you'd given me his account. I should've said something as soon as we went on that first date, but Ethan said he didn't have a problem with me working on his account. That I could Google his salary, so his earnings weren't a secret he needed to keep from me. I should've told you anyway. It was very out of character for me to not be completely upfront, and I truly apologize." The words flowed out of her at rapid speed. She didn't let him get anything in until she was done.

"You should've mentioned that you already knew him when I introduced you the first time he was in this office. I never would've handed over his account to someone he had a history with. You can see how inappropriate that would be, correct?"

"Yes. I will admit that I was in shock and not thinking clearly. I didn't expect to see him again," she said, staring Robert directly in the eyes when all she wanted to do was lower her head and slink out of this office.

"Sounds like typical Ethan," Robert said, and Penny paused.

"What?"

"Not that this has any reflection on you, but he's known for playing the field," Robert said with a half-hearted smile, and she bristled.

"I'm aware of his reputation, but at the time I had no idea who he was." She kept her voice calm.

"I'm disappointed in you for keeping this secret. Any relationship outside of the office should've been a red flag and you should've declined to take over his account."

"I know. And I shouldn't have let Ethan convince me that he didn't mind us working together, but I haven't done a deep dive of his file since it's the beginning of the year."

"You will turn his account back over to me. You cannot act as his accountant while you are dating him."

"I know. I should've come to you right away, and for that I am sorry," she said.

"Penny, we are going to clear this up now. And in the future, conflicts of interest must be addressed immediately." His words were stern, but his tone was not angry.

"So, I'm not fired…" she said, softly.

"Fired. Definitely not. While I'm not happy that you didn't come forward right away, so the rumors didn't start to begin with, we are clearing it up now and I trust that any future conflicts of interest will be addressed immediately."

"Yes. Absolutely," she said. Aside from his comment on Ethan's player status—that she was well aware of—the conversation had gone pretty well.

"Just a word of advice. You've been through a lot in the last year, and as much as I love my nephew, he's not known for long-term relationships. Not that he's incapable, it's just been a long time since he's been serious about anyone. He didn't mention your name at Christmas, but I knew he was seeing someone, and it appears that you make him very happy. But we cannot have any more rumors floating around, especially about my family. I trust that you will keep your personal and work lives completely separate."

"Of course. There should be no additional rumors. Everything is out in the open now and it will not affect my job, that I will guarantee," she said, still rattled at his comments about Ethan. He fed into her doubts, most likely without realizing, and she wanted this conversation to be over.

"That's good to hear. Please hand over anything you've printed up for his account as soon as possible and I'll let Alan know that we've taken care of the issue."

"Thank you, Robert, for your understanding. And, I am sorry for not coming to you first. I just wasn't sure what was going on between us. And please note that I am not dating him to further my career. I would never do that."

"I know, Penny. I never believed that part of the rumor for a second. So, you really met in Italy, huh?"

"Yes. Meeting him was completely unexpected. I'm not sure how that got out."

"The gossip will fade in time. Your performance at work speaks for itself. Just remember that."

"Thank you, Robert. I'll just get back to my office, then. Or, is there anything else?"

"No. That should be all."

She left his office, taking her first steady breath since Lexi had dropped that bomb on her. Her gut still churned. She needed to tell Ethan, but she didn't want him racing over and feeding the rumor monster. And she needed to think about everything Robert had said. Was she setting herself up for disappointment by continuing to pursue whatever was between her and Ethan?

Lexi caught up with her as soon as Robert's door shut behind her. "How did it go? Still employed?"

Penny let out a small laugh. "Yep. Still employed. He was surprisingly okay with it. He's taking back Ethan's account, and was disappointed that I kept it from him because of the conflict of interest, but it could've been a lot worse."

"That's great. I knew it would work out. Robert wasn't going to fire you over this."

"I still want to know who started the rumor." She glanced around the office, but no one was looking at her.

"Just ignore it. Everything will blow over. Focus on you and Ethan. On how happy he makes you and how happy you'll be not having to keep it a secret," Lexi said.

"I know. And I'm happy. So happy that I'm scared," she whispered as they reached Lexi's office.

"Don't overthink it. Just go with it and have fun. You deserve it."

She shot her friend a smile. "Thanks. Now, I need to get back to my office to make sure Robert knows I'm taking my job seriously. Can I bail on lunch?"

"Sure. But I don't think you need to prove anything to Robert."

"Yes, I do."

"Okay. If you need anything, just let me know."

"Thanks for everything," Penny said, giving her friend a hug before heading back to her office.

She'd just turned her computer back on when her phone buzzed. Amanda's name flashed on the screen.

She swiped it on, knowing that Amanda would just keep calling. "Hi," she said.

"What the actual fuck? Who am I killing?" Amanda screeched, and Penny had to pull the phone away from her ear.

"Lexi called you?"

"Of course she did. Oh my God. I want to punch someone. How are you doing?" Amanda asked.

"I'm okay now. Robert knows everything. It's a little awkward, but I'm still employed, which is good."

"Any idea how it got out?"

"No clue." She stared at her to-do list. She could get through everything and be out of the office by five. Then she could curl up into a ball and have the panic attack she desperately needed. She might appear calm, but she was a mess inside. She tried to forget the comments she'd read earlier on social media. She didn't want to be their fodder, or the subject of office gossip. She'd had enough of that when she'd cancelled her wedding.

"I'm so sorry. Are we going for a long carb-filled lunch? We can have a strategy session for hunting down the gossipy bitches you work with."

"I can't. I'm buried in work, and now that Robert knows, I need to work extra hard to prove that this isn't going to affect my job."

"They know how amazing you are at your job. It didn't suffer when you started dating Ethan, and it won't suffer now."

"I know that. I just need to prove that to everyone else."

"Who cares about everyone else."

"I do." She hated the hitch in her voice.

"Oh, Penny. I'm so sorry you're dealing with this bullshit. I'm coming over tonight. We'll get through this."

She was in no mood to rehash everything until she got a handle on it herself. "I just want to curl up and do nothing tonight. Give me a few days and then we can all vent together."

"Are you sure?"

She sighed. "Yes. I just need...I just need some time."

"You better text me if you need anything. Carbs, a shoulder to cry on, booze, a mercenary."

She laughed. It sounded watery.

"Penny, I'm so sorry you have to deal with this."

"I have to get back to work," she said, taking in a deep breath to steel herself for the rest of the day.

"Call if you need anything. Promise."

"I promise."

After she hung up the phone, she stared at her computer

again, the emails turned fuzzy as a tear plopped down on her desk. Fuck. Why had she put herself in this situation?

"Why is Amanda texting me?" Cheesy asked, setting his towel down on the workout bench between them and stared at his buzzing phone.

Ethan was halfway through his workout. Only a few guys had come in today since Coach had given them a day off, but he wanted to work on some strength exercises. Cheesy had joined him about twenty minutes ago. The guy never stopped training.

"Penny's friend?" Ethan asked, dropping the weight back into place and sitting up.

"Yes."

"The better question is, why does she have your number?"

Cheesy's cheeks turned a brighter shade of red, and Ethan would bet good money it wasn't solely due to the heavy weights he'd been lifting. Interesting.

"I gave it to her when I dropped her off at home the other night," he said, and shrugged. "But that's not important."

"So why is she texting you?" Ethan asked.

Cheesy swiped the phone on. "Something about your uncle and Italy. And that she doesn't have your number and you need to give Penny a call."

"Shit," he muttered, walking over to his bag, rifling through for his phone. Had she tried to call him? Grabbing it, he swiped it on. Nothing from Penny, but he did have a text from Robert. He'd call his uncle later.

"Weren't you in Italy last summer? What does that have to do with Penny or your uncle?"

"Long story. I need to call her. I'll talk to you later," he said. Cheesy nodded back. Ethan swiped his phone on and called Penny. The phone rang, and rang—and rang.

Shit.

He opened the messaging app and texted.

Ethan: Amanda texted me to call you. I don't have a lot of details, but I'm guessing Robert found out. I'm so sorry, Penny. I should've told him when this started. We will figure this out. I know you are probably panicking right now, but we've got this. And I'm going to keep calling until you pick up so I can make sure you're okay.

He waited a minute, no dancing dots appeared on his screen.

Ethan speed dialed Penny again. And again. On the fourth time, she finally picked up.

"I can't believe she contacted you. Ethan, I'm busy and I don't want to talk about it right now," she said. The tears in her voice sent a punch to his gut. Fuck, he wanted to hit something.

"Penny. Just tell me what happened. All I know is that Robert might know about Italy. Amanda was very cryptic."

"Someone in my office spread rumors about how we met in Italy and that I'm sleeping with you to advance my career. And there are pictures of us online. The comments were awful."

"Penny, I'm so sorry. You know I don't believe you are trying to move up at the company through me. And Robert would never believe that. He knows how hard you work, how much you care about your job."

"But I'm sleeping with my client."

"But you weren't when he gave you my account, and we've done basically nothing so far with my paperwork, so I'm not really your client yet." He tried to reassure her, to stave off the panic she was no doubt feeling.

"I know. But it's the principle of the matter. And I've never done anything like this before. I always follow the rules, and this is a clear breach. A complete conflict of interest."

"Penny, if I didn't want you as my accountant, I would've told Robert. I don't care that you see my financial records."

"That's not the point."

"So what else did Robert say?"

"He's disappointed in me and that he's taking your account back."

"I'm going to talk to him and then I'm picking you up tonight."

"I don't think that's a good idea, Ethan."

He didn't trust her tone. She was going to pull away. All of his reassurances over the last few weeks that everything would work out had amounted to nothing.

"We need to talk about this. I am so sorry this happened, but it's going to fade, and we are going to get through this. Don't listen to office gossip. They have nothing better to do."

"I just can't right now." The hitch in her voice destroyed him, and he wanted nothing more than to wrap her in his arms and pull her back into their bubble.

"I'm coming over tonight," he said.

"I don't think that's a good idea," she said, her voice low.

"Don't run, Penny."

"I'm not running. I just need some time to figure everything out."

He refused to let her slip away. "We can figure it out together. I'm going to be on your doorstep with takeout tonight. Please let me in. You can even hit me if it makes you feel better."

Her chuckle was watery, but at least they were getting somewhere.

"I don't know," she said.

"Well, I'll be there, and it would be nice if you let me in. It's going to be windy as hell tonight."

"Maybe. I have to get back to work."

"We are going to get through this, and I'm going to talk to Robert and explain that I told you to keep my account. I'll see you in a few hours. Don't leave me out in the cold." Did she hear the double meaning behind that last statement?

"Okay," she said before the line went dead. He hoped she'd open the door for him tonight. That she wouldn't run. But he'd chase her if he had to. He'd never stop.

* * *

He knocked on her door a few hours later, takeout in hand. He'd talked to Robert. His uncle had chastised him for keeping his relationship with Penny a secret, when it was a clear conflict of interest, but he'd also been genuinely happy. Now he just had to convince Penny that the rumors would fade, that her job was safe. That what they had between them was real and worth fighting for.

"Penny, open up. I brought Lanzi's," Ethan said. He didn't hear footsteps. "Please don't leave me out in the cold. The lasagna won't survive. The tiramisu might be okay, but…" he trailed off as the door opened.

"I still don't think this is a good idea, but you said Lanzi's," she said, pausing to look down both sides of the street. "I can't have you shouting on my doorstep. Enough attention has been drawn to us already, and I have no desire to add to it."

He hated her red-rimmed eyes, the tissue clutched in her hand that wasn't grasping the door. She looked around one last time, and pulled him inside while the coast was clear.

The overwhelming desire to punch something surfaced again, but he tamped it down and placed his free hand at her waist, giving her a soft squeeze.

"I'm so sorry about everything, but it's going to work out. I promise."

"You can't promise that," she whispered.

"Yes, I can," he reassured her, and she stepped back, letting him further into the house. He would do everything in his power to fix this nightmare.

Penny ached to believe him, but she'd trusted her gut before and look where it'd gotten her. Not that Ethan was like Michael in any way, but she'd fallen for Ethan, and he didn't know yet the power he held over her. How badly he could destroy her heart. Part of her screamed for her to get out now, that the logical thing, the safest thing, would be to end it before he did, and to move on.

But it was only a small part. Her heart urged her to not give up. That he—that this—was worth it. She'd hear him out. Weigh the pros and cons. Then she'd figure out how to fix this mess, if that was possible.

"I see those wheels turning. Please stop. Let's sit down and eat, and we can talk about it," he said, pressing a hard kiss to her lips before guiding her into the kitchen and spreading out everything on the table.

The aroma of amazing Italian food washed over her, and her stomach growled. She'd skipped lunch, opting for the granola bar—and a chocolate bar—in her desk to avoid leaving the office. For the most part, her co-workers had blissfully left her alone. Her closed door had helped.

"I guess I am hungry," she said, grabbing plates and silverware. "Do you want wine?"

"Maybe a glass, or water is fine," he said, coming up behind her as she took a bottle from the fridge. He wrapped his arms around her waist, brushing soft kisses behind her ear, and she sank into his embrace, enveloped in his warmth, in his protection.

"It's going to work out," he whispered against her ear. "I won't let anyone hurt you."

"I wish you could guarantee that," she said, turning in his arms, resting a hand on his chest.

"I'll prove it to you. I promise."

He took the bottle of wine, led her to the table, and then dished out dinner.

"I just don't understand the point of it all. Why would my co-workers spread rumors? Where did they come from? And why do your "fans" need to put pictures of you kissing me on social media? Why do they care? I mean, it's not like you're a celebrity," she said.

"I'm not. And if it wasn't me, if it was just another hockey player, they probably wouldn't care, but I haven't been a model citizen since I entered the pros. I have a party reputation that I'm not proud of, but it's out there. I'm trying to fix my image, but there are still going to be people who take our picture. Who comment about who I'm dating on social media. You learn to ignore it eventually. Most of what they put up there is false."

"Social media I will try to ignore. Work is another story. I can't have my co-workers thinking I'm sleeping my way to the top."

"Could it have been Kevin?" he asked, voicing the question she'd asked herself all day.

"He knows something is going on between us, but how would he know about Italy?"

"I don't know, but someone did, and they are using it against you, and I am not okay with that." He linked his hand with hers, running his thumb along her palm.

"I want to ignore it. I think that's the best plan, but maybe we should lie low for a while, until this passes." She didn't want him to agree.

"Absolutely not. We are stronger together than apart, and I'm not going to let them win." He tightened his hold on her, pulling her from the seat next to him and drawing her into his lap. He wrapped his arms around her, and she sunk into him. "We are going to act as if nothing is wrong, and it will blow over. I promise."

She nodded, snuggling into his chest. She wished she had his confidence.

CHAPTER 20

Was it five yet? Penny grumbled as she looked at her computer on Monday. Nope. But it was almost time for lunch. She needed a break. Kevin was driving her crazy. And if Jessica winked at her one more time, Penny feared she would strangle the gossipy bitch. She'd wished her secret wasn't out, but at least no one was hounding her outside of the office. Not that anyone was hounding her here—it was just the looks. They knew, and they were questioning her motives. It fucking sucked.

She'd kept to herself for the most part. Luckily, Ethan had back-to-back away games this week, so she didn't have to show her face at the arena. He'd been fired up in both, with multiple points spread between the two games. And he'd been fired up about where they stood, constantly calling her, checking in to see how she was doing. It was sweet and maddening at the same time. He'd be home tonight, and they were planning to spend the weekend together. She just had to get through today.

"Knock, knock," her mother's voice came through Penny's office door before she peeked her head into Penny's office.

Penny looked toward the ceiling. *Really?*

"Mom. Ahh, what are you doing here?" she asked, tucking her hair behind her ears, hoping she looked presentable.

"Can't a mother stop by to take her daughter to lunch?"

"A normal mother," Penny mumbled under her breath.

"You look tired." Her mother stopped at the corner of Penny's desk.

"It's been a long week. So, what are you doing here?" she asked again.

"I want to take to you to lunch. We don't spend enough time together. I haven't seen you in a few weeks."

Right. Since Christmas when they'd practically thrown Michael on her.

"You've never stopped by for lunch before."

"Stop arguing with me and let a mother take her daughter out for lunch." There was steel under her mother's smile. Her father may bluster, but her mother inspired a healthy level of fear. Not physically, of course, but her temper simmered like a dormant volcano before it exploded, and pity whoever got in her way.

Penny pulled on her jacket and smoothed down her skirt as she walked around her desk. "I can spare an hour," she said as she followed her mother out of the office.

"That's fine, dear. I just want to enjoy a nice lunch." Why did Penny doubt that statement?

They went to a café down the street from Penny's office and quickly ordered. A glass of wine and a salad for her mother. Penny wanted a cheeseburger but settled on grilled chicken on a salad. She'd need a candy bar after this lunch. Luckily, she had three of them in her desk. She eyed her mother, three might not be enough.

"How are you, dear?" her mother asked after the waiter left to grab their drinks.

"I'm good."

"It was so great to see you at Christmas. I can't wait to start planning Jill's baby shower."

"I think we can hold off on that for at least a few months," she replied.

"I know. I just get so excited. I'm finally going to be a grandmother."

"Yes, it is exciting," Penny said.

"And it was so nice for Michael to join us for dinner. I just wish you hadn't left so abruptly."

"Gee, I wonder why I left," Penny said. "Could it be because you blindsided me with my cheating ex?"

"Really Penny, there's no need to get snippy," her mother admonished.

"Are you kidding me? Why would you think that inviting the man who cheated on me would be a good idea?" she bit out. Dammit. She wished she'd ordered a glass of wine. Or maybe a shot.

"Calm down, dear. You two needed to talk it out," her mother replied before she daintily dabbed her lips with her napkin, and then draped it across her lap. Like they were having lunch at a country club or something. Appearances were everything. And a heated conversation at lunch was not appropriate.

"Why did you invite him? In fact, why are we having lunch? If it's to talk about him, Michael and I are over. Why can't you understand that? He cheated on me. I can't forgive that." Penny felt her cheeks heat. She knew that she'd raised her voice toward the end and she glanced around to see if anyone had noticed. Luckily, they were in a back corner, and the lunch rush had yet to arrive.

"Have you talked to him? Did he explain that it was a one-time mistake?"

"Wait. Did you talk to him? Is that what he told you?"

"That's what he told your father. Penny, mistakes like this

happen. We're only human. You two have a history that you can't just walk away from."

"Actually, I can walk away from it. I deserve better, and as my mother, I wish you would support that. I'm sorry that I've ruined your perfect family image, but I'm not going to take him back just to make the gossip go away at dad's office. How could you ask that of me?"

"Be reasonable," her mother said. The waiter stopped by and dropped off their drinks.

Her mother's Chardonnay looked pretty appealing at this point. "I can't believe you want me to take him back. After everything he's done."

"Yes, perhaps Christmas wasn't the best time to invite him over, but you two were so happy and I hate to see you throw away that future because of one mistake. They happen, and successful relationships are about working through the tough spots and growing together."

Penny was tired of reading between the lines. "What aren't you telling me? Why are you so determined to get us back together?"

"I never wanted you girls to know, but I cheated on your father once."

Penny gasped. Sure, she assumed someone had cheated, but she expected it to have been her father. "Why would you do that to Dad? How could you?"

"It was before you girls came along. It was a one-time stupid mistake after we'd been married for a few years. I'd miscarried our first child the year before and was so depressed and your father was always working."

Holy shit. The bombs just kept dropping.

She reached out and grabbed her mother's hand. "You never told us that you miscarried before us."

"It's not something that I wanted to talk about."

"But then you cheated and Dad forgave you?" Penny asked.

"Yes. It was a stupid mistake with a man I'd grown up with. Someone I thought was a friend, and one night, we were out to dinner and your father was at work. One thing led to another…" Her mother paused, shaking her head. "I told your father right after it happened. He was furious, but we talked it out. We went to counseling and we worked through it because we love each other and we weren't ready to throw everything we had, everything we'd built, away."

"Wow. I—I don't know what to say to that."

"I just don't want you to give up what you have with Michael. He's a part of our family and he's so sorry about what happened." Her mother looked so contrite, so sincere, but it wasn't the same situation and the further she moved away from him, away from what happened, the more she realized that he wasn't right for her. Possibly never had been.

"I'm glad that you and Dad worked everything out, but I don't want to move past this. I don't want to forgive him. Michael and I aren't right for each other. I know it makes work a little awkward for Dad, but I've moved on and I need you to accept that."

"Right. With that athlete." Her mother said, with a flippant wave of her hand, and Penny bristled. Apparently, her mother had seen the pictures.

"Yes. That athlete, who's been nothing but wonderful to me," she fired back.

"You barely know him. How long has it been? A month? Two? He's just going to disappoint you."

"You can't know that, and actually, we met in Italy. I had a wild vacation fling with him in my honeymoon suite. It was glorious." She wanted to burst out laughing at the shocked expression on her mother's face. She hadn't been able to resist throwing that last part out.

"You what? In your honeymoon suite? What does that say about you?" her mother asked.

"Me? After what you just told me about you cheating? You're going to question something I did after I ended it with Michael? And it says that I was a single woman who wanted to have a good time, and I finally found a great guy." She hated defending herself and her actions to her mother.

"But how long will it last? He's not known for serious relationships."

"And how would you know that? You can't believe everything you read online." She wanted this conversation to end. How dare her mother judge her.

"It's just a fling that will end with your heart broken again. Why not end it now? Save yourself the pain. Talk to Michael. Hear him out. You two were made for each other, and he's heartbroken about what happened."

"Then maybe he should have kept his zipper up at work."

"Penny," her mother chided. Penny glared back, refusing to apologize for her comment. It was the truth.

"We won't talk about Michael or this *athlete*. Tell me how work is going. Shouldn't they be promoting you soon? You've been there for over four years now." Story of her life. If her mother wasn't harping on her love life, it was about how slowly she was moving up in her career. God, she needed something stronger than water if she was going to survive this lunch.

"I know, and I'd hoped they would've promoted me by now, but it hasn't happened. It can be very frustrating. And now I'm training another associate and…" she trailed off. "I don't want to talk about work."

"I'm sorry you are disappointed at work. You know if you'd only pursued a law degree like we wanted, you would be a partner at your father's firm by now." And the hits just kept coming. Her parents had wanted her to become a lawyer like her father. They'd pressured her when she was in college, but she had no desire to follow in her father's footsteps. She loved being an accountant.

"I never wanted to be a lawyer. That was all you and dad. And I enjoy what I do, I'd just hoped to be further along in my career by now. I've been thinking about going out on my own, actually, but it's too much of a risk to give up my steady paycheck." Why did she tell her mother that?

"I'm sure that if you decided to go out on your own, your father would love to help you. Perhaps send a few high-profile clients your way," her mother said.

"And in return for me smoothing things over with Michael, I'm sure."

"Really dear, why must you think the worst of us? We just want to support you and help you become as successful as you should be," her mother said, but Penny could spot the requirements behind her mother's statement, and she was not interested.

"I don't want your help," she replied. Or the guilt trip that would surely come along with it.

"Think about it. And maybe you could come over for dinner again."

"So you can ambush me with Michael again? I think not."

"You're so dramatic, Penny. I still think you need to give Michael another chance. What's the harm in talking to him?"

"The harm? I don't know, maybe the fact that he cheated on me and my family thinks I should just get over that. I'm moving on, but I will never forgive Michael for what he did. Nor do I want to." Penny set her napkin down and pushed back from the table. "I'm sorry, mother, but I have to get back to the office." Before she lost her shit.

The brief attempt at compassion she'd felt toward her mother after her mother's confession vanished with each comment that Penny should forgive Michael. It wasn't happening.

"Okay, dear. Just think about what we talked about and enjoy the rest of your day," her mother said at a slightly higher decibel. God forbid the strangers in the restaurant discover that her mother had been stormed out on by her daughter. Penny shook her head as she escaped the restaurant. She needed those candy bars. Stat.

"The good luck charm is back," Sully said, sliding onto the bench next to Ethan after their first shift of the night.

"What?" His gaze immediately went to the penalty box, and he scanned the surrounding seats, but didn't see her. "Where?"

"The lower bowl, loge two, a few rows back. Where some of the WAGs like to sit when they want to be close to the action," Sully said, and Ethan spotted her.

She gave him a wave, holding up her blue-flagged book. The flags were dwindling. She'd be an expert in no time.

"Hi," he mouthed and then felt like an idiot when the guys caught him and snickered. He'd given her a security pass and introduced her to a few of the wives and girlfriends of the other players at the last game, but he loved that she'd rather watch him play up close than hang out in the WAGs room.

"Wow, she finds your playing so boring that she has to bring a book?" Baz asked with a loud guffaw.

"No, ass. She's learning about hockey because it's something I care about," he shot back, and immediately regretted those last words as Baz laughed harder.

"You two done chit-chatting, over here? I need you to focus," Coach said, nudging Ethan in the back so he'd know exactly who that comment was directed to.

"I'm focused," he muttered.

"On the game. Not the girl," Baz teased.

"Don't worry Bugsy, she's his good luck charm. We'll win now," Sully said.

"Don't get cocky. Pittsburgh is at the top of their conference, and we need these points," Bugsy said.

Ethan nodded in agreement, and slid down the bench. They were hanging out in wild card range, but a win tonight, as long as Anaheim lost, would bump them to third in their division. It was all a numbers game, which was probably why it fascinated Penny so much. He bit back a smile, not wanting the guys to tease him again, but she was so freaking adorable when she wanted to talk stats. Her interest in what he loved wasn't just superficial and that thrilled him.

"Let's get out there and show everyone how well your good luck charm works," Sully said, hopping over the boards, Ethan following behind him, tapping his stick on the ice for Millsy to pass him the puck.

The puck hit Ethan's tape, and he was off, deking past Pittsburgh's captain, and heading toward the net. Pittsburgh's goalie was a brick wall, but was weak on the blocker side, so Ethan took aim and fired. The clang of the puck hitting the pipes rang through his ears, and Cheesy got the rebound, knocking it into the back of the net. As the siren went off, the crowd roared to its feet, and Ethan slammed into the group hug, grins wide, backs slapped, before they skated past their bench, glove taps down the line.

"Guess she is a good luck charm," Bugsy yelled out as Ethan slid onto the bench.

Tonight was definitely looking up.

* * *

"You guys were amazing," Penny said as he followed her into her house later that night.

"The team wanted to say thanks to my good luck charm," he

said, pressing a kiss to her blush stained cheek. He'd had another great game, with a goal and an assist. They'd been tied until the last minute when Dom had scored the winning goal.

And as excited as he'd been by the win, seeing Penny in the stands, cheering him on, waving when she caught his eye, meant everything. They'd stayed in for the week, and he'd avoided stopping by the office to take her to lunch. She'd asked him to stay away, and he'd reluctantly agreed. He'd been tempted to show up and roam the halls searching for the rumor-starting asshole and giving them a piece of his mind, or a taste of his fist.

"I'm glad I could be of assistance," she said. That twinkle in her eyes had faded a few days ago and he was grateful to see it back. Screw her damn co-workers. Now that Robert knew the truth, his uncle was happy for him, he only wished he'd had a heads-up.

"If it gets tight toward the end, you might have to travel with us to away games," he said, flashing her a grin. The guys had suggested that tonight in the locker room after the game, and Bugsy looked like he was almost considering it.

"I don't think I'd get approved for all that time off, especially during tax season," she said.

"I know. So how is work going?" he asked when they'd settled on the couch. He slung an arm around her shoulder, pulling her close, and she burrowed into his side, her breasts pressed against his ribs. He truly had no desire to talk about work or the game.

She sighed. "It's okay. Still getting looks. Kevin's being his typical asshole self. But I'm ignoring it and putting extra effort into my job. That's all I can do."

"I'm sorry you're dealing with this bullshit. Our relationship has nothing to do with your job. You've worked hard for this promotion, and you're going to get it, if that's what you want," he said, his heart aching for her.

"But if it happens, will the rumors overshadow it? Will it always be a question of how I got it?"

"That's bullshit and you know it. You've put in your time and you've worked your ass off for it."

"Yes, I have. But does that matter at this point?" She shook her head. "I don't want to talk about work tonight."

"Okay. Just know that I'm here for you if you need anything. A shoulder to cry on, an ear to listen, a well-placed kick when we find out who started this nonsense. A mouth to kiss when you want to forget everything else."

She shifted, straddling his lap, and gave him a hard kiss. "Your list-making abilities are such a turn on."

He chuckled, and nipped her ear, enjoying the shudder that rocked through her.

"And how did you know that was exactly what I wanted?"

"Because I just know," he whispered against her mouth, sinking his hands into her hair and anchoring her head to his, deepening the kiss.

She sank into his body, her breasts pressed firmly against his chest, her hands gripping his shirt, her tongue meeting and tangling with his.

He swallowed her moan, his hands trailing down her spine, and she shivered against him. He reached the hem of her jersey and slipped his hand underneath, pulling her shirt up to reach her warm, soft skin.

She rocked against him, his cock hard between them, stretching his suit pants. He needed them naked now.

He broke the kiss, quickly divesting her of her jersey and turtleneck. The flush had spread to her chest and he leaned in, pressing kisses along the top edge of her bra, scraping his thumb over her nipples and watching them pebble under his attention.

"Oh, Ethan," she moaned, her hands in his hair, holding his mouth to her body.

He popped the clasp, and she dropped her hands, allowing the fabric to pool between them.

Her entire body trembled when his fingers met her flesh, tweaking her nipples. He dropped his head, pulling one breast into his mouth, his tongue swirling around the tip.

She rocked her hips, and he swore he could feel her heated core through the layers of their clothes, and his cock hardened to the point of pain.

She reached for his chest, quickly popping open the buttons of his shirt, trying to push it from his shoulders but his arms locked around her, stopped her, and she growled in frustration.

He pulled back, stripping off his shirt, and kissed her again as her nails skated down his chest, reaching for his waistband.

And that was when he realized she was straddling him.

"Wait? Is your knee okay for this?"

Her cheeks flushed brilliant red, and her eyes softened at his inquiry. She'd never straddled his lap before. Her injury made bending her knee painful, if not impossible, months ago.

"Yes, I've done all the therapy, and I've been practicing—"

He cut her off. "Practicing?"

"Of course. I wanted full range of motion back. I'm still nervous about it going out again, but I think I'm good," she stated. He couldn't stop his chuckle at her rational logic.

"Now, are you going to pick me up and take me into the bedroom so we can enjoy my new flexibility?" she asked, a grin playing at the corners of her well-kissed mouth.

"I always do as the lady asks," he said, standing with her in his arms. She linked her legs around his waist, her core shifting against his painfully hard cock. She was so damn adorable, he was never letting her go.

CHAPTER 21

"Why didn't you call me yesterday?" Amanda pouted as Penny walked into Lexi's house. "And it's nice to see you, too," Penny replied as she kicked off her heels. Stupid torture devices. She curled her toes into the plush carpeting in Lexi's living room before sinking down on the couch. Today had been rough.

"Bad day?" Lexi asked.

"Ugh. It started out so nicely." Maybe since she'd still been in a sexual haze from spending the weekend with Ethan. He'd stayed until this morning.

"What happened?" Lexi asked.

"Kevin is terrible. I think he spends more time looking at my chest than at the computer. How am I supposed to train that?"

"That sucks. But can we get back to you not calling me?" Amanda asked.

"I might've been busy all weekend," she said, her cheeks heating as she remembered the last two days with Ethan.

"She did have a pep in her step today when she got to the office," Lexi confirmed.

"Really? So, everything is going well? Even with all the bullshit rumors and your pictures up on social media?"

"Please don't remind me." She'd just started to forget it. Not really, but Ethan had done everything in his power to wipe her mind clean this past weekend.

"Sorry. Eventually they'll go away. I'm just happy it's working out for you two," Amanda said.

"It was fantastic. We spent all weekend together, and I'm sore in places that haven't been sore since Italy."

"Awesome." Amanda grinned. "Keep talking. What did you do? I mean, besides have tons of sex. I'm so proud of you, Penny."

Penny rolled her eyes. "Should we really be discussing my sex life with Abby in the house?" Penny looked around for Lexi's impressionable six-year-old daughter.

"Abby's with Grant's mom, so dish," Lexi replied as she filled wine glasses and set them on the coffee table.

"And don't leave out any of the good stuff," Amanda piped in.

She told them about her weekend with Ethan. Yes, they'd had a lot of sex. Possibly in every room of her townhouse, but it wasn't just that. They *oohed* and *ahhed* at all the right moments.

"You really like him, don't you?" Lexi asked.

"Yes. And it freaks me the hell out. I mean, I just got out of a relationship. Yes, it was six months ago, but Michael and I were together for years. What if this is just a rebound, and it doesn't last?"

"But you said you have stronger feelings for Ethan than you did for Michael. That should count for something," Amanda replied.

"I don't know. We've been spending so much time together, in between his away game trips. We never run out of things to say, or stuff to do." She wiggled her eyebrows for good measure, and they all laughed.

"Sounds perfect, but is it just lust and infatuation?" Amanda asked.

"I don't know." Penny paused. "No, you know what? It's not just that. Or is it just new and thrilling and I don't know what I'm doing? What am I doing?"

"You are having fun. And getting back out there with a great guy," Lexi said, squeezing Penny's hand.

"Are my feelings amplified because it's a rebound and Michael hurt me so badly? How do I not keep that in the back of my mind? I mean, it's only been like two months since we really started dating."

"Whoa. Slow down," Amanda started. "You are freaking yourself out, and I can see that overanalyzing vein popping out on your forehead."

Penny ran a finger over her brow, frowning.

Amanda laughed. "It's not an actual vein. Work with me here. You overanalyze everything. Just have fun. See where it leads. This is the happiest we've seen you in, possibly, ever. No one said your first relationship after Michael had to be a rebound. I say go for it. But be careful. You'll know in your gut if you can really trust him."

"Right. Like I knew it my gut that Michael was cheating?" Penny scoffed.

"Stop doubting yourself. Michael was a scumbag, and he hid it well. I have a good feeling about Ethan. Just be smart about it. Maybe take things slow. Like don't move in with him tomorrow," Lexi said.

Penny laughed. "It's nice waking up next to him, but I'm not ready to share my space with a boy again."

Amanda chuckled. "Yeah, they're messy slobs."

"Right, because you're a neat freak," Penny replied. She remembered their dorm room in college. Amanda always said that her mother told her as long as there was a path from her bed to the door, clutter was okay. Although Penny doubted that any sane mother would say that, but Amanda was adamant that it'd been a family rule.

"I hate cleaning," Amanda grumbled.

"Ahh, no one likes cleaning, but I have to make sure I pick everything up or else I'd spend all day tripping on things," Penny said.

Amanda grinned. "See, it pays to be graceful. It allows me to be messy."

"Very funny."

"I'm glad things are working out with Ethan. You two having a lot of sleepovers?" Lexi asked.

Penny grinned. "Define *a lot*."

Amanda let out a bark of laughter.

"Hey, it's a stress reliever," Penny said.

"I'm not knocking it," Amanda replied. "We're just jealous. Okay, maybe not Lexi, but I'm jealous."

"The serial dater is jealous?" Penny asked.

"Wait. Did you just call me easy?" Amanda asked in mock outrage, grinning.

"Of course not. Just a connoisseur of men," Lexi replied.

"Connoisseur of men? Fancy title. Is that like calling a garbage man a waste disposal engineer?" Amanda asked. Penny would never call her friend easy, she just enjoyed playing the field more than Penny and Lexi did.

Lexi chuckled. "You know what we mean."

Amanda grinned. "Yeah, and I'm not offended."

"We know," Penny replied with a chuckle.

"I still want to know why Penny knocked back that glass of wine before we sat down. If everything is going great with Ethan, what's with the bad week?" Amanda asked.

"It's Kevin, isn't it?" Lexi asked.

"Yep. He's pissing me off. He told me two weeks ago that he didn't care about learning anything because it didn't matter since once his dad retires, he's going to be handed the company. It's just gotten worse since then."

"What a punk," Amanda said.

"He tried to hit on me last Friday," Lexi added.

"Are you kidding me?"

"I politely turned him down," Lexi said.

"He asked me out for a drink the first day I met him, and I immediately said no. And the other day he made a comment about me dating Ethan. Actually, he said Mr. Knight's nephew, as if he was trying to hint that I'm trying to work my way up the food chain like he is."

"What a douche," Amanda exclaimed.

"I think he's sleeping with Jessica, too," Lexi said.

"Great. Biggest gossip in the office. I feel like I'm in high school," Penny whined as she dropped her head to the table.

"She's an idiot, sleeping with a moron. Great combination. Ignore them," Lexi replied.

"I wish I could, but the petty jabs are getting to me."

"You could quit," Amanda said.

"She can't quit. She's the best accountant we have," Lexi said.

"Actually—" Penny started.

"Please don't quit. Who would I go to lunch with?" Lexi asked.

"Glad to see your true concern." Penny grinned at Lexi. "But don't worry, I'm not quitting, at least not yet. I've been thinking of going out on my own. Not to open a CPA firm, but just to work for myself."

"That's a great idea," Amanda said.

"It is a risk, so I'm still weighing my options, but I've always wanted to be my own boss, and I'm not moving up at Knight and Welling the way that I'd hoped. I mean, how long can I stay there in the same position? Especially when that idiot is going to end up running the company."

"I say go for it," Amanda cheered.

"Thanks. I think I want to take a risk. My entire life has been about being smart and playing it safe, and look where that got me. The first time I took a risk, I ended up in Italy and met Ethan. I have no regrets there. Who's to say going out on my own won't work too?"

Amanda grinned. "Wow, who are you and where's Penny?"

"Very funny."

"I'm serious. I've been waiting for this for years now. And if I have to thank Ethan for it, then point me to him."

"I agree with Amanda. This could work. And you should take risks. Not crazy risks, but if that's what you want, I think you need to go for it," Lexi said. "And if you get busy and need someone to run payroll or admin work, you know where to find me."

"My mother hinted that my father would send me clients if I smoothed things over with Michael."

Penny tried not to laugh as Amanda's eyes widened. She knew that statement would piss them off.

"Are you kidding me? You told her you were thinking of quitting?" Amanda asked.

"She surprised me at the office last week and took me to lunch. I was angry from dealing with Kevin, and it slipped out. I told her that I would never take their help and I had no plans to smooth things over with Michael."

"Man, your parents have some big balls," Amanda said.

Penny chuckled. "Yeah, I'm sure my mother didn't enjoy me storming out on her at lunch. She told me to put the *athlete* aside and try to work things out with Michael."

"Delusional." Lexi shook her head. "You should bring Ethan to dinner one night as a surprise. Maybe they'll invite Michael."

"Wish I could see that," Amanda replied, and grinned.

"I have no plans to see them any time soon, so you could be waiting awhile," Penny said as she polished off her second glass of wine. "What time's the takeout getting here? I need to soak up the booze so I'm not useless tomorrow."

"Parents are the best," Amanda said, raising her glass.

"This is why you pick your friends," Penny muttered, taking a sip of her water. The wine would wait until after she had some carbs in her belly.

"You have me for the entire weekend, whatever are you going to do with me?" Ethan said, shooting her a wink after the waitress left their table Saturday night. Their schedules had been crazy this week. He'd had back-to-back games and she'd been swamped at work. Tax season was gearing up, so convincing her to take a break and show up at his games, which resulted in sleepovers and very little sleep, wasn't easy. She was determined to stay on top of everything, and not ask for any help at work, so no one could claim favoritism.

They still hadn't figured out who'd started the rumors, but Ethan's money was on Kevin. Ethan itched to say something to his uncle, but he resisted. This was Penny's fight, and he'd back her up in whatever way she asked, and she'd asked him to stay out of it.

"Oh, I don't know. I'm thinking movie marathon and then passing out. I'm exhausted," she said. The tiredness was evident in her eyes, but she backed it up with a naughty smile. He was on to her.

"The bedroom could play a large role in our weekend, but sleeping wasn't high on my list," he teased.

"I'm sure we can compromise." Her hand disappeared under

the table, her fingers trailing up his thigh, and he squirmed in his seat.

"Listen, troublemaker, if you keep that up, we aren't staying for dessert." He grabbed her wandering hand and leaned over, pressing a hard kiss to her lips. At least their table was in the corner of the restaurant, with a tablecloth to hide what she was doing.

"Pretty sure you started it with the sleeping isn't high on your list," she teased, scraping the thumb of her trapped hand along his palm, and calmly taking a sip of her wine as if she wasn't testing his resolve under the table.

"Complete trouble."

"You could always sit across from me instead of next to me. Keep that temptation out of my reach." She grinned behind her glass, then sputtered and coughed when he released her hand and trailed his own fingers over her upper thigh.

"Ethan, you shouldn't," she said, catching her breath. "We're in public," she admonished, and he couldn't stop his bark of laughter.

"I'm sure I could scrounge up some dessert at home. Want to get out of here?" he asked.

"Nope. We ordered a brownie sundae, and we are going to enjoy it like civilized people, and *then* we are going home to be uncivilized."

He wasn't sure what thrilled him more, the idea of what he was going to do to her as soon as they walked in his front door, or the fact that she called his house *home*. Yes, it'd only been a few months, but the idea of having her be the first person he saw in the morning and the last person he saw at night had been in the forefront of his mind more often than not.

That damn rumor had thrown a wrench in his plans to ask her about moving in. He understood her need to pull back, and keep their relationship under the radar at work. He wasn't happy about it, but he understood. Right now, she could say they were just casually dating. Moving in was a completely different story, so he'd held off. But not forever. At some point, she needed to accept that this was happening, and it had no bearing on her job.

"Promises, promises," he said, squeezing her thigh under the table, relishing in her sharp breath, just as the waitress brought over their dessert.

"Do you need anything else?" the woman asked.

"Nope, we're good," Penny said, eyeing the sundae with a bit more enthusiasm than she'd eyed him a minute ago. They'd need to work on that.

After the waitress walked away, Penny dug in.

"Yum. I mean, not as good as Ghirardelli, but still awesome," she said between bites. "So, do you think teams lose momentum with this All-Star break? You have four days off, some of the guys are taking short vacations, some guys are playing in the game. It just seems random to put an All-Star Game in the middle of a season."

Her statement came out of left field. One minute they were discussing dessert, then next she wanted to debate hockey. He loved it. She wasn't pretending to be interested, she was actually interested.

"Seriously, where have you been all my life?" he said.

"Umm, here." Her cheeks flushed and he leaned over, kissing away her blush.

"You actually care about hockey. It's not just to get in my pants." He couldn't stop the remark from spilling out of his mouth. Most women he'd hooked up with over the years only cared about the fact that he was an athlete, and his money. But Penny wasn't most women. He'd known that from the moment they'd met in Italy.

"I mean, getting in your pants is always at the top of my list, but I love learning about hockey. I'm almost done with that book. The sport fascinates me. All those numbers and stats." Her gaze took on a dreamy quality, and he chuckled.

"All sports have numbers and stats."

"Yes, but I'm not interested in watching other sports. Nothing is like hockey. Not only is it fast, but you've basically attached razor blades to your feet and skate up and down a sheet of ice, while trying to avoid getting slammed into the boards, and chasing around a small rubber disk. I've tried to skate before. Sprained my ankle all four times. So yes, I'm impressed with the sport."

He puffed his chest out in pride at her description. He wanted to take her home now and show her just how much he appreciated her enthusiasm for the sport he loved.

"And don't even get me started on hockey butt," she threw in, as calm as could be, then fanned her face with her hand. He couldn't stop laughing. "Oh, shut up, you know all about it."

"Yes, I do. And this hockey butt, along with the rest of me, is all yours," he said, pressing a hard kiss to her lips.

Her moan was soft, and she gripped his thigh again. He finally pulled back, licking a spot of chocolate from her lips. "You're not so bad yourself. Tasty, too," he said, his body tightening with need as her eyes darkened.

"Stop. We were having a serious discussion, and you're distracting me," she said against his lips, and then leaned back in her chair, putting distance between them.

"Sorry. Hockey, right?"

She rolled her eyes. "Yes. Hockey. You know, that sport you play," she teased. "Did you ever play in an All-Star Game?"

"I'm hurt that you don't know my entire Wikipedia history," he said, pretending to be shocked. Her grin was adorable.

"I might've scanned through it quickly when I first found out who you really were, but I didn't memorize it. I wanted nothing to do with you, remember?"

"How could I forget? But, to answer your question, yes, I

played in an All-Star Game a few years ago. It's a lot of fun, especially since my team won the final game of the weekend. I did place second in the accuracy competition. Took me six tries to destroy four plates. The current Penguins captain got it in four."

Hanging out with the elite in the league was an honor. Animosity was pushed aside and they hammed it up for the fans. He'd go back if they ever asked again.

"Are you sad that they didn't ask you this year?"

"Not really. And I get a break to spend the weekend with you. If you could've torn yourself away from work, we could be on a beach right now, soaking up the sun in very little clothing." He wiggled his eyebrows at her and she laughed.

"Have you seen me? I'd be loaded up with sunscreen, under an umbrella, and wearing a shirt. The sun and I do not get along."

"Then we'd spend the weekend inside. Maybe skinny dip in our own private pool." He shifted in his seat again, thinking about all her pale skin on display for his eyes only. He needed to rein it in, or he was going to put on a show for the rest of the people in the restaurant when he stood up.

"I've never gone skinny dipping. Too much of a risk. What if your clothes get knocked into the water or someone takes them? Or you get caught?" She shook her head. "Definitely too risky."

"I'll convince you one day. Just you wait."

"We'll see," she said, taking a final bite of the brownie. "Shall we get out of here?" That twinkle in her eye almost had him jumping up to flag down the waitress. He contemplated just throwing money on the table and steering her toward the door more than once since they'd sat down.

Luckily the waitress chose that moment to walk by. He had his credit card out and in the woman's hand faster than she could ask if they needed anything else. He ignored Penny's chuckle. She was definitely the troublemaker in this situation.

"Are we in a rush or something?" Her smile belying the pure innocence in her green eyes.

"You could tempt a saint, you know that?"

"Only interested in tempting you."

"The feeling is definitely mutual." He signed the charge slip as soon as the waitress dropped it off, and then propelled Penny out of the restaurant.

Her laugh turned into a huff as the cold air washed over them when they stepped outside. The wind chill tonight was brutal, but it gave him an excuse to wrap her tightly in his arms and steer her toward his car.

"Well, if it isn't the golden boy," a familiar voice cut through the brisk air. Ethan would know that voice anywhere. He waited for Julie to pipe in with her own remark, but only heard Penny's growl of irritation. Which was hot, and he wished they weren't about to be interrupted by his family. Especially his brother.

"I'm so sorry," he whispered into Penny's ear before he turned to face Darren, who was blissfully alone. Wait. Why was his brother walking out of a bar alone?

"Hello, Darren. Where's the rest of your group?" Ethan asked.

"Left them inside. Gotta head home. The *wife* needs me for something."

Ethan didn't miss the emphasis on wife, nor did it bother him to hear Darren say it. At one point in his life, he'd imagined calling Julie *his* wife. He'd dodged a bullet with that one. And he never would've found Penny if he'd ended up with Julie. That in itself was a blessing.

"What is your problem?" He was tired of tiptoeing around the issue.

"My problem? You come home after six years of nothing, and now I'm the bad guy in the family again."

"You slept with my girlfriend, who I was still dating, and then you married her and everyone just had to accept it," Ethan said. Jesus, his brother had some big balls to whine to him. Ethan had started to question just how on board his parents had been with his brother's marriage. Had he pushed them away because he didn't want to see whose side they'd pick? Had he judged too quickly and missed out on years that he could never get back?

"And you're still upset about it? Still have feelings for *my wife*?"

"Absolutely not. I moved on ages ago. I'm more pissed that my own brother thought it was okay to sleep with my girlfriend. That everyone would have to accept it and be one happy family."

"It doesn't bother you that she preferred me?" Darren sneered. A calm reassurance settled over him. It took him a minute to realize it was Penny slipping her hand under his coat, trailing her hand slowly up and down his lower back. The same thing he'd done for her when they'd run into Michael a few weeks ago.

"Let's be honest. She preferred your money. Your stable career path. I was a gamble. I might've never made it to the NHL or had a contract that brought in enough money for her." He let out a harsh chuckle. "Funny thing is, I was home early to tell her about the deal I'd just signed with New York. Guess she should've held out a little longer." The dig was immature, but he'd needed to say it. He was done with the nonsense. He had his family back. He was moving on to better, so much better.

"Oh, look. Here's a cab," he said, holding his hand out to grab the cabbie's attention. When it pulled up to the curb, Ethan held the door open. "You should get home. Sleep off the booze. Maybe we'll see you at the next family dinner." He slammed the door shut, tapping the roof of the car before his brother could say anything else.

Penny laughed softly next to him. "Feel better now?"

"Yeah, that was completely childish of me, but I couldn't resist."

"I'm glad you finally told him to shove it. After everything he's done to you, the riff he caused within your family," she trailed off, shaking her head. "I'm sorry you had to go through that, but look where you are now."

"Yes, I'm about to take my girlfriend home with me and do things to her that we couldn't do in Italy because she had a bum knee. And then tomorrow morning, we are going to wake up and do it all over again. Maybe if you're good, I'll throw in some popcorn and a chick flick."

She chuckled. "You do know the way to a girl's heart. Shall we?"

He tugged her close, kissing her with everything he had, swallowing her moan, before releasing her just as fast as he'd grabbed her.

"Let's go." He pulled her toward the car, still trying to figure out just how he'd gotten so lucky.

CHAPTER 22

"The client cannot show more in meals and entertainment than gross income," she said as she reviewed one of Kevin's files on Monday afternoon. The account had been hers, so she knew what she could deduct, and Kevin appeared to just throw random numbers into the accounting software to see what he could get by her. "You cannot show a massive increase in something like that if the gross receipts haven't drastically increased as well."

She wanted the day to end. With every question he asked, the less time she had for her own work, but she refused to let her clients suffer because she missed something or rushed the review of their files.

She already wasted a good chunk of the morning thinking about that run-in with Ethan's brother this past weekend. She was so proud that he'd stood up for himself, but would it cause more issues with his family, now that he'd put his brother in his place?

"Maybe they were wining and dining a lot of new clients," Kevin said, jabbing his pen at her computer screen, and pulling her from her thoughts.

"Not that many clients," she retorted as she pulled up her notes and changed the amount in that field.

"If you are going to continue to correct me, why don't you just do all the work yourself?" he bit out.

"I might as well," she grumbled, wishing she'd kept that thought internal as soon as she'd said it. *Boss's son. Boss's son.*

"This is a waste of time. As soon as I'm running this place, I'll never need to do this stuff, so why bother showing me?" God, he was a sniveling punk.

"It's not a waste of time. Clients expect the owners of this company to know what they are doing, why else would they trust their taxes with us? If they end up getting audited, it comes back on us." She was so tired of reiterating that to him.

"So just do the work for me, and then we won't risk an audit, since you're so perfect," he sneered.

"Please don't speak to me that way," she replied. *Calm. Calming breaths.* Holy hell, she wanted to throat punch him. She clenched her fist in her lap, willing the day to end.

"Are you going to tell on me? Or maybe you can just have Ethan tell his uncle," he said.

"My relationship with Ethan has nothing to do with my job. My personal and professional lives are completely separate. I do not appreciate what you are implying, but I have worked very hard for my position in this firm, prior to even meeting Robert's nephew."

"And Ethan isn't helping you into a new position?" His tone was lewd and she'd had enough.

"This conversation is over. If you ever think about speaking to me that way again, I will go to Human Resources and report it. I do not care what your last name is," she replied, keeping her voice as even as possible when she was about ready to explode.

"Right. HR. The department your best friend runs? You really know how to get an in with the correct people," he replied, rising from the seat next to her.

"Get out." She walked around her desk and opened her door.

"Just remember that when I'm running this place, you had better clean up your attitude. Oh, and sleeping to get to the top won't be happening." He shut the door behind him after his last parting shot, and Penny stifled her scream. *Fucking asshole.* Why did she put up with this shit?

* * *

"He said what?" Ethan growled as Penny relayed her afternoon with Kevin to him later that night. They'd settled on the couch at her place, and after tossing back a glass of wine, Penny had filled him in.

"I'm going to talk to Robert. That asshole can't speak to you that way. It's a shame I don't work in your office, maybe I could trip him on the stairs. Accidentally, of course."

"You can't do that," she said, turning to face him.

"Which part?"

She bit back her smile. "Both. That would prove Kevin right."

"I guess. What can I do? That little punk needs to be put in his place," he replied.

She put her hand on his chest. "Thank you. And while I appreciate your support, I need to ignore him and continue to do my job. Or I could quit and not have to deal with the rumors about us and all the high school nonsense that surrounds me."

"Don't quit because of him. You're stronger than that. Stay because you deserve that promotion you'll eventually get, or leave because you want to go out on your own, for your own reasons," he replied as he took her hands in his, rubbing his thumb across the soft skin. "There's steel under all this softness."

Her heart raced. "Have I told you how amazing you are?"

He chuckled. "Not today, so I guess I'm due."

"Fishing for compliments is not attractive." She grinned at him.

"I wasn't fishing. You offered."

She leaned in and brushed her lips against his. "You're amazing."

"I know." She swatted his shoulder as he grinned at her. "But in all honesty, if I can help in any way, just let me know."

"Thanks. Dealing with Kevin has made me seriously consider going out on my own."

"While I don't agree with you running away…if starting your own CPA practice is something you want, what's stopping you?"

"It's a risk. I'd have to generate my own business and dip into my savings that I wanted to leave untouched. There are so many things that could go wrong, but if Kevin keeps this up and I never get promoted, I'm not sure I can stay there." She dropped her head. "I've worked so hard to get where I am, and it feels like it amounts to nothing."

He brushed a kiss across the top of her head. "It's not nothing. And if you want to go out on your own, I'll do whatever I can. I'm sure some of the guys need a new accountant. I can highly recommend you."

"I'm not asking you to leave your uncle. If I do decide to start my own business, your account will stay with Robert. It would be too shady to quit and take you on as a client if I go out on my own."

"Then I'll send you the entire team," he said, pressing a kiss to her cheek. "And I have complete faith in your determination and organizational skills. You'd be a success in no time."

Her heart melted at his words. How long had she waited to find someone who believed in her?

Ethan charged down the ice, the puck on his stick. He'd snagged it from a Vancouver rookie when the kid had been trying to make a pass. Out of the corner of his eye, he spotted one of Vancouver's defensemen gaining on him. He tuned out the shouts, only hearing the tap on the ice. He glanced left. Cheesy was open and that damn defenseman was on Ethan's heels. He shot the puck to Cheesy, and the captain sank it into the back of Vancouver's net.

Ethan couldn't stop his momentum. He crashed into the boards with the defenseman, and then righted himself. Shit. That was going to leave a mark. Just another one to add to the many bumps and bruises. He shook his head and skated over to his teammates. They'd just leveled it with ten minutes left in the third. Plenty of time to win this game—or lose it.

"Nice shot, Cheesy," Ethan called out, giving the guy a hug and tapping him on his helmet.

They skated back to their bench, knocking gloves with the rest of the team. The next line hopped over the board and back out to the center dot for the next face-off.

In the last minute of the game, Ethan scored on a breakaway and Vancouver never recovered. His team crashed into him and after hugs and slaps on the back, his gaze met Penny's in the stands. He could see her grin from across the arena as she jumped up and down, clapping.

When the final buzzer sounded, they headed back to the locker room. Coach tapped him as one of the guys to talk to the media. When they won, the media always wanted to talk to the goal scorers. They asked the dumbest questions, as if asking such mundane and obvious questions would one day result in more than just a canned answer.

He ducked into the dressing room and grabbed his phone from his stall, firing off a quick message to Penny.

Ethan: *Tapped to do media and then I'm grabbing a quick shower.*

Don't you dare disappear without finding me. I need a good luck kiss since you refuse to stowaway on the plane. It's the least you can do.

He ended with a wink and a shamrock.

Penny: *Trying to fit in your suitcase would be uncomfortable and I have to work, but I'll gladly meet you in an alcove for your victory kiss.*

As if his adrenaline wasn't already up a notch.

Ethan: *Have to meet with Sam, too. Give me at least fifteen, maybe twenty minutes. I'll be in the office two doors down from the locker room.*
Penny: *See you then. And congrats. You were awesome tonight. Wish I could give you more than just a victory kiss. Too bad you have to get on a plane.*

She followed that with a wink and lips. He'd take the fastest shower on record just to have as much time with her as he could before he had to leave.

After rushing through his shower and providing his sound bite, he ducked out of the room. Sam said he'd have the final contract for Ethan to sign, and then Ethan was going to wait for Penny so he could kiss the hell out of her before he had to get on a plane tonight. And when he got home this weekend, he had plans. Big plans. He was tired of holding back, of waiting for something to go wrong. He was in love with Penny Connor, and it was about time he told her.

Not that he was ready to drop down to a knee, but the thought of it no longer made him break out in hives. She was who he'd waited for, and he hadn't been the same since he'd spotted her that day at the vineyard.

A copy of his house key burned a hole in his pocket, waiting for him to hand it to her, to ask her to move in, and he didn't care how fast it might be. They'd known each other for eight months, even if they'd been apart for six of those months, it didn't matter.

He pushed open the door to the office, and Sam stood up to shake his hand, and slapped him on the back.

"Great game, man. Didn't think you were going to squeeze that last one in," Sam said.

"We played great tonight, and that last shot was a lucky bounce, really. So, you have the final contract?"

"Yes." Sam gestured to the pages in front of him.

Ethan couldn't stop his chuckle when he saw the blue flags. He wondered how many Penny had left in her book.

"You heading out soon?" Sam asked as Ethan grabbed the pen.

"Yeah. Three games in Eastern Canada. We better grab a few points, at least," he said, and tossed the pen to the table. "And thanks for this. Everything looks good."

"I told you I'd get you the deal we wanted," Sam said, cocky as ever, and grinning from ear to ear.

The deal had been agreed upon earlier today, but Sam had a few details he wanted to iron out, so Ethan hadn't signed everything. Nor had the team announced anything. That would happen in the next few days.

"Yes, you did, but I had my doubts. They only signed a one-year deal for me last summer, but five years, and twenty-three million works for me. I'm not greedy," he said, chuckling. It was a huge sum for anyone, but when you signed a new contract at thirty, the amounts tended to drop unless you were a top player. Thirty was getting up there in hockey years, and the risk of getting an injury you were unable to fully recover from grew.

"Could've gotten more, but you wanted that no movement clause."

"I want to stay here. My family's here—"

"Penny's here," Sam interrupted.

"Yeah, she is." He didn't care how wistful or smitten he sounded. He wanted to take her home with him tonight so they could celebrate his news, but he had to be on a plane in an hour.

"So, this is real?" Sam asked, disbelief in his eyes, and Ethan bristled.

"Yes, it's real. How could you doubt it?"

"Because I've known you for years and settling down was never your thing."

"People change." He hated having to justify himself to anyone, his agent included.

"No they don't. They pretend to change but it never lasts. Can't teach an old dog new tricks isn't just a myth," Sam said.

"You're an ass, you know that? And who's to say that I haven't changed?"

"Sure, you aren't the same guy who was caught with Ivan's wife. But settling down? Never thought I'd see it. But she is the perfect girl for you to date. Stable job. Not a puck bunny. Not your typical type. Looks great on paper. Probably not solely interested in your money and celebrity. I couldn't have picked someone more perfect to get management to see that you're not the party boy you once were. I'm sure the owners loved that you were *settling down*. They fought the bigger deal a lot harder before you started bringing around your good luck charm. Guess she's good for all aspects of your game."

Ethan glared at the guy. He was skating on damn thin ice. "Dating her has helped my game, I can't deny that, but—"

A gasp cut him off before he could say anything else and he spun, his heart freezing in his chest as Penny stared at him in horror.

Oh, fuck.

CHAPTER 23

Perfect girl to date. Looks great on paper. Ivan's wife. Bigger deal. Dating her has helped my game.

The words rattled around in her head as her heart stopped, unsure of how to process each crushing comment she'd heard. She'd known everything was too good to be true, and Ethan not refuting anything his agent had said just drove that point home with brutal clarity.

How could she have been so stupid, and so naïve? She hadn't missed the scorn in Sam's voice when he'd joked about Ethan settling down. And who the fuck was Ivan? Did he have anything to do with Ethan's abrupt trade? Ethan never told her what exactly caused the move.

"Penny, how much did you hear?" Panic was clear in his eyes. Panic, not remorse. Well, maybe a little remorse. He moved toward her, and she stepped back.

"Enough," she croaked out. Her eyes welled with tears, and she needed to escape before a single one fell. She'd thought he was different. She spun on her heel, clutching her book to her chest, armor to hold in her breaking heart, and bolted.

"Shit," she heard him shout, his voice fading as she pushed

through the side door, into the stairwell, and then paused. She had no idea how to get to the parking lot, and she was not going back to find someone to ask. She headed up the stairs, hoping it would put her on the correct level to get the hell out of there.

She concentrated on each step, her vision blurry, the possibility of faceplanting a real dilemma. Fuck. What had just happened?

The door slammed below her, his voice echoed around, and she wished she could disappear. She didn't want to talk about it, to hear his excuses. She'd heard them before. From Michael. Not that he had any place in this moment. But there it was, proof again that she was a horrible judge of character.

"Penny, stop," he said, his steps pounding behind her. She wasn't sure how she heard them over her rapidly beating heart.

He finally reached her, grabbed her hand and forced her to turn and face him on the landing just outside the door to her hopeful salvation. She'd been so close. "Ethan, please. Just let me go," she said.

"Sam was being an ass and none of what he said was the truth."

"But you agree with him," she said, hating the pain in her voice. She refused to look at him and yanked her hands from his. He released her easily.

"Penny, please. I was just about to tell him to shove it. He was out of line and I am so sorry you heard any of that."

"Why? Because you didn't believe anything that he said or because you didn't want me to hear the truth?"

"None of that was the truth," he repeated, but it sounded hollow in her ear. She was tired of excuses.

"Please. It's just a game to you. Everything is about the game, and playing a game. And who's Ivan? Why were you traded?" She couldn't stop herself from asking, but she didn't want to know. Not if it was going to crush her heart even more. Had he been a cheater? Were all men cheaters? She started to shut down, wishing she could curl up in a ball and wake when the nightmare of falling in love with another liar was over.

He grasped her hand again, and she tried to pull back, but he held strong. "I'll be honest, my trade was because of a misunderstanding. The trainer's wife threw herself at me, and her husband walked in on us. But I never started anything. I would never pursue a married woman—an attached woman. She kissed me, that's it. You have to believe that."

"Why should I? Your team didn't." Her chest clenched in pain. Why hadn't she questioned the trade? Why hadn't she done more than just a cursory search online when she'd discovered who he really was? She would've known to steer clear, regardless of how many times he claimed that most of what was online was false. Rumors started from somewhere, a kernel of truth that exploded into the ridiculous in some cases, but there was always some truth in most rumors.

"It was an excuse they used to trade me. They needed the cap space for one of the guys coming out of his rookie contract. I was easily expendable because my numbers sucked and my behavior caused a lot of grief with PR. But I didn't pursue this woman, and the truth eventually came out. Penny, you know me. I would never do that…"

"Do I? Until this moment we never talked about your trade. You never wanted to tell me what happened. Was it because you were ashamed? Did she really throw herself at you? Did you really pursue me because I *looked good on paper*?" she asked. He sounded so sincere, but was it a game? How could she trust him?

"I was pissed about the trade and since the story wasn't out there, I didn't want to rehash it and tell you about it. They swept most of it under the rug when they found out what really happened, so it never hit the media, but I swear to you, nothing happened. I'll give you Ivan's number. He'll confirm it if you don't believe me. But I need you to believe me. I'm not proud of who I was, but I've worked hard to fix my image this season."

She wanted to trust him. To look into his blue eyes and believe the sincerity and hurt they currently held, but she'd been played before.

"Maybe you're just dating me to get back at me for leaving you in Italy. I should walk away before you hurt me even more." There. She'd said it. That idea that had niggled in the back of her brain, that called out to every doubt she'd ever had.

"How could you think that of me? After all this time? You're panicking, so you're grasping at anything, no matter how ridiculous. Sam was talking out of his ass," he said.

She ignored him. "So you didn't date me to get a better contract? Pretending you're settling down didn't help your career? I've seen the pictures online. You never stay with the same woman for very long. It was only a matter of time for us." With each word from her mouth, her heart tightened a bit more. Had she learned nothing from Michael?

"That had nothing to do with it. I love you."

Her heart stopped, and she took in a quivering breath. He looked so earnest. But how could she trust him? Trust herself?

"Now you say it? Of course you say it when we are fighting. Where were your words before? You could've told me last night. This morning. Any. Other. Time. Saying it for the first time during an argument is a guilt mechanism, not an actual feeling."

"That's total bullshit. I was waiting for the right time. I'd planned to tell you tonight, when I gave you the key to my house and asked you to come over whenever you wanted. Maybe move in, if you wanted."

"I don't believe you. It's too convenient," she whispered, hating the pain in her voice. This wasn't supposed to happen again. And so soon.

"I don't want to do this now. You're reading way more into that conversation than was there. Sam was an ass. Yes, I have a track record that isn't the best. Yes, I did things in New York that I'm not proud of. But I'm not that guy anymore. And you're different. You've always been different." She would not acknowledge the pain in his eyes. It was easily faked.

"I'm sure you say that to all the women who question their importance in your life," she shot back, refusing to back down.

"There's no one else I ever wanted to say that to."

"Even Julie?" she scoffed.

"Julie has no place in this conversation. And we were kids when we dated. She was never as important to me as you are. I never had feelings as strong for her as I have for you. You have to believe that. Believe that I truly love you."

"I just don't know," she said, trying to tug free, but he held on tighter.

"And now I have to get on a fucking plane, and I don't know how to fix this. I'm not just trying to save face here. I love you."

She looked away. "I don't know if I can trust you, Ethan. I'm not like the women you've dated before. I'm just me. And you're a star athlete. Why would you settle for me when you have so many options?"

"I was never settling for you. I settled for them. They were never what I wanted. Goddammit. I want you, Penny. Why can't you believe me? Trust me?"

"Because I don't want to get hurt again," she said, stiffening when he pulled her close.

The shrill ring of his phone echoed through the concrete walls and he angrily swiped it on.

"Give me a minute. I'll be there," he barked into the phone before ending the call.

"Fuck. And now I have to get on a plane with this—with us—up in the air."

"Just go, Ethan," she said, breaking free from his hold.

He tugged her back, locking his arms around her. "This is not over. Don't think for one minute that we aren't going to figure this out. Trust me, Penny. Trust us. This started between us when we didn't know who the other person was, how intertwined our lives already were before that first kiss in Italy. That has to count for something."

"I can't do this now," she said, a sob breaking free, and he cursed again in pure frustration.

"This isn't over. And we are going to talk about it when I get back. Don't push this aside because of what you thought you heard, what my stupid agent said, that I didn't agree with. I never agreed with his statement."

"And you never disagreed," she whispered, finally breaking his hold.

He reluctantly let her go, and she pushed through the door, giving him one last look before it closed behind her. Tears ran down her cheeks and she tried to catch her breath as she made her way out of the arena.

She wanted to trust him, to trust her own gut, but it scared the hell out of her. What if she was wrong again? She'd survived Michael's betrayal. She wasn't sure she'd survive Ethan breaking her heart.

He needed to punch something. Preferably Sam. And now he had to get on a damn plane, and he wouldn't be back to fix this mess for four days. He headed back to the scene of the crime to grab his bag. Sam was seated at the table. He stood when Ethan walked into the office.

"Did you talk to her? Everything good?"

"Nope," he bit out, clenching his fists at his side to resist giving into his urge to inflict bodily harm to the man in front of him.

"I'm sorry, man. Sorry for mentioning New York. And, I had no idea you actually cared about her."

"Seriously? I was never *that* bad."

Sam snorted. "Yeah, you were. But you were single and the women knew upfront that it was never going to be anything more. Guess you didn't have that conversation with Penny."

"No. It was always more with her," he said, his shoulders slumping for a brief second, before he straightened up. He refused to believe it was over. He'd get her to trust him again, no matter what he had to do. Fuck. This was a disaster.

"I am sorry about what I said. Should I talk to her?"

"No. You've done enough. She probably wouldn't listen to you anyway. I'm going to fix this. I have to."

He grabbed his bag and headed to meet up with the team. The chartered bus was leaving in a few minutes for the airport, so he had to hustle.

"Let me know if you need anything. Apology, booze, a face to punch," Sam called out.

"I'll keep that in mind," he said, walking down the hall, moving further away from his car and the overwhelming urge to say fuck it and go after her. But he had a job to do, a team to support. She had to understand that.

The key he had made for her burned a hole in his pocket. Maybe if he'd waved the thing in her face, she would've believed him.

* * *

By day four, he was a healthy combination of nervous, disappointed, and pissed. Mostly pissed. He'd told her he loved her. Why didn't that count for anything? He'd only told one other woman that he loved her and that woman had turned around and married his brother. And Penny thought she had trust issues.

Sure, he hadn't picked the best moment to say those three words, but he'd panicked. And he hadn't been lying. He loved her. More than he'd ever loved anyone else. More than he thought possible. And what had she done with that? She'd bolted. For someone so clumsy, she was good at running away.

How could they make this work if she ran when she panicked? How could she trust him so little to not hear him out? Would she run every time things got tense?

Those questions had played on loop in his head for the last four days. Four days of her ignoring his calls and his texts. Four days of him playing like total shit on the ice. They'd squeaked out a win last night, but had lost the first two games of the road trip. Luckily, one had been in overtime, so they'd walked away with three out of six points. He'd gotten a lucky bounce last night to win the game, but his head wasn't in it, and that was a major problem.

They'd announced his new contract the first morning of the road trip, and he'd repaid them by playing like crap. The league analysts were already circling, questioning if he deserved a deal that big, that long. He wasn't getting any younger. It pissed him the hell off. He'd earned that contract, those guaranteed years of playing with the Strikers. His heart was messing with his head, and he needed to get it together.

He'd never had a woman affect his play and that shit had to stop now. Yes, he loved her. And no, he wasn't ready to give up on what they had, but he could only go so far. She had to meet him halfway. She'd thrown his trust, and his love, in his face. How many times was he willing to put himself out there for her?

And he needed to focus on his career. He'd put that mindset into place last night, and it'd paid off. But he needed to do better than scoring one goal on a lucky bounce. He had to contribute, get back to how he'd been playing before she'd bolted. This was his job and if he had to push her aside, he would. She clearly didn't care enough to fight for them.

But right now he wasn't thinking straight. He was exhausted from the long flight. They'd left Montreal in the early morning hours, and it was still morning when they landed in San Francisco seven hours later. He needed his bed and blackout curtains, but he hated getting on the wrong sleep schedule, so he'd try to stay awake at least until the afternoon. They didn't have a practice scheduled until tomorrow, and no games tonight or tomorrow night.

Monday was the first home game back. Would she be there? He shook his head. Why would she? He hated how melodramatic he sounded, but the ball was firmly in her court, and he resisted the urge to text her and remind her of that.

She wouldn't be able to dodge him forever. He'd almost called Robert. His uncle knew exactly how Ethan felt about Penny, but roping her boss in to help Ethan's love life was not a good idea. She'd freak and bolt for good, so he'd held back.

When the plane touched down, the guys exited to their waiting cars. Goodbyes were grunted, a few guys mentioned meeting up for dinner, but they steered clear of him. He hadn't been subtle in his frustrations, and he wasn't happy with the number of heads he'd bitten off in the last few days. They were giving him space.

Even Baz hadn't teased him. That was saying something.

CHAPTER 24

"Spill," Amanda said when Penny opened her door that weekend.

"What?"

"You've put us both off for two days now, and something is going on, so we are ambushing you and demanding answers," Amanda said.

"And we brought pizza," Lexi said, holding up the box when she walked in behind Amanda, shooting Penny a small smile.

Penny had successfully avoided talking about it for the last three days since Ethan had left. Her shoulders slumped. Sam's words. Ethan's laugh. They echoed in her head, drumming up every doubt she'd ever had. She'd tried to find anything about Ethan and the trainer's wife online, but nothing came up. At that point she'd begun to doubt her doubts.

"I think I've made a mess of things," she said, shutting the door behind them. She walked into the living room to plop down on the couch. They knew where everything was if they were thirsty.

"I knew something was up," Amanda said.

"What happened?" Lexi asked, grabbing a bottle of wine and glasses from the kitchen.

She told them about that night. About Sam and Ethan. About why he left New York. About Ethan running after her, trying to explain. She should've listened to him. After dwelling on it for a few days, and reading the texts he sent her each night, she'd known she was wrong to assume. She bit back her snort. What did they say about assuming?

"Oh, Penny. He didn't agree with his agent, did he? And you didn't find anything to substantiate the rumors, right? You should know that rumors are just that—rumors," Lexi said.

"I know. And he told me he loved me. But that doesn't count when you're in a fight, especially when it was the first time he'd said it," Penny said, picking at the pepperoni on her pizza.

"Or it could mean that he loves you and just hadn't found the perfect time to tell you," Lexi said.

"You're just saying that to make me feel better," Penny grumbled, but her heart told her to believe him. To believe in them.

"Stop making excuses, Penny. And stop avoiding him. I've watched you together. It's not a game to him. You're scared that you found something worth hanging on to. Michael screwed you up, and your parents didn't help matters, but Ethan is the real deal. Sure, he doesn't have the best track record, and it might not work out, but what if it does? Why not hear him out? Let him explain," Amanda said.

"I know. I panicked. I'm not proud of it. And he's been texting…" she trailed off.

"How often? What's he saying?" Lexi asked.

"Every night, and that he can explain, and he's sorry. God, I'm an idiot. But I'm still scared. I love him. Like, more than Michael, and I was going to marry Michael. It would destroy me if it didn't work out with Ethan."

"Look, no relationship is perfect. You're going to argue, say stupid shit. And you work at it because you can't imagine your life without that person. Can you imagine your life without Ethan?" Lexi asked.

"No."

"So knock this nonsense off and talk to him now," Amanda said.

"He's not home yet. I was thinking of apologizing at the game tomorrow night." It was the right decision. She wasn't going to give up on them so easily.

"Then we are going to need to make a sign," Amanda said. "Got any poster board?"

Penny laughed, it was the first in days, and her nerves began to fade away. She loved him, and she was going to fight for him, even if she had to fight against her fears.

She squashed down her nerves as she knocked on Alan's door. He'd requested a meeting and she had no idea why. When she walked in, Robert was sitting in one of the chairs, and her stomach turned into a knot.

"Penny, please take a seat. We wanted to talk to you."

Oh God, were the rumors ramping up again? More pictures online? She took a steadying breath, willing her breakfast to remain where it was—in her stomach.

"Is anything wrong?" she asked, taking a seat and twisting her fingers in her lap.

Alan smiled at her. "No, not at all. We wanted to talk to you about taking on a new role at the company. It hasn't escaped our notice how much you do for our clients and how you always go the extra mile to help train new colleagues. My wayward son included."

"Thank you," she replied. Not sure what else to say, besides *it's about freaking time!*

"You manage some of our largest clients, which we know is

no easy task," Alan continued.

She nodded in agreement.

"And with that in mind, we want to move you up to an Accounting Manager position. You'd have your own team of accountants that will report directly to you. You can keep your own clients or they can be moved to other colleagues."

"Wow. Umm." This is what she'd been waiting for and her words failed. She'd worked so hard to get here, and instead of jumping up and agreeing, something held her back.

"So you'll take the position?" Alan asked, just as his door opened, and Kevin poked his head in.

"Ready for lunch, Dad?" he asked, taking in the room. "What's going on?"

"Kevin, now is not the time. Please wait in the hall, and when I'm done, we can go to lunch," Alan admonished.

"Let me guess. She's getting promoted?" he sniveled, ignoring his father, and glaring at her. What the hell was this asshole's problem?

"Excuse me," she bit out, clenching her fists and attempting to keep her temper at bay.

"Dad. You know she's screwing Robert's nephew, right? Trying to sleep her way to the top," Kevin said.

Penny gasped. "How dare you imply that I have not earned this position," she said.

"What position were you in when you *earned* it?" he asked, pure malice in his voice.

"I don't know what I did to make you hate me, but I'm done trying to figure it out. And the entire office is aware that I am dating Robert's nephew. And my personal life has nothing to do with my professional life," she said, trying to remain calm while itching to stab him with a pen.

"Sure it doesn't. When I'm in charge, your behavior will not be tolerated," Kevin said.

Alan's eyes widened, and Penny could only be grateful that Alan was witnessing his son's horrendous behavior.

"When you're in charge? Planning my retirement a bit prematurely," Alan said, his eyes hard.

"But—" Kevin started.

"No. Your mother convinced me to give you this job, and while I would love nothing more than to pass it down to you, eventually, your behavior today makes me question why I thought this would be a good fit. Penny has worked hard for this company for years. Well before she probably met Ethan. We've been looking to promote her for some time, and it has nothing to do with whom she might be dating. You could learn a lot from her, but I have a feeling all you've given her is grief."

"But she's—"

"You called in sick on Friday. Came in late today. And treated your new manager with complete disrespect. Now go home and think about how you can be an asset to this company you think I'm just going to hand over to you."

Kevin spun on his heel and stormed out of the room. Penny almost felt bad for the dressing down Kevin had received from his father. *Almost!*

"Penny, I am sorry that you've had to deal with his complete unprofessionalism. Alan, we need to have a conversation if he can even have a place here. I know you are trying to please Susan, but this is too much," Robert said.

"Yes, we will. I'm extremely sorry on behalf of my son, Penny," Alan said as he turned to face her, embarrassment clear on his face.

"Thank you for supporting me," she replied, unsure of what else to say, especially since that outburst had made her decision for her.

"I do hope you take the position. I will make sure he is assigned to another manager," Alan said.

"While I have loved working here over the years, and have

worked for this promotion, I'm going to turn it down." She rose from her seat. A mixture of panic and exhilaration rushed through her, but this was the right decision. The only decision.

"Wait. What?" Robert asked, his focus back on her.

"There will always be questions, the rumors, the doubt. And why did it take so long for you both to realize that I deserved to be promoted? I've brought in more clients than anyone else, and my error rate is miniscule." Her confidence flowed through her. She was going to resign, and she was going to be okay with it. Happy, actually.

"Ignore the gossip. It means nothing. You are a highly-valued employee, and it was our oversight waiting this long," Robert said, his expression calm, but his voice held the faint tremor of panic.

"I've thought about it for a long time, and I'm tendering my resignation. I'll have a letter on your desk within the hour."

"Penny, you don't need to do this," Robert said, the tremor in his voice growing.

"Yes, actually, I do. I want to go out on my own. I will not poach any of your existing clients, Ethan included. I am fully aware of the non-compete clause in my contract, and I'm fully prepared to start my business from scratch." She was surprised at how calm she sounded, and how peaceful she felt.

"Is there anything we can do to convince you to stay? I'll gladly fire Kevin," Robert said.

"Yes, Penny, you are our best employee. What can we do to convince you to stay?" Alan asked, looking chagrin, as well he should. Kevin was an entitled, spoiled brat, but she wouldn't tell his father that. It wasn't her place.

"Nothing. It's been a pleasure working here for the last six years, but it's time for me to move on. I'll give you the standard two weeks, unless you want me to leave now?" she asked.

"No. Two weeks is fine."

They both looked shell-shocked, and she couldn't blame

them. She'd had no intention of dropping the bomb today, but the moment had felt right, and now all she wanted to do was find Ethan and tell him. And tell him what an idiot she was and how much she loved—and trusted—him. But that would happen tonight at the game.

"I'm going to go back to my office then. Thank you again for the opportunity. I'll make sure each of my files has very detailed notes for the next accountant." With one last nod, she exited Alan's office.

"What the hell just happened?" Lexi asked, poking her head into Penny's office ten minutes later.

"I just got the promotion...and then I quit."

"I'm sorry, you what?" Lexi asked, plopping down into the chair on the other side of Penny's desk.

Lexi's rage grew as Penny told her what had happened with Kevin.

"Holy shit. But do you really have to quit?"

"You know it's for the best. And I've been thinking about this for a while now."

"I'm really proud of you, Penny. Don't let them convince you to stay," Lexi said with a smile.

"I won't."

"So, are you nervous for tonight?"

"Nope. I'm ready to fight for what's mine," she said. She was totally lying to herself, and her nerves came back in full force. But in a few hours, she was going to prove to Ethan how much she loved him. He'd stopped texting yesterday, and she tried not to think about what that meant. The ball was in her court and she was running with it. She was going to get everything she wanted. She refused to hold back on her dreams any longer.

CHAPTER 25

Ethan skated out onto the ice, focused solely on the warm-up puck currently on his stick. He would not look up into the stands, searching for the woman who refused to respond to his texts. He had a game to play, he had to prove to everyone that he deserved to be here. That he could help his team edge closer to the playoffs.

They were currently in the second wild card spot, but Edmonton, the team below them, was only two points behind the Strikers. One measly game could change the standings since Edmonton had games in hand, and they were playing tonight against a flailing Vancouver.

Cheesy skated up to him, shooting a practice puck on net, sinking it behind Gally. "How are you doing tonight?"

"Fine. Just want to get started and beat Tampa tonight. Keep Edmonton on our heels," he said, dropping down to stretch his hips. The left side was sore from a hard hit into the boards the other night.

Cheesy sank down next to him, twisting at his waist to loosen up. "You sure?"

"Yeah. I'm good." He couldn't stop himself from scanning the harsh, and she flinched. "Sorry, I didn't mean for it to come out that way."

"Umm." She dropped her gaze and tucked an errant curl behind her ear, then rolled her shoulders back and looked up at him, her gaze no longer tentative. "I came to apologize for last week. To tell you I miss you and I'm sorry."

"I missed you, too," he couldn't stop himself from saying.

"For fuck's sake," he heard Bugsy mutter as he brushed past Ethan, "you have ten minutes, Harty. We need our good luck charm, so fix whatever shit you caused and make her happy."

Penny's awkward laugh rang through the tunnel. "It's actually me who has to apologize. Ethan's been nothing but perfect." There was a wistful tone in her voice and a few of the guys who'd stayed to watch the show chuckled. Shit. He'd get ribbed for this for a while.

"Let's grab an office and talk," he said, steering her away from his teammates.

"Nope. I'm doing this right now. I love you and I'm sorry. And I should've said it earlier, as soon as I knew, but I was scared. Hell, maybe I fell in love with you in Italy. I definitely gave you part of my heart all those months ago, and now I want you to have the rest of it." She rushed toward him, her voice lowering. "If you still want it."

He pulled her into his body–she'd have to deal with the sweat–and he dropped his gloves, needing to touch her face. He cupped her cheek, and leaned down, further than usual since his skates added extra inches. "Of course I do," he said, then sealed his lips to hers.

Her hands snaked around his waist, the sound of her book hitting the ground echoed through the hallway, mostly muffled by the sounds of clapping and a few *woo-hoos*.

"Get a room," Baz called out, and the guys laughed.

He broke the kiss on a soft groan, wishing he could take her lower bowl, looking for Penny, but the seats next to the penalty box, her favorite, were filled by someone else, and he didn't see her pressed against the glass, book in hand. He refused to acknowledge what that did to his heart.

He bit back that thought. He had no time for it. He had a game to win. Teammates to support.

As the puck dropped twenty minutes later, Ethan easily won the face-off and focused on the game. Everything else had to be pushed aside. The game—and his love for it—was all that mattered right now. He was living his dream, so why did it feel hollow?

* * *

"Great first period, boys," Cheesy said as they headed down the tunnel toward the locker room at intermission. One down, two to go. They were up one to zero thanks to a goal by Dom ten minutes in. Ethan might not have any points yet tonight, but his game was back. His focus sharp and determined. Tonight was going to be a good game, even if their lucky charm was absent.

None of the guys had said anything, and he'd stopped looking for her after his third shift. He'd really thought she'd show up tonight. It pissed him off, but he channeled his anger into his playing, and it'd paid off so far.

"I see the good luck charm is back," Cheesy said. Ethan spun around, following the direction of Cheesy's pointing finger.

How had he missed her? She held that damn book to her chest, a tentative smile on her face, her cheeks pink, as she nibbled on her lip. What did she have to be nervous about? She knew exactly how he felt. Him, not so much. But this had to be a good sign.

"Hi," she said, her voice soft.

"What are you doing here?" His tone was unintentionally

home right now, but he had fifteen minutes left before the next period.

"We'll be right back," he said, towing her toward an empty office, shutting out the catcalls as the door slid shut.

"Sorry, maybe there was a better place to do this, but I was late to the game, so I couldn't get you before warm-ups, and I wanted to tell you in person, and I should've texted you back or called or—"

He cut her off. "No, this was perfect. God, I missed you," he said, sinking his hands into her hair and pulling her close again. "But you can't run again. I'm not perfect, and no relationship is easy."

"I know. And I'm sorry. I panicked, but I trust you and love you. I'm not running again, I promise. I love you more than anyone else in my life. You brought me back to life and helped me realize what I want is you. With all my heart," she said, and he crushed his lips to hers.

When he broke the kiss, he whispered against her lips, "I love you, too. Even if you drive me crazy."

She huffed out a laugh. "The feeling is mutual. Do you have to get back to the locker room now?"

"Probably," he said, straightening up. "Sorry, I got you sweaty."

"I don't care."

"I see all the flags are gone," he said, motioning toward the book she'd dropped down on the table.

"Yes, and I'm still here. I'm sorry, I don't know why I said that," she said, gripping his hand.

"It's fine, Penny," he said, squeezing her hand back. "But now what are you going to work on, if you've become a hockey expert?"

She pulled a small book out from the middle of the hockey book. Green flags decorated this one.

"I have a new list," she said, showing him the cover.

Twenty-two ways to show Ethan that I love him. And it had a picture of her wearing his jersey and blowing him a kiss. He was man enough to admit what that picture did to his heart. Not to mention how freaking hot it was.

"Did you make this?"

"Yes. I'm not a total expert on showing you how much I love you, but with each task, I get to remove a flag," she said, her cheeks bright pink. He snagged the book from her hands.

Her words warmed him down to his toes. This was what he'd always wanted. Sure, there'd been bumps he hadn't anticipated along the way, and he hadn't been looking for her, but now that she was truly his, he was never letting her go.

"And what exactly are these tasks?" he asked with a grin as he flipped through the pages.

Penny's cheeks heated again as that crooked smile she loved so much grew. Yes, she'd listed a few naughty items. More like love coupons. Not actual pictures or anything, but his grin made her belly flutter.

"We can get to that later," she said, snagging the book from his hands. "You have a game to finish."

"I still have a few minutes," he said, tugging her closer. She sank into his embrace, tilting her head up to meet his kiss as he surrounded her. Why had she ever doubted him? Every nerve disappeared as he consumed her mouth, his tongue tangling with hers. She dropped the book to the table, and his hands gripped her waist, lifting her.

She wrapped her legs around his hips, and he groaned

against her mouth. She wished they could go home now so she could show him just how much she loved him.

A knock on the door broke them apart.

"Five minutes left, Harty," a voice called out.

"Dammit," Ethan grumbled, pressing a kiss to her forehead before lowering her feet back to the floor.

Her chuckle was breathless, and her heart raced.

"Meet me back here as soon as the game ends. Then we are going home," he said, his eyes glittering with determination and lust.

Holy hell, he was hot.

"Only if you get a hat trick for me," she teased.

"Those aren't easy, you know," he said.

A few hours later, she straddled his lap on the couch. They'd arrived home ten minutes ago. *Home.*

He'd pressed a key into her hand and asked her to move in as soon as they'd walked in the door. Yes, it was way too early to live together, but part of her—a large part of her—wanted to say yes. She'd moved into her townhouse a week after coming home from Italy. She hadn't turned it into a home yet, so moving was no hardship.

"Move in, Penny," he said between kisses. "I mean, I did get that hat trick for you tonight."

She grinned. Yes, he had. They'd trounced Tampa five to one and she was annoyed with herself for not being prepared with a hat in case he did follow through with her ridiculous request. She'd had nothing to toss onto the ice for him.

"I'm thinking about it." She leaned in, nibbling on his lower lip. "I mean, it would be good since I'm going to be unemployed in two weeks."

He pulled back. "What?"

"Today's been a big day for me. I finally told you that I love you, and I quit my job this morning."

"Back up. What happened?"

"They promoted me, then Kevin made an ass of himself, and I knew that staying wasn't an option. I don't want the questions. I've proven myself time and again, and I wanted to start fresh. So in two weeks I'll be unemployed."

"That sniveling little prick. Want me to kick his ass?"

She laughed. "No. It's not worth it."

"Did Robert panic?"

"A little, but I hope it doesn't make family functions weird. I mean, if I'm invited." How was she still questioning that?

"Of course you are. And you should definitely move in. You don't even have to work. I signed that big deal, remember? And then you could follow the team around like a good luck groupie," he said, grinning.

"Not work? I'd be bored in an hour. And I'm not stowing away on the team plane to help you win."

"Fine, fine. How about I send every hockey player your way? I'm sure they need your accounting skills. You're amazing at your job. You didn't even make me review or sign anything," he said, and then smiled.

"I was your accountant for a split second, and tax season hadn't ramped up yet, so you were safe. I wouldn't say no to a client or two being sent my way, but I don't want you to think I'm using you to start my business," she said, keeping her tone serious. She would never take advantage of her connections. He had to know that.

"Penny, relax. I know you aren't looking for my help, but I'm offering it anyway," he said, gripping her hands and pressing a kiss to her lips. "Now, if you're done talking about work, I believe there are twenty-two ways you were planning to show me how much you love me? Should we start with number one and work our way through, or jump around?"

"Obviously, we are going to start with the first one. I put them in a specific order," she said, her voice calm while her belly fluttered with nerves and need and a love that she'd never felt before. It knocked her off balance, but she wouldn't have it any other way.

EPILOGUE

Two months later

"How was your first day, dear?" Ethan asked, pressing a kiss to her cheek before dropping his hockey bag just inside the front door.

She grinned. "Great. Someone sent me three amazing clients today. I wonder how I should repay him?"

"I'm sure there's something in the book that would do the trick," he said, tugging her close and kissing her hard.

She pulled away a few breathless minutes later. "You didn't have to help. I've got feelers out for new clients."

"I didn't force them. It came up in conversation."

"It came up? You typically discuss accounting at team meetings?" she asked, laughing at his innocent shrug.

It'd been six weeks since she'd walked away from her stable job. Four weeks since she'd moved in with Ethan. And three weeks since she'd proudly introduced him to her parents. Her mother had politely said hello, and her father had shaken Ethan's hand. Her father's smile had been genuine and supportive and Penny had wondered just how much her father had truly pushed for her reconciliation with Michael. Families were a work in progress, and they were getting there.

She'd found a small office space a few streets over from Knight and Welling so she could still grab lunch with Lexi, and Lexi could fill her in on any work drama that she was missing. They'd finally found out who started the rumors. Nosy Jessica had overheard Penny and Lexi talking about Ethan and Italy and then relayed the story to Kevin, who'd started the actual rumor.

Penny almost felt bad for Alan. *Almost.*

Robert had refused to keep Kevin on as an employee after that. She could hug the man, and now that he was no longer her boss but just her boyfriend's uncle, she fully intended to do just that.

Ethan guided her to the couch, tugging her down into his arms, and snuggled her close.

"Now, about that book," he said, wiggling his eyebrows.

She laughed, and wrapped her arms around his neck, getting lost in the crooked smile that had captured her attention all those months ago in Italy.

She shifted, straddling his lap, and bit back her smirk as he groaned, his hips rocking against her. Heat pooled in her belly. "I think we are up to number seven." She leaned in, pressing a hard kiss to his lips. "It's a dirty one."

His chuckle was strained. "I will never get enough of you."

"That's the plan," she said, then sealed her lips with his, grateful that what happened in Italy didn't stay there.

AFTERWORD

Thank you for buying this ebook.
To receive special offers, bonus content, and news about my latest books, sign up for my newsletter today.
Sign up today!
Just for signing up, you will receive a free novella.
What Happens in Italy – what exactly happened when Penny and Ethan met in Italy?

AUTHOR'S NOTE

This note is going to be a long one, so sit back. I promise it's funny.

In late 2011, I convinced my husband to get married in Gretna Green, Scotland, home of the runaway weddings featured in the Regency romances I loved so much. I planned it perfectly. Ceremony in the original marriage room at the Blacksmith's Shop, and a three-week honeymoon through Europe. Funny things happen when you think you've planned things perfectly… they're never perfect.

In early May 2012, one week before we left to go overseas, my friends threw me a bachelorette party. You know those nights when you just want to drink your face off and dance like a crazy lady? Yep, that's what I did. Until my knee gave out on the dance floor. I'd had the same injury in college, dancing the night away in a London club during my semester abroad, so I knew exactly what had happened. Unfortunately, there was no hot guy to catch me this time, so I landed on my ass.

And the line that Penny said about taking three shots because she went to college…yep, I said it. Still not sure why, but it made sense at the time, well, as much sense as anything can make when you're wearing a veil in a bar.

I did pick myself back up and hobble over to the bar, requesting another martini to numb the pain and a cup of ice to reduce the swelling. I tossed back that martini and urged my friends to keep dancing. Didn't want to call it a night just yet. That was the booze talking.

A week later, after daily physical therapy sessions, the swelling had slightly reduced and I was down to just one crutch, so I pulled on my compression sock for the plane ride and John and I headed to Scotland. That perfectly planned wedding was still on, even if I'd end up hobbling down the aisle instead of walking gracefully.

I did leave that crutch in the honeymoon suite, for future injured brides. I like to pay it forward.

We survived the wedding and started our honeymoon, traveling through France and Italy, until an earthquake struck outside of Siena while we were on a train headed to Florence, and we ended up stuck on the tracks for a few hours, across from another American who was kayaking through Italy with friends.

Yes, you thought that was crazy, didn't you? Who would kayak through Italy? Well, it happens. You never know what you're going to hear when you strike up a conversation with a stranger.

After we made it to Siena, we spent the rest of our honeymoon wine tasting and walking through museums *slowly*. At the time, I had not plans to turn my injury-filled adventures into a book. Had I know, I probably would have asked the kayaker more questions.

But a year later, on the anniversary of that ill-fated bachelorette party, I wrote a Facebook post:

A year ago today, I was getting ready for my bachelorette party. Little

AUTHOR'S NOTE

did I know that by the end of the night I would have a dislocated kneecap from too much dancing—and too many cocktails—and that I would end up having to take crutches with me on my honeymoon. I learned many valuable lessons that night: never wear a veil in a bar, never take three shots in a row just "because you went to college," and if you do find yourself flying overseas, crutches gets you through border control super-fast! Ahh memories!

It was off the cuff. Just a funny post that I never expected would go anywhere, but my friend, Penny Watson, told me that this was the start of my contemporary romance. Pretty sure I told her to shut up because I wrote historicals. And how would I even turn this into a contemporary romance. I'd gotten married. No drama—aside from the knee.

But the next day, I sat down with a notepad, and jotted down a few ideas. This wasn't going to be a retelling of what actually happened on my honeymoon. Sorry kids, this isn't a tell-all! It's fiction, pure and simple. Now I had to figure out what happened with my heroine. Why would she still go to her bachelorette party if she was no longer getting married? And did I really want to leave the world of dukes and duchesses and ballroom dancing?

But I love Penny and Ethan, and the characters that have popped up along the way. And I no longer have to deal with those pesky chaperones that kill the mood.

And now I get to write about hot hockey players. Lumberjacks on skates. Seriously, if you haven't looked up a few of these guys by now, what are you waiting for? I recommend Patrice Bergeron, Kris Letang, Tyler Seguin, and Jamie Benn to start. And join the Sin Bin Facebook group. The best place to satisfy your love for hockey and hockey romance.

Happy Reading!

ABOUT THE AUTHOR

Stephanie Kay has always loved a good romance. Reading them, writing them, and watching them on TV. She got hooked on the dirty ones at the tender age of 14, when she told her mother that if the cover wasn't a bodice ripper, then there was no sex in the book. As an avid mystery reader, her mother never checked to see if Stephanie was lying. Twenty years later, Stephanie's most prized possession is her Kindle, and she may have a Hallmark movie obsession.

Stephanie loves strong, swoony heroes and independent heroines that go after their dreams. She married her own strong, swoony guy, and convinced him to get married over the anvil in Gretna Green, Scotland, so she could live out her historical romance dream. Since he agreed, she decided he's a keeper.

She has called California, Maryland, and Rhode Island her home, but now lives in New Hampshire with her husband where she asks him incessant questions until he escapes to go hiking in the mountains. That's the only time she can get him out of the house so she can get her writing in. Married couples shouldn't both work from home!

Stephanie loves to hear from her readers. Please sign up for my newsletter for upcoming releases and exclusive excerpts. You can also email me at stephanie@stephkaybooks.com or find me on Twitter or Facebook. For more information, please visit my website, www.stephkaybooks.com. You can also join my reader group on Facebook, Stephanie Kay's Sassy Readers. We discuss books, romance, dessert, and hockey butts.

I hope you enjoyed Breakout and reviews are always welcome!

BOOKS BY STEPHANIE KAY

Love by the Bay – Romantic Comedy

Unmatched

Last Call

About A Boy

San Francisco Strikers – Hockey Romance

Breakout

Skating the Line

Delay of Game

Faceoff

All I Want – Strikers Holiday Novella

Going All In

Rookie Move

Defensive Zone

Steelwolf – Rockstar Romance

Fractured Rhythm

Keeping Time

Made in the USA
Middletown, DE
02 July 2021